SHADOW PACT

AN IMMORTAL ROMANCE SERIES NOVEL

SHADOW PACT

TALLY ADAMS

BROWN BOOKS
PUBLISHING GROUP

Shadow Pact

Brown Books Publishing Group
16250 Knoll Trail Drive, Suite 205
Dallas, Texas 75248
www.BrownBooks.com
(972) 381-0009

A New Era in Publishing®

Names: Adams, Tally.
Title: Shadow pact / Tally Adams.
Description: Dallas, Texas : Brown Books Publishing Group,
    [2019] | Series: A shadow series novel
Identifiers: ISBN 9781612542850
Subjects: LCSH: Missing persons--Fiction. | Sisters--Fiction. |
    Vampires--Fiction. | Werewolves--Fiction. | LCGFT:
    Fantasy fiction. | Romance fiction.

Classification: LCC PS3601.D3973 S53 2019 | DDC 813/.6--dc23

ISBN 978-1-61254-285-0
LCCN 2018947715

Printed in the United States
10 9 8 7 6 5 4 3 2 1

For more information or to contact the author, please go to
www.tallyadams.com.

This book is for Morgan and Robyn.
Those two girls are nearly as invested in these
characters as I am. Love you both!

Here's To Pie In the Sky

CHAPTER 1

Emily parked her car outside of the warehouse and waited. She was terrified but determined. It was a chilly autumn day. The small trees that lined the road had lost most of their leaves as they prepared for winter, giving them a somewhat skeletal aura. Above, gray skies stretched out, blotting the sun in a heavy weight of dreariness. It mirrored her mood nicely.

At another time—what seemed like a lifetime ago—she'd loved the fall. The colors, crunchy leaves, and the hint of warm apple cider in the air. It'd always filled her with a sense of happiness. Of contentment. Now, in this place so far from home, it was just a cold reminder of hard months ahead.

Any minute, the warehouse employees would be leaving the building. She was going to confront *him*. She'd never seen him in person. The passenger seat of her car was littered with pictures and documentation from a private investigator she'd hired six months ago. Right after her sister suddenly disappeared. He'd been expensive, but finding Amber was worth any price.

She hadn't ended up with as many details as she'd hoped for, though, since he'd just up and disappeared one day, as well.

While not as well informed as she'd hoped to be when the investigator vanished, she was able to use the information he'd already supplied to pick up the trail right where he left off. His last batch of pictures had contained several shots of her missing sister— proof positive Amber was still alive—and a single five-by-seven of the man who had her. Enclosed was a two-page letter Emily had first thought to be a tasteless joke.

It read like the rambling of a madman. One word recurred again and again in excited print.

Werewolf.

On the day he was supposed to call and give her an update, she'd been waiting by the phone, ready to blister his ears and demand her money back. How dare he blame her sister's disappearance on his delusional fantasies?!

But the call never came.

It was only a few days later when she'd been politely excused from two different police stations. As soon as the officers pulled Amber's information and saw her sordid history, they shrugged off her disappearance, saying she'd likely run off with the man in the photo, and there was simply nothing to indicate otherwise. Then, in a roundabout way, informed Emily she was better off to let it go and move on with her own life. Unfortunately, the local police knew Amber.

Well.

They also knew this wasn't her first disappearance. But Emily couldn't just walk away and move on. While her relationship with her sister was . . . strained, to say the least, Amber was the only family Emily had left. Their mother had passed a few years ago, leaving her two daughters all that remained of their little family.

A few days after her ill-fated attempt to contact authorities, Emily got her first glimpse of the monster the investigator had warned her about. It was a night she'd never forget. She bore the deep grooves on her arm from the beast's claws for weeks after the attack. The human man that accompanied the creature claimed it was a warning to let it go and leave it alone.

Idiots.

It was the attack that spurred her to start doing her own research. Months later, the research had led her here, to this quiet small-town street in Maine. Now she was waiting for the pack leader to leave work so she could follow him home and hopefully find Amber. She'd stared at the picture of him so many times in the past months, his face haunted her dreams. She'd know him anywhere.

When the whistle that announced quitting time finally blew, her heart seemed to grow cold with nervous excitement. She slumped down in her seat to avoid notice as the workers began to file through the door and scatter into the parking lot.

She paid no attention to them, because the moment he walked through the door, she locked onto him like a radar. Nothing could break her focus. She was surprised her hot stare didn't burn a hole in the side of his head as he walked along the sidewalk that hugged the building and led into the employee parking.

She had a moment of panic when he stopped suddenly and looked around, then tipped his head up and seemed to take in a deep breath. Smelling, no doubt. He was a hunter, and something had clearly triggered his instincts. That she knew it was her—while he didn't—gave her a small thrill of satisfaction.

His behavior only lasted a moment.

Not long enough to be noticed by anyone around him. He seemed to dismiss it as he continued toward his truck.

Emily waited as the old truck pulled past her before she started her car. She wouldn't have much trouble following the truck since it was white with a big orange stripe down the side, and something in the engine knocked loudly.

Using the rush of workers as cover, she pulled into the flow of traffic almost a block behind him. She was comfortably hidden by the vehicles through town, but every few blocks more people turned down side streets, slowly dwindling her cover until there was no one left to act as a buffer. His blinker indicated a left turn onto a country road, and Emily quickly decided to go straight through the four-way stop instead of following him directly.

She was so close.

She crossed through the intersection and turned her car back around as soon as he was out of sight. With a deep breath to calm her jangling nerves, she turned onto the country road he'd taken and began to follow the cloud of dust left in the wake of the ancient truck.

It was even easier than she expected since the old gravel road gave her nearly half a mile worth of dust cloud, which was plenty of distance to go unnoticed and acted as a perfect cover. It wasn't a long drive, maybe fifteen minutes at most, but it seemed like forever to her.

She passed by the property he pulled into without even slowing down. It only took a glance for her to mentally map out the lay of the land. Two buildings stood apart by maybe two hundred feet. One was an old farm-style house, run down, with peeling paint and at least one broken window covered with plywood. The other structure looked like a large yellow workshop-style metal building. It appeared much newer than the house itself and was in better repair.

What worried her was the number of vehicles in the driveway. Counting the old truck she followed, there were five in total. The number suggested there might be a lot more people there than she was prepared for.

Her original plan was to wait until tomorrow when he'd be back at work and Amber might be alone. But with so many vehicles present she had to rethink quickly. Either something was happening—which certainly didn't bode well for Amber—or there were always people there.

In case it was the former, she quickly decided to go ahead and get Amber out today, now, before it was too late. If she made it this far, and got this close, only to have Amber die at the hands of her captor on the eve of her rescue, she'd never be able to live with herself. If her sister was in that house, she was either going to get her out tonight or die trying.

Just under a mile from the house, she pulled her rented car onto a service road and parked. She saved the coordinates on her phone and turned it to silent before she slid it into her back pocket, then closed her eyes for a moment to gather her courage. Nothing was going to stop her from finding Amber. Since the police had already proven they had no intention of helping, she was on her own.

Her new plan was simple. Find Amber and get them both out undetected. She had no delusions of grandeur. It wasn't like she was She-Man the Warrior Woman. She tipped the scale at a whopping one hundred and forty pounds—much of it muscle, she told herself firmly—and she had no chance of taking on a werewolf, though she had come prepared, just in case.

She opened her eyes, pulled her gun out of the glovebox, and slid it into the waistband of her pants. In her front pocket was a gaudy silver cross necklace covered in rhinestones of all colors. Her other pocket held an extra clip of silver bullets. She'd acquired a small bullet-loading machine to design her own ammunition and made a surplus in preparation.

When she had everything she thought she might need, she took a final deep, resolved breath and left the relative safety of her car. It was only a few steps to cross the road and get into the line of trees on the other side. It wouldn't do for her to come walking up the road and give them plenty of time to prepare for her arrival. With luck, she could sneak up to the house and look in the windows unnoticed until she found Amber, then smuggle her out with no one the wiser. Maybe extra people was a good thing, she decided while she made her way toward the house. Maybe it would keep Amber's captor distracted while she mounted a rescue.

If the car ride following the leader had seemed long, the walk toward the house seemed like eternity. Every breaking twig, every movement from the corner of her eye put her more and more on edge until she was such a tight bundle of nerves that if a butterfly brushed her arm, she might just scream in terror.

Somewhere, she'd heard that real courage meant being afraid and doing something anyway. With that in mind, she decided she was the bravest woman on the planet. Now, if she could just get her knees to stop knocking, she might be able to sell herself a little more on her courage.

With trembling fingers, she touched the gun in her waistband. The metal was cold and comforting. A class on firearms and countless hours at the range meant she knew how to use it.

She wasn't helpless.

She pressed her back against the rough bark of a tree and took a few deep breaths to slow the rapid rhythm of her heart. Once she felt her nerve a little more steeled, she searched the house across from her. No movement indicated alarm. A window sat facing her, and she decided it was as good a place to start as any.

Head down in determination, she pushed off from the tree and headed toward that window at a dead run. When she arrived at her destination, she didn't even pause to breathe. Who needed to breathe with so much fear in their veins?

She stood on tiptoes and peered into the room. It was a dark space with very little furniture except for a bed with a bare mattress in poor repair in one corner and a plastic dresser beside it. No sign of Amber.

A quick look around showed no sign of anyone coming her way. She slid down the house to the next window and found a similar empty space, then the next one. She waited beside the glass for a moment, straining to hear any sound from the room.

There was something.

It was a sound she couldn't quite place. Not a voice, exactly, but a soft whimper came again and again.

Amber.

Emily slowly leaned over just far enough to see in the room. It was furnished much like the other ones had been, with cheap furniture. On the bed she could make out a shape that could only be her missing sister.

A jolt of excitement flew through her.

She tapped on the window, trying to get the person's attention. But the figure never moved. Thinking she may have been drugged, Emily tried the window. It was old, and the frame had years of paint layers holding it down. With her nearly frantic fingers, she was able to pry it lose after a few attempts.

It didn't open quietly, however.

Giving a screech that sounded louder than a gunshot to Emily's ears, the window reluctantly slid on the track. She didn't consider the danger as she wriggled through the small opening. Not until her feet hit the uneven wooden floor and a hand clamped around her mouth from behind.

CHAPTER 2

William sat at the butcher-block table in the small kitchen of the house he shared with Paoli. He stared at the paper before him—scripted in Paoli's neat handwriting—with open surprise. On the page was a single name and species along with location.

"Are you sure this is right?" William frowned at the paper.

"It's right," Paoli confirmed without even glancing at him on his way past.

"When was the last time we had a female were-wolf?" William raised a skeptical brow, and his gaze followed Paoli around the table.

"It's rare they're marked," Paoli agreed. "But it happens."

He took the chair across from William and propped his bare feet on the edge of the table for no reason other than it bugged William.

Paoli was one of the oldest vampires William had ever met and by far the least conspicuous. He stood only about an inch shorter than William himself, which put him just shy of six feet. Where William's hair was raven and cropped short, Paoli's was a dark blond and long enough to rest on his shoulders. He had none of the dark characteristics a person would usually associate with a vampire—especially a vampire as old as he was. Instead of being intimidating and tortured, Paoli was always the first to laugh and the last to take anything—including himself—seriously. He had a lighthearted and fun-loving nature that kept him very popular with the opposite sex, which—according to Paoli—accounted for his light-hearted nature.

"We haven't had one in the last . . . what, hundred years?" William reached out and flicked the end of Paoli's toe hard enough to send an electric jolt of pain halfway up his leg.

Paoli howled and snatched his foot back. Humor glittered in his eyes as he cradled the injury. "Now that just wasn't nice," he proclaimed.

"Keep your nasty feet off the table." William gave him a pointed stare. "If we're going after a female wolf, you need to focus. She probably has a whole pack surrounding her. You'll have to help this time. It's going to be dangerous."

Paoli gave him an impish grin and folded his legs neatly under him before he offered an indifferent shrug. "I don't mind hunting werewolves," he said offhandedly. "It's the vampires that give me the creeps."

William shook his head at the irony of that statement. "How can vampires give you the creeps? You *are* a vampire."

"Not that kind of vampire," Paoli shuddered dramatically.

"Sorry, I forgot. You're a *nice* vampire," William said with a derisive snort.

Paoli ignored the slightly mocking tone.

"That's right," he confirmed. "I'm like a mosquito. I take just what I need to survive and don't kill anyone."

William gave him a look.

"It's more than you can say," Paoli pointed out.

"I'm not a vampire," William reminded him.

"You're not completely vampire, but close enough to be forgiven for that," Paoli said. "Everyone has their own struggle in this world."

"What's your struggle?" William wanted to know.

Paoli scoffed.

"You think it's easy being your conscience? Or this good looking?" he asked with a waggle of his eyebrows.

"Or that humble," William added under his breath. He tapped the paper in front of him to redirect Paoli to the matter at hand. "We'll have to use stealth," he mused.

"They'll never know I'm there." Paoli moved his arms in his best ninja imitation.

"Do you know anything about the pack?" William asked thoughtfully.

A female wolf being condemned was all but unheard of. Normally, the pack defended them so they had no need to spill blood except the monthly animal hunt. Which all but eliminated the chances of them losing their humanity and being condemned. Hell, they *were* the humanity in a pack.

"What's on the paper is all I know," said Paoli as he stood back up and headed for the fridge across the room.

William leaned back and sat silent for several moments, thinking.

"Are you sure we should do this tonight? It's a full moon and this place is almost a two-hour drive from here." William didn't mention he had plans for a full moon run himself.

"Where are wolves during a full moon?" Paoli asked over his shoulder, his head in the fridge. He grabbed a bag of red liquid and tore open the top. He poured it into a mug before throwing a questioning look at William.

"Two for me," William answered absently while he considered the question. "Wolves hunt during the full moon."

It was a piece of common knowledge that werewolves were at least partially controlled by the moon. Even he could feel its pull.

Paoli finished pouring more liquid into a second mug and set them both in the microwave to warm. "Exactly," he said finally.

"Which means this might be a good chance to get her alone," William concluded slowly, trying to make sense of Paoli's logic.

"Maybe not alone, but at least not as well guarded as usual." He waited until the microwave dinged, then grabbed both mugs.

He set one down in front of William before re-claiming his seat.

William took a drink and savored the flavor as the liquid warmed him. It might not be as good as it was fresh, but at least it came without the guilt. And without the nagging from his conscience across the table.

For the next thirty minutes, they discussed strategy and alternate strategy in case they found themselves with more opponents than expected. Several plans were made, depending on whether their target hunted with the pack or waited somewhere else. Eventually, William was satisfied they had a plan for each possible scenario.

They loaded the car down with the usual cache of weapons, making especially sure they had plenty of silver-tipped ammunition. From personal experience, William knew the crippling agony of silver. No immortal could fight with the pain searing through their veins, which was why he used it when he was forced to play his role of executioner. Nothing took the fight out of immortals like a silver-based injury.

Finally, he turned his phone off—grateful for an excuse to power down the bright screen—and headed for their target. He hated cell phones. It was far too easy to track them. And he always worried about having his on him when hunting. It would be just his luck for the annoying device to start beeping and give away his position at the wrong moment. While dying wouldn't bother him, he didn't want it to be because of something like that. He wanted a real death; a warrior's end. Dying in battle was an honorable and proud thing. Dying from sheer stupidity was just embarrassing.

William killed the lights and pulled off the road and into a clearing. It was a decent-sized area; clear of trees but full of holes and uneven ground, which made it less than ideal for driving—a fact he only realized once they were halfway in. Any high-grass area could easily conceal a hidden stump or deep rut, though they were fortunate enough not to find one.

Their hiding spot was just over a mile from the farmhouse that acted as home to the pack. There was no way to know which direction the wolves had gone to hunt, but there was no sign of them there, so it was the safest place to start. They got out of the car cautiously and closed the doors slowly to keep them from making any sound.

The house they were headed to was surrounded by corn fields on three sides—all thankfully late to be harvested—which gave them the luxury of cover they hadn't expected.

Paoli breathed an audible sigh of relief as they silently started to make their way through the field at the back of the property, moving carefully through the corn to avoid giving away their presence. Recent rains had made the ground soggy, which meant their every step made a slight sucking noise. Light from the shining moon spilled across the land, casting eerie shadows and making the corn look like silent sentries.

"I don't care what anyone says," Paoli whispered, ducking to avoid a stray leaf that seemed to be reaching for him. "Corn is a seriously creepy vegetable."

William stopped, motioned aggressively for him to be silent, and gave him a look that threatened violence.

Paoli raised his hands in mock surrender and mouthed 'sorry.'

William continued to glare at him another minute.

Paoli needed to understand the severity of the situation they were in. Wolves had excellent hearing, and the last thing they needed was for his big mouth to give them away. There was no telling how many wolves might be around, and it was important they have the element of surprise if they were going to get the execution done and get out with minimal incident. William might be an excellent fighter, but even *he* wasn't capable of taking on an entire pack of wolves.

William was still glaring at Paoli when a smell caught his attention. It was very faint at first, like a whisper.

A promise.

It was there for only a second, then gone.

His head snapped around, and something inside him became very alert.

"What's wrong?" Paoli whispered, closing the distance between them to stand at his side.

"Did you smell that?" William closed his eyes and inhaled, chasing the elusive scent. It was gone, and he couldn't pick it back up.

Paoli gave him a look, then sniffed and shook his head.

"I don't smell anything," he said.

William stood for another moment without moving a muscle. He used all his senses, but he couldn't identify a danger anywhere. There were no scents in the immediate area except the two of them and the corn.

Besides, it hadn't smelled dangerous.

It smelled . . . good.

Comforting, somehow.

Confusion edged his every step when they resumed their advance. There was something so familiar about the smell, and yet not. Almost like a memory playing on the edge of his mind that he just couldn't bring into focus. It drove everything else out of his immediate concentration.

He was aware of Paoli watching him with concerned eyes, but he had no explanation to offer, so he ignored it and continued forward. They had a job to do. No matter what else was happening, he needed to remember the job. Somewhere nearby was a female wolf with a sentence of death. He had to get his focus back on that before his fractured concentration led both he and Paoli into trouble.

Just a few more steps brought the scent again, stronger this time. He breathed in the subtle aroma, trying to figure out why it had such an alluring effect on him.

"Are you seriously telling me you don't smell that?" he hissed at Paoli.

Paoli frowned, his face growing even more concerned. With his eyes still on William, he breathed in the night air very slowly. After a few seconds, he shook his head and gave William a look of mixed confusion and annoyance.

"I don't smell it," Paoli said a little defensively. "I'm a vampire. My sense of smell isn't as good as yours. What does it smell like?"

Peace. Joy.

"I don't know how to describe it." William took another lungful of air. "But it's different than anything I've ever scented."

Better. More.

"I don't like this," Paoli said, his eyebrows drawn together in worry. "Maybe we should come back tomorrow and try again. This is dangerous enough without something unknown complicating it further."

"Tomorrow won't be a full moon," William pointed out. "This may be the best chance we'll have for a month. Do you really want to wait that long?" He gave Paoli his full attention and raised one sardonic brow.

"Don't look at me like that," Paoli said with as much attitude as he could manage at a whisper. "Better to wait a month than walk into a trap. I don't want to turn to dust at sunrise and blow away after they kill us. Well," he added offhandedly. "I'd blow away in the sun. There's no telling what'll happen to you."

William would have conceded his point, but there was something about the scent that called to him in a visceral way. It brought out a need to . . . protect. Guard. Provide. There was no hint of malice.

"This doesn't give me the impression of danger," he said.

He hoped his voice didn't sound as befuddled as he felt. What was happening?

He began to move again. Paoli was still watching him closely, but he couldn't bring himself to care. He just needed to find the source of the unusual smell. It seemed to leech into his mind and push out everything else. His mission was all but forgotten. He let his nose guide him on toward the house, Paoli following closely behind.

After what seemed like forever, they broke through the last row of corn and were near enough to the farmhouse for an unobstructed view.

Without warning, the scent seemed to saturate him like honey. As if a spell had been cast, it dragged the instincts of his beast forward. All capacity for the tight reign of control he fought to hold on to was gone. Paoli was talking, but none of his words penetrated the blind fog in William's mind. There was nothing in the entire world but that smell and the unknown promise behind it.

"William?" Paoli's voice was hesitant and questioning. "What is it?"

His gaze darted in all directions, as if expecting to see wolves descending from somewhere. There was nothing.

William barely responded at all, and when Paoli gripped his arm, the eyes that snapped toward him were liquid gold and hungry. William was no longer in control.

"Oh no!" Paoli exclaimed. "This is not the time to go all wolfy. You have to fight it before you get us both killed!" His voice was a tight hiss.

Without a word, William jerked away and flew toward the house, leaving Paoli no choice but to follow. He gave a loud, strangled groan and stayed right on William's heels.

William knew only a fool would rush in this way, but he was helpless to stop himself. His body trembled with the effort he put into fighting the compulsion, but he could barely even manage to slow down.

Old wood creaked as he stepped onto the back porch, but all he heard was the female scream from inside.

He tore through the back door of the dilapidated house like a crazed animal. Not for a second did he stop to consider what he was doing. He was beyond rational thought, the beast within having taken complete control for the first time in years. He located the origin of the scent immediately.

It was coming from a small woman who stood in the doorway of a hidden room, blocking the entry. In front of her was a large man with shaggy blond hair clad only in dark jeans. He held her arms in a painful grip and pulled her forward so far she was on her tiptoes. William's nose instantly marked him for what he was.

Werewolf.

CHAPTER 3

Emily was doomed. She was aware of the fact with a quiet acceptance. Surprisingly enough, it left her with no fear. The man who'd grabbed her when she managed to get into the room with Amber was named Brian.

He was the one she'd followed here, to her place of doom.

He was also the one who held her now and had pulled her so close to his face the acrid stench of his unwashed body and bacteria-laden breath assaulted her nose.

She met his turbulent gaze levelly, refusing to be cowed by him. If she was to die at his hands, she'd do it with a brave face.

If she had just a pinch more courage, she would have spit at him. But evidently, her courage tapped out after one yell of "let me go." Now the best she could manage was a level stare. Oh well, she decided. At least he wouldn't get the satisfaction of seeing her crumble at his feet in terror. It may have been a minor victory, but a victory nonetheless.

A sound from beside them changed everything. The back door flew open with enough force to slam into the wall with an ear-splitting crash. The only light in the room was a bare bulb hanging from its electric wires, and it was sent swinging, throwing dancing shadows across everything.

Emily's attention snapped over to see what the commotion was, and she found two men standing the doorway, framed by the aged wood. At first, she could only make out their silhouettes in the darkness, and a hint of features as the light swung their way. Then they moved more fully into the room, and she got a clear view of them.

One was very nice looking, with long, blondish hair caught up at the nape of his neck. The other one was the most striking man she'd ever laid eyes on. His hair was inky black and cropped in a short, careless style. His face was rugged and strong with a long, straight nose over his wide slash of lips. His eyes were an amazing shade of gold, and just now they sparkled with the dark promise of death.

Almost too fast to follow his movements, the dark-haired man crossed the room with its crumbling plaster walls and stood behind her captor with two curved, ornate hand sickles already in his hands. The soft ringing of metal resounded as he swung with expert precision, not even brushing her hair with his blades while he decapitated her tormenter.

The head that had just been level with hers went one direction, while the hands gripping her arms fell away and the body toppled to the floor on her other side.

Her mouth fell open in stunned horror, then clamped firmly shut again as she was sprayed with blood.

For William, his blind rage dissipated almost immediately when he gazed into her wide eyes, as purple as the dawn. Her face—now splattered with blood—was paralyzed in shock, but she was perfect.

In an instant, the beast relinquished control. For the first time in his entire life, it seemed to sleep, leaving him with a feeling of control and calm serenity. Everything in the world was right, and there was nothing but the two of them, frozen in a timeless moment. It could have been seconds, or hours. He stared at her in awe, both amazed and confused by his reaction to her.

He could smell the level of her fear, but until he killed the werewolf, she'd shown no outward sign of it. Almost like it was a normal thing for a human—and his nose told him she *was* human—to be standing in the middle of a houseful of monsters under a full moon.

Yep, just another mundane day.

Her features were gentle, with high cheeks and a small nose with a slight curve at the tip, set above a perfectly bow-shaped pair of lush, full lips. Her square chin jutted defiantly forward, despite the situation and the fear she couldn't hide from his astute nose. With her exotic eyes and the wavy dark hair that bounced halfway down her back, she looked almost like a vampire herself.

"William, we're not alone in here," Paoli's voice intruded, pulling William's attention to the werewolves pouring in from three doorways to partially surround them. Paoli pulled his blade, clearly prepared to fight their way out.

William groaned inwardly. There was only one reason the wolves would have abandoned a hunt and returned together. The newly decapitated man must have been their alpha.

Of course he was, he thought wryly.

They were going to have a hard time explaining that one later. If—that was—they survived for there to *be* a later.

"William!" Paoli barked sharply when William remained still.

There was a small swishing sound as Paoli's small sword found its mark on the first wolf to rush him.

It was the slight edge in Paoli's voice that finally snapped William back to himself.

In one swift movement, William stepped protectively in front of Paoli and the girl. He swung first one blade, then the other with almost lightning speed and the deadly accuracy of centuries of experience. One werewolf fell at his feet, not yet dead, but mortally wounded from the gaping hole in his throat. The other took the bite of William's blade and spun away, splashing both William and the wall with blood before he slid to the rickety wooden floor and was silent.

Still more wolves kept coming, and William realized they were about to be too outnumbered to hold their ground.

For just a second, he stood completely motionless in the chaos and closed his eyes to feel the energy of those in the room.

Most of the wolves were new and weak, with a few dominants scattered in the mix. None anywhere near as dominant as he. Then again, he had yet to encounter one who was.

"Paoli, bring the girl," he commanded, his voice already low and rough with the stress of the coming change.

Then he burst free of his human form. In a flash, he practically exploded. He went from being a man to a gray wolf about half the size of a small car. His massive form filled the room, and his sheer power sizzled like electricity, making the air feel heavy and charged.

One by one, the werewolves backed up nervously. A few bowed their heads slightly in a classic submissive pose.

William held his head low, long teeth bared. A deep, continuous growl rumbled from his chest.

A warning.

A challenge.

He maintained eye contact with the other wolves in turn, forcing them to feel the power of his dominance. His sheer will, and his willingness to kill them all.

"He's a werewolf?" Emily gasped incredulously, staring at the biggest furred creature she'd ever seen.

She wasn't sure why it hit her with such shock, all things considered, but she hadn't been prepared for that. Something in his eyes when he'd looked at her made her think he was the good guy. Not another monster. But she was seeing the truth for herself, and it made her feel almost . . . betrayed.

"Nothing so simple," the blond man said.

He gave her a friendly smile and held his hand out in an old-fashioned gesture, as though helping a lady of old into a carriage.

"Shall we?"

She hesitated, staring at his outstretched hand without making a move to take it. Her eyes darted back and forth between him, the giant wolf, and their surroundings.

Monsters or not, these two were definitely a better gamble than her current circumstances.

Still, she'd come here for a reason. She wasn't about to leave without Amber now.

"I can't leave without my sister," she said finally, the slightest crack in her voice.

He stared at her blankly.

"Excuse me?" he said in disbelief, as though he may have heard her wrong.

"I'm not leaving this house without my sister," she repeated with more force, squaring her shoulders.

"This really isn't a good time for negotiation." He waved an arm pointedly to encompass the room and all its inhabitants.

"I'm sorry," she said quickly.

She really was. But there was no way she could walk away and leave Amber to her fate.

"I'm not trying to be difficult. But I can't leave without her," she said.

She didn't know what she'd do if he shrugged and wished her the best. But, if she left with them and didn't take Amber, the guilt would eat her alive.

After staring at her another minute, he finally closed his eyes and gave an exasperated groan.

"Where is she?" he asked in a resigned tone, as though doing so caused him physical pain.

Emily's heart gave an excited leap at the surrender in his voice. She turned toward the room at her back.

"In here," she said, leading him through the doorway.

He followed her closely but stopped short when they entered the room. It was small, lit only by the streaks of moonlight through the window, and was empty except for the narrow bed in the corner.

Lying atop the blankets was Amber, flashing back and forth between human and wolf forms. For a split second, she was in human form and let out a soft cry, then the sound merged with an animal whine as she shifted to wolf. It was almost like she was short circuiting.

The man watched in silence for a while, his expression horrified.

"She's condemned," he said finally, his voice apologetic.

"There must be a way to help her," Emily said, her voice edged with desperation she couldn't quite banish.

"It doesn't matter. She's marked for execution," he said.

He produced a small dagger and stepped toward the bed. Moonlight spilled across the blade and made it clear what he planned.

"No!" Emily cried, putting herself between him and Amber.

Her heart was in her throat, and her gaze flicked back and forth between his face and the knife in his hand.

He stopped and looked at her, a note of impatience in his eyes.

"He can't hold them forever," he said, jerking his head toward the door, indicating the power play in the next room. "Time is of the essence."

Impotent tears sprang to Emily's eyes, but she ignored them. She met his gaze unwaveringly.

"I didn't come here tonight to watch her die. I won't let you hurt her," she said.

Even with the tears in her eyes, her voice was level and determined.

"Please," she added with a touch of desperation. "She's my sister."

"An order was given against her life," he pointed out reasonably. "Besides, look at her. She's in pain." His voice was gentle and persuasive.

"I won't accept her death. Not after . . ." Emily's words trailed off and she took a deep, steadying breath.

Not when she was this close to saving her, after so much time.

"There has to be a way to fix it. Please help me get her out of here." She paused, then added, "Alive."

The growl in the next room grew stronger and more dangerous, which seemed to make up his mind.

"You can take this up with William," he said.

He sheathed his knife irritably, then crossed the room with quick strides.

"There's no time to spend arguing with you," he said.

He lifted Amber from the bed in one arm.

Emily breathed a sigh of relief, but he strode past her and toward the door with a doubtful shake of his head.

"Let's see if you think it's such a good thing after you face *him* on this," he warned darkly.

Back in the main room, the wolves continued to ring the huge one in the center, but they didn't appear any closer to him than when they'd left.

Emily watched as the man carried Amber to the large wolf and threw her across his broad back. When the wolf rewarded him with a low growl, he growled back in clear frustration.

"The other one wouldn't come without her," he snapped. "And I'm *not* getting in the middle of this one."

Emily stiffened her spine while he got Amber situated. She made her way along the wall to the dead man on the floor, keeping her eyes firmly on the wolves. Her gun protruded from the waistband of the dead man's pants, and she wanted it back. With everything happening around her, she had a feeling it would come in handy.

Careful not to look at the gory stump where his head should have been, she knelt down beside the body. With her face twisted in a grimace, she pulled the gun free and stuffed it into her own waistband. She tried to hide a shudder when she got back to her feet and headed toward the others, careful not to move too fast and look like she was fleeing.

"Don't fire that gun in here. The sound will deafen him," the man warned when she stepped beside him.

She started to nod in understanding, but without so much as a warning, he threw her atop the wolf's broad back behind Amber, a bit unceremoniously. She grabbed at the fur to keep from flying off the other side and threw him a dirty look, which he ignored.

"Sorry," she whispered into the nearest furry ear, then scooted up as far as she could manage to make room for the man.

He gave her a slight smile and shook his head.

"I have my own way," he said cryptically. "Just don't be afraid of me. If it bothers you, don't look."

With those words, he seemed to dissolve into a thick stack of black fog. His face peered from the center and took on a horrifying, almost demonic appearance with glowing red eyes and elongated features made of the same fog.

Emily opened her mouth in a silent scream, but the only sound that emerged was an almost inaudible squeak.

"Don't look," he commanded, his voice sounding like a haunted howl of wind. "Hold on tight," he cautioned as the group barreled through the line of werewolves and into the night.

CHAPTER 4

Emily gripped with her knees and buried one hand deep into the thick pelt to keep herself from falling off. Her other hand was clamped around Amber's ever-changing waist in a desperate effort to keep her upright so Emily could use her body as a brace. It was sort of like the world's most dangerous juggling act, with the threat of certain death if any of her body parts gave out too soon.

Her thighs began to shake with the effort of holding on, but the sound of howls closing in as the wolves gave chase seemed to lend her exhausted muscles the strength she needed.

When the massive wolf came to a sudden halt, she nearly flipped over his head. She was only saved by the appearance of strong hands on her waist. She jerked away in surprise and turned to find the blond man standing beside her, a *man* again.

With reluctance and a wary look, she allowed him to pull Amber down. It was only when she saw him move toward it that she realized they were standing right beside a gray car. It was nothing impressive, just a plain sedan. But right then, it looked like a haven to her.

"Come on," the man ordered, stuffing Amber into the backseat and following her in.

Emily had no idea how close the wolves chasing them were, and she had no intention of waiting around to find out. She swung her leg over the wolf's head and slid to the ground.

The force of her landing brought her to her hands and knees in the mud, but she was scrambling toward the car even before she had fully settled onto her feet.

She jerked the passenger door open at almost the exact same time the dark-haired man opened the driver's door. With a start, she looked back to where the wolf had just been standing a moment ago. Of course, it was gone.

She knew it would be, since the man on the other side of the car *was* the wolf, but she couldn't imagine how he'd gotten back into human form, fully dressed, and around to the driver's side in the time it took her to stand up.

"Get in," he commanded with his rich baritone voice, following his own advice.

She didn't need to be told again. Even though she had a weird feeling she was sealing her own fate, she leapt in and slammed the door firmly as the engine fired to life.

"Hold on," the dark-haired man advised as the car began speeding in reverse, mud and rocks flying as it spun back onto a dark road.

Through her window, she watched the pack break through the corn right behind them.

She swallowed hard.

One of the wolves was close enough she could have reached out and touched it if she wanted.

She did not.

She was slammed back against her seat as the car shifted into drive, and the distance between them and their pursuers began to grow rapidly. In the matter of a few seconds, the wolves were no longer visible. They were left far enough behind to be nothing more than an unpleasant memory.

Still, Emily stared through the window at the darkness in silence, afraid to believe it was actually over.

"I'm William," the dark-haired man said, breaking into her musing and reminding her she hadn't escaped *all* the monsters yet.

She turned toward him slowly. His arm that was nearest to her had scars that ran from his wrist all the way up until they disappeared under his sleeve. They were too numerous to count and created a strange crisscross pattern across the muscles and skin.

"That's Paoli," William said, inclining his head toward the backseat.

"I'm Emily," she heard herself say in a voice that was shocky and hollow. She cleared her throat nervously before continuing. "That's my twin sister, Amber." It was her turn to motion her head toward the backseat.

"Well, that could *not* have gone more differently than I expected," Paoli suddenly piped up. "Can you please explain what the hell happened back there?"

He scooted forward and perched both arms on the seats in front of him, his head right between the front passengers.

Emily shrank back against her door to keep as much space between herself and Paoli as possible. She had a strong suspicion she knew what he was and wanted him nowhere near her neck.

With a quick glance at her, William answered the question. "I don't know."

"You don't know?" Paoli repeated, his voice incredulous. "I've never seen you so out of control in an execution. You barreled into that house without paying any attention to what you were getting into . . . getting *us* into."

"I am well aware," William said in a tone that clearly meant "drop it."

Paoli watched William for a moment. Then his irritation disappeared, and a much more concerning look sparkled in his eyes.

Mischief.

Without warning, Paoli's attention turned to Emily, and he gave her a boyish smile.

"You said you were twins?" he asked in a voice that was too innocent to be believable.

"Yes," Emily said. "Fraternal, not identical. Obviously."

"Delightful. Now that we're all acquainted, could you look at my eyes for a second and tell me what you see?" Paoli asked, leaning toward her.

"No!" William cried, but it was too late.

The instant Emily looked into the depths of Paoli's gaze, she was lost. Her eyes glazed over, and her posture went relaxed.

Paoli waved his hand in front of her face and got no reaction.

"I just love that," he said with a chuckle, turning to face William. "It's the simple things that make life worth living, don't you think?"

"I think you better release her before I help you shuffle off your immortal coil," William said, surprising himself with the fierceness of his own reaction.

Paoli hadn't harmed her, he knew. But for some reason, her being under the power of someone else triggered the rage in his wolf.

Paoli gave a surprised smile to his would-be attacker.

"Oh, relax," he said, rolling his eyes. "It's not like I'm going to make her cluck like a chicken or anything. You know I don't like to treat humans like meat puppets."

"Then release her," William demanded.

"After we talk," Paoli agreed, ignoring William's dark tone. "What's the deal with this woman?"

William looked at Paoli, then away.

Silence stretched out while he considered the question. The truth was, he couldn't explain it. It wasn't something he knew how to put into words. It was more about feelings and instincts than logic.

He glanced toward Emily and looked at her, long and hard. There was no denying she was beautiful. But he'd known many beautiful women in his long life.

This was different.

More.

It wasn't about sex. He hesitated, his gaze drifting over the curve of her throat to the outline of her full breasts, straining against the material of her shirt. Her creamy skin looked satin soft. He turned his attention back to the road and cleared his suddenly dry throat.

Well, he couldn't deny he wanted her in that way, too. But it was more than that.

"I just need . . ." he trailed off and shook his head, unable to find the words. "I don't know."

Paoli looked at him with a frown. "You've never had a human in your company for anything good. Tell me you didn't bring her for a midnight snack."

"I don't know why I brought her," William said defensively.

Except that he couldn't have left her if he'd wanted to.

"If you just risked both our lives because you're feeling peckish, I'm going to knock you in the head. I won't sit back and watch you kill an innocent woman. Humans have value, remember?" Paoli demanded, and what promised to be a full-blown rage began to gather steam.

The very idea of her death left William with a cold knot in his stomach.

"I'm not going to hurt her," he said with certainty.

"Are you serious?" Paoli's tone was clearly skeptical. "You aren't exactly known for your control when it comes to humans. I hate to point out your history, but your record isn't exactly good."

William couldn't argue with that. "This one's different."

"Why?" Paoli asked doggedly, watching him as if trying to ferret out something he wasn't saying.

"I don't know," William said in exasperation.

Leave it to Paoli to never stop asking questions.

"You better figure it out, and fast. We've now stolen a woman from a pack of werewolves and kidnapped a woman we were supposed to execute. This is getting messy in a hurry. When the Coven finds out—" He shook his head. "I don't even want to *think* about it. Maybe we should just finish the job we were ordered to do. Then you can figure out what the deal is with the other one." He pointed to the woman in the backseat. "I mean, look at her."

Instead, William looked past Paoli to Emily. He considered Paoli's suggestion and quickly discarded it. If she woke from the trance to learn they'd killed her sister, she'd be crushed. She'd never forgive him.

"No," he said firmly.

Paoli gave a deep, frustrated groan and threw himself back against his seat.

"All right, but if it comes down to her or me, I'll kill her myself," he warned. "It'd be doing her a favor, if you ask me."

"It won't come to that," William promised.

"It must be nice to be so sure," Paoli said, his voice dripping in sarcasm. "This is the Coven we're talking about, remember? The immortal government. The ones who *own* us. They aren't going to be forgiving about their orders being ignored."

Having his own concerns voiced aloud made William's temper flare.

"You think I don't know that?" he demanded impatiently. "You just have to find something to stop the shift. Then we might be able to get the sentence rescinded."

Paoli slid forward so that his head was level with William's again and stared at him, mouth open.

"That's a big *maybe*," he said with a scoff. "And what do you mean by *I* have to find something?"

It was William's turn for a frustrated groan. "You have a ton of herbs in your damn fortune-telling shop—"

"New-age bookstore, thank you," Paoli corrected matter of factly.

"Fine," William conceded irritably. "New-age bookstore." He looked at Paoli pointedly. "There must be something in there that can help."

Paoli was quiet for a minute.

"I hadn't thought about that," he admitted. "And I'm not saying it's a bad idea."

His voice was thoughtful, his brow furrowed in a look of consideration.

"I have books on every herb and healing plant. It's possible there might be something in there. But even if we stop the shift—" He paused and looked at William. "And that's a big *if*, mind you," he said, before he gestured to the woman in question. "She's still marked for death, and we still failed to follow an order."

Paoli was right. As much as he hated to admit it, the Coven didn't tend to take individual situations into consideration. Even if they managed the impossible and found a way to reverse the change, there was no guarantee the Coven would care. An order had been given, and the Coven tended to see in black and white.

"Then we can take her to the Coven and ask them to reconsider," William said.

It was the only chance they had.

"Are you serious?" Paoli gasped. "You want to walk right into the belly of the beast? You know how they feel about you."

William did know how the Coven felt about him. But there was no other way.

"It's been centuries," he said, remembering the last time he went before the Coven.

It had been after a human kill he wasn't exactly . . . discreet about.

"But we have to try." He glanced at Emily again, unable to stop himself.

Paoli followed his gaze and gave a loud huff.

"You've been near this woman for half an hour, and you're ready to risk the wrath of the Coven for her? What if she's bait for some trap?" Paoli said.

"I don't think so," William said confidently.

His wolf would have smelled a trap.

"Well, let's wake her up and ask her," Paoli returned haughtily.

"Let me do the talking," William ordered.

Paoli made a rude noise, flipped him the bird, then snapped his fingers and waved his hand in front of Emily's eyes, breaking the hypnosis.

Most people came around drowsy and disorient-ed. She surprised them both.

CHAPTER 5

Emily had read everything she could get her hands on about the world her sister disappeared into in the months she'd been missing. While perhaps not a full-blown expert, not a lot of people knew as much about the legendary creatures of the night as she did. Therefore, as soon as her mind cleared, she knew exactly what had been done to her.

She'd been enthralled . . . by a vampire.

They were the only creatures capable of such an act.

She'd been right about Paoli.

He was an honest-to-God blood sucking vampire.

Not really alive, but not dead.

He was undead.

There was no telling how many innocent people he'd killed.

Well, she wasn't about to be added to his numbers.

Without giving a single warning, she jerked the gaudy silver cross from her pocket and shoved it against his forehead.

Paoli let out a howl of shock and pain. His face contorted demonically, his features twisting into a horrifying mask. He was no longer remotely handsome. Instead, he looked like something right out of a nightmare. His eyes were wide and gleaming with a red light, his mouth open in a scream, revealing the length of very long, white fangs.

Emily stared at those fangs in morbid fascination, unable to look away. She wondered that she hadn't noticed them before.

Had he sunk them into her while she was unaware?

Just the thought enraged her further.

When he shrank into the back seat, she stayed with him, climbing over the armrest of the car to maintain the contact.

She was no one's victim.

William grabbed her arm and pulled her away from Paoli even as he maneuvered the car off the side of the road.

Just before they came to a stop, Emily jerked her arm free and jumped through the door in a flash.

With an uttered oath, William threw the car into park and leaped from the driver's side to give chase. His vision was perfect at night, and he had no trouble locating her, though she was moving faster than he'd ever seen a human go. Annoyance warred with respect as he made three leaping steps to land directly in her path.

Emily almost ran right into him.

One moment, she was running for her life—her heart hammering so hard she could scarcely breathe—but sure she could use the cover of trees to escape the horrible death they had planned for her.

The next moment, he was right in front of her, just appearing out of the dark like an apparition. She came to a stop so suddenly her legs slid out from under her and she landed on her backside right at his feet with a painful thump that knocked the breath right out of her.

Before she could scramble away, a massively strong arm picked her up, and she found her back pinned against his large chest while her legs dangled off the ground. His arm was firmly locked just under her breasts, and she was well and truly trapped.

Panic lent her strength.

She kicked for his shins and swung her head backward just like they taught her in self-defense class, hoping to make contact with his nose. Her instructor would have been proud. She screamed and snapped her teeth toward his arm like a wild piranha, determined to take a chunk of flesh.

If her dead body was to be discovered here, she wanted to die knowing she'd inflicted damage, at the very least.

Meanwhile, William held her fast, fighting his own battle as he waited patiently for her to wear herself out.

Her hair flew in his face, saturating him with her wonderful scent. It surrounded him and drew him in. Nothing had ever smelled so wonderful, so tempting. Her squirming was enough to test his control in other ways, so he was trapped in a torturous hell of desires and needs.

It had been so long since he'd had a woman, or even any interest in one. Now, the years of celibacy seemed to weigh on him, and his manhood strained enough to make him grateful his pants were made to stretch.

He was holding on to his control by the thinnest of threads. Which made his voice sharper than he intended when she finally started to slow down.

"Are you quite finished with this foolishness?" he demanded harshly.

"Let go of me!" she cried, her voice on the edge of hysteria.

"What's wrong with you?" he asked, giving her a small shake that jarred her teeth.

"You were supposed to be my savior from the werewolves. But you just took me from them to attack me yourselves," she accused.

Another booted foot swung into his shin. Her head flew backward toward him again, and William worried for a moment she may hurt herself trying to do him harm.

With his free hand, he braced her head against his shoulder to keep her from using it as a battering ram. He held her until she couldn't struggle any longer and went limp and panting in his arms. He couldn't stop himself from running his nose along the sensitive spot right behind her ear and breathing her in.

She went very still.

"Let me make a few things very clear to you, Emily," he murmured, letting his hot breath lick against her skin. "First of all, I am no savior. I am no hero, and I'm not the good guy. Secondly, neither me nor Paoli has attacked you. Yet."

The last word hung in the air, heavy with double meaning.

"You're lying," she hissed, but her voice sounded less sure.

"I'm not," he whispered.

His lips brushed the pulse beating like humming-bird wings in her throat, and he heard her sharp intake of breath. It would only take the smallest pressure.

Just a taste.

He turned his face and tried to breathe away the impulse.

"He did something to me," she accused, her voice now a husky whisper.

"He did," William agreed distractedly, continuing his exploration of the hollow behind her ear.

Her involuntary shudder and following gooseflesh made him smile hungrily.

"He put you in a brief trance so we could have a private conversation. That's all," William murmured throatily.

He brushed his mouth against her throat again, unable to stop himself. Her skin was velvet soft.

"He's a vampire," she said.

It wasn't quite a question, but he decided to treat as such.

"He is," William agreed.

There was no reason to deny it. Under normal circumstances, Paoli preferred no one know what he was. William respected that and would never reveal his secrets. But the car incident proved she already knew the truth. If she'd been merely suspicious before, Paoli's reaction to her cross had surely solidified the knowledge.

"But you're safer with us than anywhere else in the world," he said.

It wasn't until they were spoken that he realized how true the words were. Even with his body on fire and his need to pierce her throat riding him hard, he would never hurt her. Taste her, yes. He would taste her very soon. But never hurt her.

It was a strange revelation for him, considering his self-control had always been lacking with humans. But with her, it was different. He didn't know why or even how it was different, just that it was.

"We'll do our best to help your sister. And you have my word, I'll keep you safe," he said.

Emily went very still.

He might be willing to keep her safe from others, but who was going to keep her safe from him? Or from herself? She was responding to the pressure of his body against hers and the brush of his lips like a hormonal teenager.

Five minutes ago, she'd been convinced he was about to have her for dinner. Now, she was feeling warm and far too heavy in his arms, very aware of the pressure of his forearm right under her suddenly aching breasts. Every sane thought seemed to be flying out of her head, leaving her a breathless puddle of pathetic.

It was disgusting.

She wasn't a woman to lose her head over a man or let her loins guide her, and she intended to keep it that way. That was more in Amber's wheelhouse.

A stab of guilt gripped her chest.

Amber.

She'd fled for her own life without even giving Amber a second thought. Now, one of her would-be attackers offered to keep her safe, which just served to make her feel worse.

"Why?" she heard her own voice ask in an embarrassingly throaty tone.

It was a fair question. Why would he want to keep her safe? Why had he helped her at the farmhouse, instead of letting the werewolves tear her apart? Why?

William was intoxicated by her soft skin and the overwhelming scent of her essence surrounding him. He was ensnared in a world of his own desires, having some of them reawakened with a vengeance after many years dormant. It didn't occur to him to be anything but truthful.

"I want you," he said simply, though there was nothing simple about it.

"Helloooo!" Paoli's voice broke the spell of the moment just before he appeared beside them, saving Emily from having to try and speak after such an admission.

For one awkward instant, Paoli just stood there and took in the scene, his eyes growing darker and more suspicious the longer he looked at them.

"I was coming to make sure you were *both* all right," Paoli said, his voice thick with accusation as he looked at William.

"I'm fine, thanks," she heard William retort and had to bite back a smile. "We were just discussing your actions in the car, which scared her into thinking she'd been attacked," William continued in a slightly accusatory tone now himself.

Comprehension widened Paoli's eyes when he looked at her.

"I'm sorry about that," he said, and his voice sounded honest and pained. "Humans usually don't even know when they've been hypnotized."

She gaped at him a moment, unable to believe anyone could see it as acceptable to steal someone's free will as long as they didn't know it.

"That doesn't make it right," she said with heat.

Despite the fact she was dangling from William's arm like a rag doll, she still managed to sound authoritative.

"You're right," Paoli agreed without a fight. "Please accept my apology, as well as my guarantee I will never hypnotize you again."

Emily snorted derisively. "How can you expect me to take your word for anything? You're a vampire."

She spat out the last like an insult.

Paoli's casual demeanor disappeared and was replaced with a very formal one. He straightened regally, his eyes flashing but his voice very cold.

"I am," he admitted slowly. "I have been for a very long time. It wasn't my choice, and I won't apologize for it. This night, what I am, what *we* are," he amended with a quick nod toward William, "saved not only your life but your sister's as well."

Beneath the icy tones, he sounded resigned and somehow sad, like she'd hurt him deeply.

Emily felt small and petty for her harsh words.

He was absolutely right.

She owed them a debt she could never repay. Instead of thanking them for saving her, she'd attacked him both physically and verbally. She looked at him from under her lashes in a suddenly contrite pose.

"Did you take my blood?" she asked.

She hadn't meant to speak the worry aloud, but the words tumbled out of their own accord. She had to know.

"Absolutely not," Paoli answered, clearly aghast.

The look of horror on his face was almost insulting, and Emily bristled at his tone.

"You're under our protection," he explained, his tone sounding slightly exasperated. "Don't be offended that we *didn't* feed on you. We didn't bring you as a food source," he said. "We brought you to help you. And like it or not, you need our help."

She let out a long, deflated breath of defeat.

"You're right," she admitted. "I'm in way over my head here. You guys saved me tonight."

She offered a weak, apologetic smile, which he returned readily enough, his usual demeanor having been restored. "I'm sorry about the cross."

Paoli chuckled at that, his eyes twinkling.

"If I hadn't scared you, it never would have happened. So, I guess I had it coming," he said, waving her apology away. "Besides, I heal quickly."

He threw her a small wink.

"Are we all friends again?" William spoke up from behind her.

"You can put her down now," Paoli confirmed.

Emily breathed a little easier once her feet were back on the ground and William stepped away. With his admission still ringing in her ears, she needed some distance from him.

A lot of distance.

And time to get her body back under control.

While Paoli made her nervous for her life, William affected her in very different ways.

He was clearly the more dangerous of the two, judging by his actions at the farmhouse. But his eyes when he first saw her had a possessive heat that made her uneasy. Eyes that seemed to see into her very soul.

She swallowed hard at the mere memory. He was dangerous to her, indeed.

"Here," she said as the trio made their way back to the car.

She held out the cross as a peace offering to Paoli and felt a fresh rush of guilt when she noticed him flinch just slightly, though he played it off as surprise.

He stared at the large necklace for a moment, then looked over her head at William on her other side.

"You keep it," he told her finally. "In fact, go ahead and wear it for now, so you'll know you're safe from me."

Back at the car, she checked on Amber before she got back into the passenger's seat.

She pulled down the vanity mirror and fumbled to fasten the clasp on the necklace. Both Paoli and William pretended not to notice her check her neck discretely, though she could feel their eyes watching her.

Still looking in the mirror, she glanced in the backseat at Paoli. His reflection smiled and waved at her in the mirror.

"Sorry," she mumbled, her cheeks blooming with color at having been caught checking his reflection.

"Don't be," William told her, definite humor in his voice.

"There's no reason to be sorry," Paoli agreed. "In fact, this is a good time to get to know one another a little better, wouldn't you say?"

As usual, he ignored William's warning growl.

William could smell her apprehension increase and wanted to kick Paoli. She'd already been through enough for one night. Clearly what she needed was a shower and sleep.

After everything that'd happened, her head must be spinning.

Unbidden, an image of her lying in bed, asleep and vulnerable, rose into his mind's eye.

He squelched it immediately, but not before he had to readjust his position in his seat irritably. After having no desire for a woman in more years than he could remember, his manhood was suddenly determined to make its presence known.

"All right," Emily's voice agreed reluctantly, and he focused on the conversation at hand. "What do you want to know?"

"What were you doing at the farmhouse? You're obviously not a werewolf," Paoli said. "Or a vampire," he added with a teasing note.

She gave a slight chuckle.

"No, just a plain ole human, I'm afraid," she said.

She gave William a look full of meaning.

"And I intend to stay that way," she added firmly.

Then she turned back to Paoli.

"I tracked Amber to that location and went to find her," she said.

"She was missing?" Paoli's voice had gone from simply conversational to interested.

"For almost a year now," Emily confirmed. "She ran away with some guy she met. I've been searching for her since then."

"What was his name?" Paoli asked.

"Brian was his first name, but I never found out his last. He was the one you—" She broke off, looking uncomfortably at William.

"Killed," William finished for her. "Do you know anything else about him?"

As much as William hated to start questioning her too, they needed to know as much as possible. This night was bound to have a nasty fallout.

Paoli was right.

The Coven was going to be angry, and they needed all the information they could get to mount a defense.

"Not much," she said with a small shake of her head. "It took a long time to find out where he worked. I followed him back to the pack from there. Amber has a long history with men and—" She broke off suddenly and fell silent. "Poor choices," she said finally.

"What kind of poor choices?" Paoli wanted to know, seemingly oblivious to the prying nature of his question.

Emily looked uncomfortable again. She was chewing the edge of her lip nervously.

"We're sorry to ask such probing questions," William said. "But we need to know everything. We broke some rules tonight, and we'll have to answer for it soon. The more information we have, the better."

Emily nodded in understanding and gave a deep, resolved sigh.

"Amber's long line of bad decisions plagued our mother until her passing and has controlled most of my adult life. She got into drugs, prostitution," she shrugged. "You name it. I can't tell you how many times I've had to bail her out of jail."

She scoffed and gave a small shake of her head.

"When she said this man could change everything, I didn't pay much attention. It seemed like every other day there was a new man who could change her life. After a while, I just learned to tune her out."

There was a long pause.

"We weren't exactly on speaking terms when she disappeared," she admitted, her voice sounding somehow small.

"Do you know what they did to her?" Paoli asked.

"All I know is they bit her and something went wrong," Emily said.

She spared a glance at her sister's sorry state.

"Is there any way to help her now?" Her voice broke just the slightest bit.

William's eyes met Paoli's in the rearview mirror, but neither spoke. They were dancing into dangerous territory, and the question of what would happen to the condemned woman was one they would have to discuss at length.

Privately.

Paoli patted Emily gently on the shoulder; a move that was rewarded with a dark stare from William.

"We'll try," Paoli said.

It was the only promise they could offer.

CHAPTER 6

William leaned against the door with his head near the partially open window for the last part of the drive. His body hadn't fully cooled from having Emily in his arms, and the wind helped to dilute her scent somewhat.

He breathed a sigh of relief when he finally pulled into the garage and got out of the car. Emily got out, looked around, and gave him a look of surprise from across the car roof.

For the briefest of seconds, her surprise puzzled him. Then it dawned on him, and he gave her a knowing smile as he closed his door.

"Were you expecting something else?" He quirked one teasing brow.

Emily froze. She didn't want to offend them.

Again.

But she hadn't covered her surprise well enough, and it was too late to deny it.

"Yes, actually," she admitted. "Like castles and moats—"

"And a guy in a cape who 'vants to zuck yer blood'?" Paoli asked in his best Lon Chaney voice as he carried Amber past them and into the house.

Her face flushed warm again. Maybe not the last part, but she certainly didn't expect them to be living in a completely normal split level just outside of a small town.

She really had a lot to learn about the world she'd tumbled into.

Her embarrassment kept her silent as she followed William to the room Paoli laid Amber in. After Paoli got Amber situated, he considerately pulled the plush blue chair right up to the bedside for Emily. She sat down with a fleeting smile of thanks, but Paoli's demeanor kept her wary.

He seemed uncomfortable, and he was looming.

"We need to be honest with you," Paoli said once she was seated. "We have to discuss some things you may not want to hear. But there are things going on here you must understand. You need to know the truth we're all facing so you can make your own choices. Informed choices," Paoli said.

Emily didn't like the sound of that. She swallowed a lump in her throat and tried to sound normal.

"Like what?" she asked.

To her surprise, she managed to pull off merely curious. But she fingered the silver necklace under her shirt nervously.

"Like what's going to happen with your sister." Paoli's voice was gentle and patient.

"What do you mean?" Emily asked, her voice growing stiff.

"The Coven said she's to be executed," William supplied from the doorway he was leaning against.

Emily sucked in an audible breath, but her voice was level when she spoke.

"What is 'the Coven'?" she asked.

She'd only heard the term for a group of witches, but she suspected that wasn't what they were referring to.

"The government of our world," Paoli explained.

She nodded after a moment of thought. It made sense for them to have a separate government, she supposed. It wasn't like a vampire could appear in a normal human court. But she got the distinct feeling there was more.

"OK," she said slowly, trying to process the new information. "So, we need to keep her away from your government people until we figure out what to do."

It seemed simple enough to her.

"It's too late for that," William said.

A long moment stretched out before he admitted, "I'm the Coven's executioner."

It felt like someone just punched her in the gut. She stared at him in disbelief for a heartbeat, then sprang out of the chair and to her feet. Far too much anger welled in her for any fear, and she stormed up to William and stood toe to toe with him.

"Did you bring us here for an easier kill?" she demanded. "Because if you expect me to stand aside and let you kill her, you're in for a real surprise."

She thought of the gun at her waist. Could she do it? Could she really kill a man, *this* man?

"No," he said, and honesty shone in his intelligent, now-gray eyes.

She hadn't noticed his eyes had changed colors before. They were now a beautiful steel gray.

"But we can't ignore orders from the Coven," he went on.

His answer gave her some degree of relief. She didn't want to find out if she could bring herself to kill him. But the relief was a fleeting thing. If they couldn't ignore orders from the Coven, how could they possibly save Amber?

"Are you saying they never change their minds?" she asked.

She wasn't about to just sit back and let some faceless group make the decision to kill her sister.

Paoli and William exchanged a heavy look but said nothing.

"What?" she demanded.

She looked at William, then at Paoli, and back to William.

"I saw that. What aren't you telling me?" she pressed.

William gave her a hooded look, his face carefully expressionless.

"They reversed their decision once, but it came with a high price," he said.

He took a step back from her, putting distance between them.

"I don't care about the price. I'll pay any price there is to save her," Emily insisted.

Her purple eyes flashed with challenge and determination. She meant every word.

"You're not in the human world anymore, young Emily," Paoli interjected.

He carefully guided her away from William. It was something that didn't escape her notice.

A glance back at William showed he seemed to relax subtly.

"I don't care about human world or world of whatever you are," she said.

She was beginning to yell, but she couldn't stop herself. He wasn't going to make it OK for Amber to die. Nothing could make that OK. Not after they gave her hope.

"Settle down and listen to me," Paoli said calmly in the face of her anger. "You have no idea what you're saying. There are prices you can't even begin to guess at."

"I don't care," she said stubbornly.

She really didn't. There was nothing she wouldn't do if it could save Amber, and she didn't want to hear about the worst-case scenario.

"Now, are you going to help her or not?" she asked, staring Paoli right in the eye.

"I'll try," he said. "But the point we're making is her overall fate cannot be decided by either of us."

"But if you can help her, she'll have a chance, right?" she asked.

She needed to hear there was a chance. She couldn't accept anything else.

Paoli held her hopeful gaze with a look of sympathy that worried her more than anything else.

"I won't give you false hope. It's going to take a miracle, but there is a very slim chance," he said.

And just like that, Emily could breathe again. She squared her shoulders and looked at him levelly.

"It's better than none," she said.

For a moment, he just looked at her. His eyes showed something akin to respect. Then he gave her a nod of agreement.

"I'll see what I can do," he said heavily.

He shot a look at William and left the room.

Silence stretched out, broken only by Amber's constant moaning.

"He's not like I would have pictured a vampire," Emily said finally.

William gave a small smile.

"No," he agreed. "But he gets that a lot."

"So, you're a werewolf?" she asked, trying to sound casual.

"Not exactly," he said, a little hesitation in his words.

She noticed the hesitation. A thoughtful little crinkle appeared between her brows.

"But you turned into a wolf," she pointed out.

He gave her just a hint of a nod.

"I'm complicated," he said.

Another silence stretched out.

What did that mean? He either was a werewolf or he wasn't. What was the point of being obtuse about it?

"Do you kill people?" she asked bluntly, her voice almost a whisper. "Humans, I mean?"

A tight smile crept across his face and didn't reach his eyes.

"You're safe with us," was all he said.

She nodded almost absently.

"So yes," she mumbled.

There was a heavy feeling of disappointment in her gut, but she refused to examine it. She needed to keep her distance from him. She could never be involved with someone who killed people, no matter how attracted to him she was.

He was a killer, and she needed to remember that.

"Not if I can help it," he said heavily.

"Prop her up," Paoli instructed when he reentered the room, a small vial in his hand.

Emily did so without question. She watched with bated breath as he poured some vile-smelling concoction down Amber's throat.

Amber coughed and sputtered, covering Paoli in frothy spittle, but the transformation continued, unchanged.

"Well, that was disappointing," he announced dryly.

He wiped his face with a grimace, then hustled back out of the room.

"What if he can't fix this?" Emily asked William in a small voice. "Then what happens?"

William held her gaze.

"You already know the answer," he said darkly.

"I told you, that's not going to happen. I won't let you kill her," she said.

She met his eyes boldly, as if daring him to challenge her.

He said nothing, but continued to watch her. Like she was a bug.

"Stop looking at me like that," she said, squirming uncomfortably.

"Like what?" He cocked his head to the side, a look of puzzlement on his face.

"Like you're a cat watching a mouse," she said.

She jabbed an accusatory finger in his direction.

William grinned at her. It was a guilty look.

"What's funny?" she demanded.

"You walked into a werewolf den under a full moon without a thought, but someone watching you makes you uncomfortable," he chuckled.

Emily glanced at Amber.

"I didn't consider the moon," she admitted. "I just knew she was there, and I was afraid for her."

William sobered, becoming instantly serious.

"Did you know she was with wolves?" he asked.

"Yes," Emily said, watching Amber again.

"Then you should have considered the moon," he admonished. "You're lucky to be alive."

Emily plucked at the blanket, uncomfortable at being scolded, especially when she knew he was right.

"I know," she said softly.

"Let's give this a try," Paoli said, his voice very serious when he returned.

A gold necklace dangled from his hand, and the reeking smell of whatever was inside the charm made William back away, a scowl on his face.

"What the hell is that?" William demanded when Paoli crossed the room and slipped the necklace over Amber's head.

"Wolfsbane," Paoli said over his shoulder.

As the trio stood watching, the transformation gradually slowed.

Several minutes later, it stopped completely and Amber was left in exhausted human form. She crumpled in on herself. One last moan escaped her lips before she fell into a blissful state of unconsciousness.

Relief washed through Emily with enough force to make her knees weak.

"You fixed her," she whispered breathlessly, her eyes tearful.

"Not exactly," Paoli disagreed.

He held his hands out to ward her off when she stepped forward like she wanted to hug him.

"Cross," he reminded.

"Oh, I'm sorry!" Emily cried.

She quickly stepped back. Then a frown crossed her face when his words sank in.

"What do you mean 'not exactly'?" she asked.

"Wolfsbane won't cure lycanthropy. All it does is stop the wolf from being able to take over the body. All the rage is still there, but now it has no outlet," he explained.

"What does that mean for her?" she asked.

She didn't like the way that sounded. Amber wasn't exactly known for her even temperament before.

Paoli looked back at William, who was now standing in the hallway to avoid the wolfsbane.

"I don't know," he admitted. "I'll keep looking for something more permanent, but at least this will buy her some time. It's almost sunrise, and we all need to rest. There's another bedroom down the hall."

"I'll stay with her," Emily said absently, her eyes on Amber's worn-out form.

At least she was human again. Sort of.

"No," William said sharply.

Both Paoli and Emily turned and stared at him.

"Until we have a chance to see what her mental status will be, it may not be safe," William explained.

Paoli seemed to consider it, then nodded in agreement.

"That's true," he said. "Something like this may have left her . . . different."

"But she's my sister," Emily objected. "We may have a troubled relationship, but I can't imagine she'd ever actually harm me."

It was ironic to be arguing about her safety with two men who killed people.

"We need to see if she's still your sister when she wakes up. For tonight, you need to be safe so we can all rest," William said.

He held his hand out to her and waited.

With a heavy sigh of surrender, she stroked Amber's damp forehead one last time and left the room to meet up with him. She gave his outstretched hand a distrustful look and waved her own arm toward the hall, instead.

"Lead on," she said with clear irritation.

CHAPTER 7

William led her to the spare room, trying to keep his mind clear of the images it seemed determined to show him.

Emily followed him around the room, politely nodding when he indicated the bathroom in the corner. He was *not* picturing her within the shower, naked and soapy.

He was not.

A sudden dry lump formed in his throat and he swallowed hard. With more speed than courtesy, he indicated fresh shirts in the drawer and left the room as quickly as possible. Being alone in a bedroom while not touching her was like torture, and he didn't want to push his shaky control too far.

He closed the door behind him and found Paoli waiting in the hall, his expression uncharacteristically serious.

"We need to talk," Paoli said solemnly.

A glance toward Amber's room showed a wind chime on the knob of the closed door. It was low-tech, but they'd hear the sound in a dead sleep.

Satisfied, William followed Paoli silently down the stairs and into the kitchen.

William settled into his favorite chair at the table and waited for Paoli to join him.

Paoli was never this quiet, so William braced himself for the worst. He watched Paoli heat two glasses of red liquid and visibly gather himself for a conversation he clearly didn't know how to begin.

William took the glass Paoli handed him with a nod of thanks and gave an impatient sigh.

"Will you quit stalling and just come out with it?" William demanded shortly.

"I think we have a problem," Paoli said finally.

He walked back to the sink and leaned against the cabinet, facing William.

William just stared at him for a moment, then offered a questioning half smile.

"Do you mean other than the condemned woman now resting upstairs?" he asked.

"Yes," Paoli said slowly. "The problem is Emily. Well," he hesitated, his face looking torn by indecision. "Not a problem, exactly. From what I've read, it's actually a good thing."

"I have no idea what you're talking about, but I'm more concerned about the condemned woman we're harboring instead of executing," William cut in with a trace of sarcasm.

He tipped his glass and drained half the contents in a single swallow.

Paoli watched him in silence, his expressive face still uncertain.

"Quit stalling, old man," William prodded.

When silence continued, he decided to put Paoli's mind at ease.

"If you're worried about the Coven, rest assured. I'll carry through with their orders like I always have if they decide the execution stands. I'd never let them have you. Surely you know that," he said.

Paoli gave him a pained smile.

"I do know that, and I appreciate it. But my concern isn't for me," he said.

Paoli took a deep breath and seemed to reach a decision at last.

"As you know, I've been reading on werewolves tonight. I think I've come across something that might explain what's happening between you and Emily," he said.

Paoli turned and retrieved a heavy tome from the counter behind him, then walked over and sat it in front of William.

It was a beautiful book with a handwoven navy-blue front cover. It was decorated with ancient magic symbols, long forgotten by all but a select few. Paoli opened the book with one hand and pointed out the section.

"Here," he said.

William leaned forward and read the yellowed pages of a book that looked old enough to have been scripted in the dark ages. Smelled it, too.

He stared at the page for several minutes and felt the cold hand of dread grip him.

"This can't be right," he said.

Paoli nodded slightly. "I knew what was happening as soon as I read it. She's your mate, William."

"No," William said flatly. Stubbornly.

Paoli hesitated.

"I don't think you really get a choice," he said. "According to this, your wolf will recognize her immediately and move in to claim her. I think that's what happened in the cornfield tonight. Her scent got your wolf's attention."

William just scowled at him.

Paoli huffed in response.

"How do you feel around her? Because here," he pointed out a section, "it says the wolf's mating drive will be triggered."

Well, that was certainly one way to put it, William thought irritably.

Paoli must have seen something on his face—which was unusual, since William had perfected the art of neutrality.

Paoli pushed on doggedly.

"See, according to this, it's going to get worse, not better," he said.

"That's only *if* she's my mate," William responded finally. "But it says here," it was his turn to tap a section, "that both people involved will be werewolves in a mate situation. She's human. She can't be my mate."

He shrugged, as if that settled the matter. He was simply too long without having a woman and he was . . . amorous.

Paoli gave him an exasperated look.

"You're only half werewolf, so I'm going to guess your situation won't necessarily follow the script," he said with a hint of impatience.

William glowered at him.

"Well it's true," Paoli insisted in response to William's dark countenance.

"Look," Paoli sighed a moment later. "It says something in her will respond to your wolf if she's your mate. So, test my theory. Take her in your arms. If she screams bloody murder, I'm wrong, and you have my apologies. If I'm right, she'll melt like putty in your hands."

William continued to remain silent, but the mental images those words brought up were not going to help his resolve to stay in control of his needs.

"If you don't do it while the man in you is still in control, eventually the wolf will take over. It's going to happen, either way," Paoli insisted.

"I don't care," William said.

He read the passage again, a little desperately. Sure enough, it didn't say anything about a choice. But he couldn't have a mate. He wasn't a pure werewolf, and he was owned—*owned*—by the Coven. If he had a mate, they'd own her, too.

He'd be helpless to protect her from them.

Emily's face flashed in his mind. He wouldn't do that to her. He wouldn't force her to be enslaved. Besides, a wolf had already tried to change her sister—her twin sister—and the results were disastrous.

He groaned inwardly.

As if the situation wasn't already bad enough, this new knowledge just made it worse. Every word in the book proved Paoli right, whether he wanted to admit it or not. It was the only thing that made sense. She was his mate. A mate he'd never even thought to hope for, and she was right here, in this very house. But he couldn't have her. With a vicious growl, he shoved the book away and stalked from the room.

William lay wide awake in bed, hours later. His hands were tucked behind his head, and he stared intently at the ceiling. His lack of knowledge was frustrating. He and Paoli had always been isolated from other immortals because William didn't exactly fit anywhere in their world. That, and his job made him more or less the boogeyman of the immortals.

No one except Paoli was comfortable around him, which kept him set up as an outcast. He'd never considered the downside of it. Now he was faced with a wolf problem, and Paoli had no more knowledge or understanding than he did, since mates were specifically a wolf issue. His lack of basic knowledge had never been so glaringly obvious.

For over an hour he'd searched Paoli's books before he tried the internet and read everything he could locate on the subject. There was precious little to be found.

He needed to talk to a werewolf.

There was only one he knew well enough to ask about something so personal, but Empusa had become a guard to the Coven about a century ago. Since William was currently hedging orders from the Coven, calling Empusa was not a good idea. He wouldn't put Empusa into a position to either lie or betray a trust.

William caught himself straining to hear sounds from the room on the other side of his bedroom wall. He groaned in frustration and sat up, too full of restless energy to be still.

What he needed was a hunt to distract him. It was the end of the full moon cycle, and he could feel his wolf's driving need to heed her call. Besides, it would do him good to head into the woods and find something he could sink his fangs into.

With the thought of fresh, dripping meat in mind, he padded on bare feet into the hall. He glanced at Emily's door and paused, staring intently at it for several minutes.

There was more than one way to rid himself of excess energy.

Paoli's suggestion came back into his mind and tempted him further. "Take her in your arms," he'd said. William had never wanted anything more. But if he took her, there was no turning back. For either of them.

Still, the thought of her lying in bed, his oversized shirt hiked up to bare a glimpse of her rounded—he jerked his thoughts away. With a growl, he snapped his teeth together at the door and forced himself to leave the house.

As soon as his feet hit the front porch, he slid effortlessly into his wolf's form, feeling his skin give way to different muscles and the smooth slide of fur over him. He launched himself from the porch with his strong back legs and headed into the woods.

There was something so freeing about losing the mantle of humanity and letting the wolf have free reign. In wolf form, his mind remained intact, but changed in subtle ways. The concerns that weighed on him were as nothing. He was able to let the wolf instincts guide him and lose himself in the thrill of the hunt.

A deer ran somewhere ahead. He picked up on the scent and tracked it ruthlessly, his body held low and quiet. It took some time to locate the buck. The forest covered several acres, and the animal had clearly been there a long time, leaving scent trails in several different places.

Finally, he located it, bent low over a spot of thick vegetation. Keen senses detected his presence too late. By the time the animal realized the danger, William had already brought it down and killed it, quickly and efficiently. Long fangs tore the carcass apart, and for a while, William lost himself in the aftermath of a fresh kill and the joy of the night.

When he eventually shifted back into human form, the first rays of dawn were pushing back the blanket of darkness. A new day was beginning. He stopped at the porch railing and watched the gray slowly fade away the shadows, wondering at the significance for the first time in many years.

It was a new day, indeed.

He made his way back upstairs with exhaustion riding him hard, took a quick shower to clean himself of the hunt, and lay down to sleep at last. Exhausted and sated, sleep came blissfully quick.

CHAPTER 8

E mily woke much earlier than usual, feeling trapped and claustrophobic. She made her way to the bathroom and splashed cold water on her face, then noticed her reflection looked as exhausted as she felt. Her eyes were bleary with dark patches beneath them, and her skin was much paler than normal, which gave her an unpleasant pause.

How sure was she that no one was feeding on her?

She leaned forward, checking her throat carefully in the mirror. There didn't appear to be any bite marks, and the cross was still protectively around her neck, which made her feel better.

Somewhat.

Cautiously satisfied she was simply suffering from sleeplessness, she got dressed in last night's clothes. What she needed was some space and fresh air to settle herself. Her nerves weren't about to let her get more sleep, and she felt like a caged animal in her room. After a long moment's indecision, she slipped her gun into the waistband of her jeans. Considering the fiasco of last night, it wouldn't hurt to keep it with her, just in case.

She half expected to find the door locked, but the knob turned easily in her hand. She made it all the way to the front door and turned the deadbolt to make her escape. Then, with no warning, William simply appeared between her and the door. She let out a small shriek of surprise and jumped back, her heart hammering in her throat.

"Where are you going?" he demanded, his voice rough and suspicious.

His dark hair was tousled slightly, and his eyes were hard and glinting.

Emily recovered herself from the surprise quickly, then bristled at his tone. She stiffened her spine and narrowed her eyes.

"Am I a prisoner?" she demanded.

He frowned at her for a moment, as if considering the question.

"Not exactly," he said carefully.

"Good," she answered shortly and moved to step around him.

William caught her arm in a gentle but firm grip.

"Where are you going?" he repeated.

She looked at the hand on her arm pointedly, then back to his darkly handsome face, set in stubborn lines. She tried to take a step away from him, but he moved with her. It was then she noticed he wore nothing more than a loose pair of athletic shorts, which gave her a perfect view of his bare chest, since it was at eye level.

It was an impressive chest; wide and strong, giving way to his broad shoulders and well-muscled arms. He looked like the perfect specimen of man, without an ounce of fat on him. All muscle and power. Not that she was about to let that stop her temper. If anything, it seemed to add fuel to the fire.

"I'll be back in a little while," she said stiffly and gave a little pull to indicate he needed to release her.

Amber was here, so it wasn't as if she'd run away. His grip never faltered.

"After last night, the pack will be out searching for you. It isn't safe," he said.

His hand slowly moved from her wrist to her forearm in a gentle caress, and the atmosphere changed drastically.

His touch felt far too intimate, and her skin seemed overly sensitive where he touched.

"I've managed on my own a long time now, William," she said, her voice a little thick.

She used his first name deliberately—like a schoolteacher might—to show she had the authority to do so and was at least his equal.

His eyes took on a golden glint and a heat that made her pulse rate ratchet up another notch. With his free hand, he reached out and ran a single finger down her cheek in a featherlight touch.

"You're so fragile and you don't even know it," he said silkily, his voice a low, throaty murmur.

She swallowed hard and tried not to lean into his touch like a cat. His words of the night before floated through her mind, and she felt the color rise in her cheeks.

He wanted her.

He'd told her so outright.

That made his touch now very dangerous, indeed. Her reaction to the contact seemed way out of proportion. It was nothing that should have caused sudden heat to build in her midsection and beyond. She needed to get control of herself before things got out of hand. With a small, forced laugh to dispel the moment, she shrugged nonchalantly.

"I'm not nearly as fragile as you seem to think," she said.

To which he chuckled. It was a deep, rich sound.
Then his gaze pointedly raked over her from head to
toe appraisingly.

She refused to look away from his eyes. Instead, she
raised a single brow mutinously, daring him to mention that her head barely reached his chest or that the
gun in her waistband hung halfway down her thigh.

Instead of saying anything, he took a step toward
her, crowding her away from the door and against the
wall with his large frame, forcing her to step back.

Emily retreated a single involuntary step, but no
more. She stood firm, determined to face him down.
He might deliberately intimidate her—though she
wasn't really sure it *was* deliberate—but he wouldn't
hurt her.

She didn't know what made her so certain of that.

After all, she'd seen him decapitate a man without
a word only a few hours before. But somehow, she just
knew she was safe with him. So, she stubbornly held
her ground. He had to stop eventually or walk over
the top of her.

He didn't stop advancing until his legs were
against hers, and she became very aware of the sheer
size of the man. With one hand, he cupped her chin
and tipped her head up, then bent to brush her lips
gently with his own. The pressure from his lips was
barely there for an instant before he pulled away.

"I understand you want to leave the house. Give
me a few minutes to get dressed and we can go
wherever you want," he whispered thickly, his mouth
a mere inch from her own.

Emily watched him walk toward the stairs without
saying a word, wondering that her knees still held her

up. She was dumbfounded and rocked to the core of her being. As soon as she heard the door to his bedroom click shut, she turned and ran from the house for all she was worth.

She had no idea where she was going.

She needed time and space to think.

So much had happened, and her life seemed to be spinning out of control. She needed to find a way to get her feet back under her so she didn't feel so helpless. That would start with a clear head.

If William went with her like he intended to, it would completely negate her ability to think. Her head was muddled even worse in his presence.

He was too big, too handsome, too ... male for her comfort. She responded to him in ways she'd never experienced before, and it scared the hell out of her.

She needed time to sort it out.

Once she stepped off the porch, she stared at the only car parked outside of the house. Her own rented car had been abandoned last night, she realized with dismay.

Well, she thought with a sigh, *there goes the deposit*.

She gave an exaggerated groan and started down the road on foot. Town was only a couple of miles, and the walk would help to clear her head. If any werewolves were lurking about, she had her gun loaded with silver and no qualms about shooting them.

Although, from what she'd read on werewolf lore, the pack would be in ruins until the new pecking order was established. This knowledge made her confident they would be too busy dealing with their own mess to worry about her too much, no matter what William thought.

It was a beautiful day for this late in the year. Cool air brushed lazily across her cheeks. The leaves provided the perfect crunching sound as she walked along, determined to think about nothing except the sound of the world around her and the success of yesterday.

No matter what else had happened, she'd found Amber, just as she promised herself she would. Against all odds, she'd rescued her from a pack of werewolves. Granted, she'd had unexpected help, but that didn't stop her from being able to claim success.

Hopefully Amber would see it as the rescue it was.

Even after their last conversation had ended as so many before it—Amber screaming undying hatred for her and storming out—Emily refused to consider the possibility of anything other than a happy reunion. Maybe this rescue would finally bring Amber around and make her realize the error of her ways.

Emily snorted aloud at her own foolishness.

It had never occurred to her Amber might have done something irrevocable until she saw it for herself last night. While Amber had always been troubled for unknown reasons, she really went out of control in their late teen years.

Their mother did everything she could think to help her troubled daughter, which only seemed to make it worse. As her behavior continued to spiral, Amber had grown bitter and resentful of her sister, and the gap between them had become a gulf Emily couldn't breach. Emily couldn't remember the last time they'd had a civil conversation. But Amber was her sister, and Emily refused to give up on her.

There was good in Amber.

There *had* to be.

It was the roar of an engine that pulled her from her musing.

Without looking up, she knew who was flying down the road. Her eyes jumped to the trees beside her. They were a good ten feet away—too far to hide herself before he spotted her—and she didn't think it would be a good idea to make him chase her through the woods.

Again.

When she glanced up at the approaching car, it took every bit of her self-control not to run anyway.

William's face was clearly visible through the windshield, and he looked furious.

The car came to a stop beside her and the passenger door flew open almost violently.

She peered inside with a nervous smile and found William staring at her, his eyes a glittering shade of amber instead of cool gray. .

Something told her that wasn't a good sign.

"Get in," he growled.

With one hand on the door, she glanced over her shoulder and wondered if she really *could* escape him in the woods. It would take him a minute or so to free himself from the car, and if she timed it just right—

"Don't even think about it," he warned dangerously. "I'm not fully in control right now, and giving a wolf something to chase is asking for trouble."

Well, didn't that just build her confidence?

She swallowed loudly and climbed into the car.

After a single deep breath to calm her nerves, she decided not to cower in the face of his anger. She couldn't exactly plead weak and helpless, not after the

speech she gave him at the house, so she decided to go
on the offensive, instead.

"Why are you so determined to come with me?"
she asked irritably as she closed the door and he
pulled back onto the road.

"Because you're m—" He paused, and a muscle in
his jaw twitched. "My responsibility," he finished.

She waved a dismissive hand at him.

"No, I am *my* responsibility," she argued.

He grunted and gave a shrug that clearly said he
didn't care what she thought.

"I disagree," he said simply.

And with those words, she went from pretending
not to be afraid of him, to being too angry to fear
him.

"I hate to break it to you, but no matter what you
think, I am a free woman," she declared. "Capable of
my very own thoughts and making my own decisions."

"Not when it comes to your safety," he snapped.
"Not anymore."

She eyed him a long moment, fighting back the
urge to reach out and punch him in the side of his
oh-too-handsome face.

"I went for a walk," she said between clenched
teeth. "To get some time to think. You're acting like I
was on my way to slay dragons or something. Which,
just so you know—" She jabbed a finger at him to
emphasize her point. "I could do if I chose."

"Where did you want to go?" he asked causally,
ignoring her words as if she wasn't about to burst into
a temper.

Emily had to take a few deep breaths to keep from
screaming in frustration.

"I need to get my rental car and a change of clothes if I'm going to be staying at your house for a few days," she said with deliberate slowness once she had her temper under better control.

"Where are your clothes?" he asked.

"My hotel is about an hour that way," she said, pointing through the window.

Amusement flitted across his face.

"You were planning to walk there, huh?" he asked.

Actually, she'd intended just to buy a new outfit since she was on foot, but if he was determined to drive her around . . .

She gave him her best innocent look, wide eyes and everything.

"Of course," she said.

Still smirking, he headed in the direction she indicated.

"Where did you leave your rental?" he asked after they rode along in companionable silence a while.

"Close to the wolf's house," she answered. "Or den, I guess."

Didn't wolves live in dens?

"Paoli and I will pick up the car when he rises," William said. "You don't need to be anywhere near that place."

At her narrowed eyes, he gave a slight shrug and a long-suffering sigh.

"I'm sorry if I'm being bossy or . . . overbearing," he offered. "But your safety is very important to me."

"Why?" she asked, frowning at him.

"I already told you," he said. "You're my responsibility."

"OK. But why?" she asked.

William was quiet for a moment.

"It's complicated," he said finally.

"Of course it is," she said dryly.

William laughed at her tone.

"I'm not trying to be difficult," he said. "But there are things even Paoli and I are still trying to figure out. I promise to tell you when the time comes."

"And meanwhile, I just sit quietly and trust you to look out for me?" she asked in a dangerous tone.

"Well . . ." William said slowly.

He cast a quick glance in her direction and sighed loudly again.

"It's not a woman thing, if that's what you're thinking. It's a human thing. You're a lot more fragile than we are," he said quickly.

When she gave him a look that clearly said she didn't believe a word he was saying, he sighed.

"If Paoli's arm were ripped off by an enemy, do you know what would happen?" he asked.

She blanched slightly at the mental image but shook her head.

"He'd regrow it. Now, if *your* arm were ripped off, you'd likely bleed to death in just a few minutes. See the difference? Humans are fragile. That's why they're our natural—"

He broke off and gave her a look of discomfort that was hilarious to see on his face because it looked so out of place.

"Prey?" she supplied in a falsely sweet voice.

"Yes," he said after a long hesitation. "Humans are our natural prey. But Paoli and I try very hard not to kill."

"Why?" she asked curiously.

Then—considering her own circumstances—she raised her hands before he could say anything.

"I'm glad of that, all things considered," she said quickly.

She gave a slightly nervous chuckle.

"But I'm curious why you don't just go around munching people if they're your natural prey," she said.

"It's—" he began.

"Complicated," she cut him off irritably, then fell silent.

Several moments passed while she pointed out turns to get to her hotel.

William didn't voice any complaints, but his eyes burned.

He needed sunglasses.

While the sunlight may not harm him the way it would Paoli, years of living with a vampire had kept him in the dark long enough that the bright of the day was blinding and his skin felt overly sensitive. All the light made him feel strangely exposed.

His wolf stirred with unease, and he had to focus to keep it controlled, especially with Emily so close.

When he parked the car in front of the hotel and saw all the people around, he groaned inwardly. He was in no shape to be so close to that many humans.

Something must have shown on his face, because Emily gave him a slight smile.

"You wait here. Don't want you eating anyone," she said.

Then she hopped out of the car and jogged across the parking lot to the front door of the building.

He stared after her in silent surprise.

Had she been teasing him?

He threw an arm across his face to hide his eyes and rested back on his seat with a satisfied smirk. She *had* been teasing him, he decided.

And the wolf settled.

CHAPTER 9

"What have you done!?" screamed a shrill, angry voice.

The blood-curdling sound woke everyone at once, followed by the loud jangle of wind chimes as the bedroom door was jerked open.

Emily leapt from her bed—instantly wide awake—and rushed toward Amber's room, her heart in her throat. She hadn't made it two steps when she heard a dangerous growl, and William stepped out from the doorway of his own room to block her path. Before she could open her mouth to demand he move, Paoli was lifting a kicking and fighting Amber into his arms further down the corridor.

Paoli carried her back into the room and left Emily alone in the hall with William.

William's feet and chest were bare again, and his eyes were sparkling a predatory gold as they fixed on her, unblinking.

She backed away from him, uncertain.

William had practically flown out of his room with only one thought on his mind—Emily.

He'd fallen asleep earlier with his body on fire after spending the day in a car with her. All evening he'd fought his every screaming instinct to go to her, and she'd even haunted his dreams.

To wake from a fitful sleep to such a horrible scream had gripped him in a fist of terror, her safety his only concern. Now, she stood right in front of him, perfectly safe, and he felt he could draw breath again. She was wearing nothing more than his long-sleeved tee shirt, standing right outside of his bedroom door. Her legs and feet were bare, her beautiful hair falling all around her like a cloud of dark silk. To him, she looked like an offer from the gods.

It would be so easy to claim her. It would stop the raging fire in his blood and give him a mate.

Which would give him peace.

She would be the gift of humanity he'd always lacked.

Without even realizing it, he moved toward her like a moth to a flame.

Emily took another step back. He took another step forward. There was something going on she didn't understand. His eyes were golden and hungry, and she wasn't sure how safe he was. The doorjamb to her lower back stopped her retreat, and just as she thought of calling Paoli for help, she was pinned between the door and William's heavy body as he leaned against her.

"You are mine," he said, his mouth mere inches from her own.

It was in no way a question.

His voice sounded deep and gravelly, as if the words were torn from the pit of the earth itself.

Her heart hammered strangely at his declaration.

Her breath seemed to come in shallow pants.

With a low growl, his lips captured hers in a kiss that was anything but gentle. It was hungry and full of need; a mad onslaught of desire. His arms wrapped around her, dragging her against him.

She froze for a second, having been taken completely by surprise.

Then something in her answered his need, and she met his kiss with a heat of her own.

His mouth was warm and dry, but hot and open and invading hers with an expert tongue.

Her arms wrapped around his neck and she pressed herself against him, feeling his strength; his power all around her.

He cupped her head with one hand and pulled her leg up to his hip with the other.

She could feel the thick bulge of his erection pressing against her, giving her just enough friction to drive her need for more.

They were separated by no more than the thin cloth of her panties and the material of his athletic shorts. The only thought in her head was accepting every inch of him that was male.

"We have a situation in here. Are you two coming or what?" Paoli's voice called impatiently.

His demanding tone washed over Emily like cold water, and she pulled away and stiffened in William's arms.

William tore his mouth away and pressed his face against the wall, hiding his expression.

She had the suspicion he was fighting a battle she didn't understand.

Finally, his arms released her, and he took a step away, though he continued to keep his face averted.

"I'm sorry. It seems I may have overestimated my control where you're concerned. Please get dressed before you go in there," he said at last, his voice still sounding too deep.

She fought the urge to say, "You and me both," and instead moved away from him and back to her room on wobbly legs to comply with his request.

She hadn't even considered her lack of clothes. She pulled on a pair of pants before she headed down the hall to Amber's room.

William was thankfully gone when she reentered the hallway.

"Take me back!" Amber demanded loudly.

Those were the words that greeted Emily when she entered Amber's room.

Paoli looked at Emily with undisguised censure.

"Did it never occur to you to mention she didn't *want* to be rescued?" he asked.

Emily stared at him for a moment, at a loss for words.

How could she tell him her sister hated her, and had for years? How could she admit that to anyone, let alone a stranger?

Amber was propped up in the bed but struggling to rise.

If looks could kill, Emily would have been a puddle on the floor.

"You're not well," was all Emily could think to say, looking back at Amber.

She couldn't even bring herself to address Paoli's question, so she sidestepped it and turned all her attention to Amber.

"You need to rest," she said.

"I hate you. Brian's dead because of you. So help me, Emily. I'll make you pay for what you've done," Amber said in a voice that was laced with venom.

Emily swallowed hard, determined not to tear up.

She wouldn't cry.

Not this time.

Amber's hateful words were almost a staple of her personality.

As children, they'd been close.

But that was a long time ago.

"I couldn't leave you like that," Emily said almost pleadingly, her voice resigned to the worst. "I thought they were holding you against your will."

"You never should have been there. I don't want you in my life. It's not like I haven't made that clear by now. Leave me alone and become a nun or something. Do whatever perfect people do, and stay away from me," Amber spat.

Emily took it in silence and made no outward sign the words bothered her.

Paoli gave Emily a look that bordered dangerously on pity and only served to make her feel even worse.

"Remember, I warned you. With no outlet, the wolf's rage might cause personality changes," he said gently.

Emily gave a small, humorless laugh.

"This isn't a change from her normal, Paoli," she said quietly.

"If she hadn't been there," William's voice suddenly announced as he entered the room and crossed to Emily's side, "I would have killed you. So, maybe you should suppress your nastiness and show a bit of gratitude instead."

His voice was like a chip of ice and full of authority.

Amber glared at him.

"Go to hell. Brian's dead because of her," she snapped.

"Brian is dead because of me. Not her. You're alive thanks to Emily," William said, his voice low and dangerous. "I was there to kill you."

"Who was Brian to you?" Paoli asked Amber.

She didn't seem to have heard him. Her eyes were glued to William.

"Why would you want to kill me?" she asked, and there was a definite note of nervousness in her tone.

"There's an order of execution against you," William said.

Amber paled. She stared at William for a long moment.

"Are you the executioner?" she whispered, her voice now fearful instead of angry.

William nodded.

"The Coven ordered my death?" she asked, her eyes wide and full of horror.

"They did. I can't understand why Emily wants you spared. But we promised to try to help you," William said.

He glanced at Emily, who was standing at his elbow.

Emily reached out and brushed his fingers subtly in thanks.

He gave her a very subtle look of surprise.

After the space of a heartbeat, he gently wove his fingers through hers without a word.

"Like William said, we promised to try," Paoli interjected suddenly, breaking into the tension.

He clapped loudly, then held out his arms and shrugged.

"That's all we can do," he said.

He gave a loud sigh, as if that settled the matter.

"Now, everyone get ready to go. We leave for the Coven tonight," he said.

He turned and left the room without a glance, as if not noticing the rush of shock that ran through the room's occupants at his pronouncement.

William followed him into the hallway.

"You want to leave tonight?" he questioned. "Are you sure that's a good idea?"

"Nope," Paoli said quickly.

He started walking toward the stairs, and William kept pace beside him.

"But there aren't any other options, are there?" Paoli said.

He didn't stop to wait for an answer but went on to explain himself.

"I thought we'd have a few days. I wasn't expecting Emily's sister to be like *that*," he said.

He indicated the general direction of the bedroom with a wave of his arm.

"Do you want a woman with that much hatred for your mate to be in the same house with her?" Paoli asked.

William thought about it as he and Paoli made their way through the house.

He considered the execution that wasn't done, Amber's behavior, and his own situation with Emily.

"Not really," he had to admit. "But going before the Coven won't be easy."

Paoli stopped when they reached the library and gave a bark of laughter before he dropped into his office chair and looked up at William.

"We're bringing them a human and a malfunctioning she-wolf who should be dead. We'll be lucky if any of us walk out of there," he said.

While said lightly, it was a true statement and gave William pause.

"Maybe we should leave Emily here," he suggested.

It would be a mistake to take her before the Coven. They saw humans as having a single purpose on earth.

Food.

"Maybe you should just stop fighting it and claim your damn mate," Paoli returned smartly. "Before your wolf takes over and claims her without you there to gentle him."

"You think I don't want to?" William growled. "I can't think of anything else since I laid eyes on her. Hell, since I first *smelled* her. This is nothing short of torture. But I have no right to force my kind of existence on her. Besides, you saw what happened to her sister when they tried to change her."

Paoli hesitated.

"That's a valid point. I wonder why that happened," he mused aloud, clearly unperturbed by William's agitation. "I've never heard or read about anything like it."

"I don't know." William said irritably with a shrug. "But it's not a risk I'm willing to take. And I don't want her anywhere near the Coven. That's just asking for trouble."

Paoli rolled his eyes and snorted in derision.

"Do you really think her loving sister will leave her out of this mess? And if the Coven learns a human knows as much as she does, they'll send goons after her. It won't end well, especially if we're stuck there while she's here, alone and unprotected."

It was an idea William couldn't even allow himself to think of.

"If we just completed the execution, we wouldn't have to go at all," William said thoughtfully.

Paoli shook his head.

"Not true. I guarantee the wolves will complain to the Coven about their alpha being killed and a woman being stolen from their pack. Get that idea out of your mind," Paoli said.

Just the thought of her being at the Coven was enough to make William's chest tight.

But her alone and unprotected was worse.

She had to go.

"I don't like her being there, but I see your point," he said grudgingly.

She wouldn't leave his side for a minute while they were there, he decided.

"I don't like the idea of *any* of us being there under these circumstances," Paoli said with complete sincerity. "But this is where we are." Then he added, almost as an afterthought, "Tell her not to bring that gun of hers. It's sure to be noticed, and someone will be offended. The last thing we need is to give them an excuse."

CHAPTER 10

Emily stood, unarmed, on an airplane runway between a vampire and a "complicated" man who could turn into the world's biggest wolf. She was feeling slightly dazed and unreal. Everything happening seemed to have a dreamlike quality.

Behind them, a small white hanger stood in shadows. In front of them, a small plane taxied to a halt like a weird cab. The hatch opened to show a man she'd never seen.

His hair was long, similar to Paoli's, shoulder length, though not nearly as well kept.

She wondered absently if that meant they were from the same time period.

She turned to look at William, wondering about his age, and found he was scowling at her for some reason. She scowled back in response and returned her attention to the pilot, who made his way quickly to them.

Once he stopped and exchanged greetings with Paoli, his attention turned to her in a way that was just unnerving. His body didn't seem to move, but his head looked like it was rotating on an axis, and there was something she didn't like in his eyes.

The man gave her the creeps.

He stared at her with a smile that looked more reminiscent of a fat man at a buffet.

His long fangs were clearly visible.

Vampire.

Again, she glanced at Paoli, who was, after all, a vampire as well.

But where Paoli was friendly and light and carried his condition effortlessly, this man looked much more like what a person would expect a vampire to.

Especially his eyes. They were dead, hungry eyes.

Unconsciously, she moved closer to William's side.

"This is the girl I was referring to," Paoli said, pulling the man's attention back to him as he indicated an obviously tranced Amber, who was standing like a zombie on his other side.

The man moved over to look more closely at Amber.

He hunched down so he was eye level with her and moved his hand in front of her face, as if checking to see how well tranced she was.

Apparently satisfied, he straightened back up and looked at Paoli.

"And you want me to take her to Lycaon's people?" he asked.

He waited for Paoli to nod in agreement.

"All right. I'll keep her in the cockpit with me, then, and manage her for you when we arrive," said the creepy pilot.

"Perfect. Thank you, Walter," Paoli said, politely but dismissively.

The three of them watched Amber be led onto the small aircraft by a night-flying vampire.

Emily found herself shaking her head at the strangeness of it all.

Two days ago, her life had seemed so much of the same. She was simply chasing her sister into yet another mess she'd gotten herself into.

Now here she was.

She felt a bit like Alice down the rabbit hole.

But this was it.

It was the last time.

If she got out of this one, Amber was on her own.

Nearly half her life had been spent chasing her; finding her when she ran away from home, bailing her out of jail, coaxing her out of a cult. Each time it seemed she, Emily, was the one who got the worst of it while Amber flittered off again to the next disaster.

It was time to sever the relationship.

Past time, really.

This one last time, she would muster her courage and put on a brave face.

But honestly, she was terrified. She couldn't help feeling there may be no coming back for her this time.

William's eyes had been gold all evening, and she'd figured out that meant his wolf was close to the surface.

William was ready for trouble.

Paoli had been forcing smiles and was overly talkative, which she quickly understood meant he was nervous, as well.

Couple all of that with the fact she was being whisked away on a rickety little aircraft to fly halfway around the world to the government of the world's monsters, and terrified was putting it lightly.

Her legs were like rubber.

She wondered again how she'd ever let them talk her into this.

Then she remembered Paoli's warning that she could either come of her own accord, or he and William could bring two enthralled women.

Either way, she was coming.

She'd quickly decided she preferred to remain in control of her own body, so poof!

Here she was.

She spared a dark glare at Paoli.

William's warm hand was on the small of her back—such a small, but somehow comforting thing—and he gently urged her toward the steps of the plane.

Paoli walked, or *glided*, was a better word—apparently he forgot to act human when he was nervous—ahead and turned to offer a hand to her when her feet touched the first step.

Her own hand trembled when she reached for his, and he gave her a gentle and somewhat encouraging smile as he helped her onto the plane.

It was a tight little craft with only three rows of seats and just enough room for six passengers and two pilots, though tonight they only had one pilot and Amber in the front.

It was certainly not a craft designed for comfort, or to make a person feel particularly safe. Maybe they'd fall out of the sky and not have to worry about the Coven at all.

Emily settled nervously into a seat with William right beside her and Paoli across the aisle.

William was staring out of the window into nothing, clearly lost in thought.

It didn't escape her notice he was carrying an arsenal of weapons, including the twin hand sickles he'd used at the wolf's den. When she questioned him about it, he'd simply assured her it was purely precautionary.

Somehow, she wasn't buying it and resented that he could carry enough weapons for an army while she wasn't allowed as much as her gun for protection.

The trio was silent during takeoff, but when the plane righted itself and the flight became smooth again, she could bear the weight of silence no more.

She wanted answers.

She turned to Paoli and opened her mouth to speak, but found he was facing forward, his face slack, and his eyes completely white.

For a second, she was taken aback.

Her quick jerk away from him must have disturbed William's brooding, because he leaned across her and smacked Paoli in the back of the head.

Immediately, the white cleared from Paoli's eyes, and he seemed to almost . . . reanimate.

His head snapped toward William, and there was clear annoyance in his gaze.

"Knock it off," William said, ignoring Paoli's irritation. "You're scaring Emily."

Paoli spared William another dirty look before he turned his attention to Emily with an apologetic smile.

"I was just looking for . . . something," he said vaguely. "I didn't mean to startle you."

He gave his elegant apology, then shot yet another dirty look to William, who returned it with a tight smile.

Emily gave them both a quizzical look but decided they had more important things to discuss than Paoli's odd behavior.

"Are we heading into certain doom here?" she tried to break the tension by asking it as a half joke.

"Not certain," Paoli returned in the same light manner, as though they were discussing nothing more important than the weather.

"But it could be . . . let's just say unpleasant,"
William added.

His tone lacked the lightness of the others.

"The Coven isn't exactly known for their leniency.
An order was given, and they expected it to be followed.
This is the first time I've ever failed to follow an order.
We really don't know what to expect," William said.

Emily considered his words. "Not known for their
leniency" didn't sound good to her.

"Are you saying we could all be killed because of
Amber?" she asked.

"It's a little more complicated than that," William
told her. "For me, this isn't about your sister. It's about
you."

He held her gaze, and there was a deeper meaning
in his eyes than she understood.

"What do you mean?" she asked with a frown.

"If not for you, I would have executed Amber and
gone on my way," he answered simply.

"And now, because of me, you're prepared for
war?" she asked.

If something happened to either of them because
of her, she'd be forced to live with that knowledge. If
the Coven people let her live at all, that was.

He held her gaze for a long moment, and she felt a
thrill run through her belly.

"I'm ready to protect the things that matter to me.
It's just a precaution," he said.

There was no doubt in her mind he meant her.

"How scared should I be?" she asked of Paoli
specifically.

William was likely to say something cryptic to
make her feel better, and she needed the flat truth.

Paoli seemed to consider the question for a moment.

"Remember when I told you there were prices you couldn't even guess at?" he asked.

He waited for her to nod.

"I hope you really meant it when you said you'd do anything," he said.

Emily swallowed hard and leaned back against her seat. Maybe she didn't want the flat truth, after all.

"Is it too late to ask for the sugar-coated version?" she asked with a tight laugh.

William brushed her fingers with his own, and the contact sent a tingle all the way up her arm.

"You aren't alone. We'll defend you to the death, if it comes to that," he said.

Her eyes sought first William's steady gaze, then Paoli's. She saw nothing but raw honesty in both men. It wasn't just empty words. They were ready to risk their lives for her. It was a very humbling feeling.

"Why?" she asked in a small voice. "You barely know me."

William ignored Paoli's presence and cupped her face in his hands. His gaze bore deeply into hers.

"This isn't the human world, Emily. Things are different for us. Look into my eyes and tell me you don't already know the answer you seek. You may not have the words, but you know, just the same," he said.

She couldn't look away from the intensity in his eyes.

His hands were large and rough against her skin, but so gentle when he touched her.

She'd seen him take a life without hesitation.

She'd seen him *kill*.

But never in her life had she felt so protected, or like she simply . . . belonged.

It made no sense, especially in light of the situation she found herself in.

She was flying off to enter the government of monsters, unsure if she was to live or die, but the truth was right there in his eyes. She may have just met him—and Paoli, too—but they were willing to die to keep her safe.

She had more questions than answers.

But that, at least, she knew.

"I don't understand what's happening," she whispered, and for some reason, tears stung her eyes.

"I'm a little lost here, too," William admitted.

The rest of the flight went by amazingly fast.

Paoli told her it would take eleven hours to reach their destination, but it went by in a blur and was over almost as soon as it started.

At least it seemed that way to her.

She dozed off at some point. A change in the feel of the plane disturbed her rest.

When she woke up, Paoli's face was slack again, his eyes far off and white.

William was staring through the window again.

She took the opportunity to just look at him.

He was like the darkest fantasy of every woman's mind. Dangerous, mysterious, and too handsome for words.

"We've landed," he announced suddenly, then looked at her and gave a knowing smile.

Emily's cheeks burned when she realized she'd been caught staring at him.

Luckily, her embarrassment didn't last long.

William quickly ushered both she and Paoli from the plane.

She stepped out into the unexpectedly freezing Romanian air and gasped at the cold blast that bit at her. Her nostrils seemed to freeze together, and she had to breathe through her mouth. It was so cold, it made her eyes burn.

"Why, oh why couldn't the Coven be based somewhere tropical, like Tahiti?" she grumbled, her chin bouncing as she shivered.

William chuckled.

It was too dark to see much of the landscape, and she was too cold to really care, but she froze on the spot at the sight of the foreboding castle lit up in the distance.

It was like glimpsing something from ancient times.

Even as far away as they were, it was massive.

Towers seemed to be everywhere, ringing the structure and lending it an even more unearthly feel. It loomed before them like a giant, dwarfing everything else.

Each step she took away from the airplane seemed she was slipping further and further into the past. She vaguely heard Paoli talking to the pilot about separate transportation for Amber, then he was on one side of her and William was on the other.

A small car awaited them, but even that didn't deter from the feeling of leaving reality behind.

She sat in the back seat with William, and Paoli took shotgun.

She stared out at the darkened countryside and thought about every vampire movie she'd ever seen as the car made the short trip to the castle. They drove over an honest-to-God drawbridge and pulled through what once would have been a small village to arrive at the doorway of the castle.

William and Paoli flanked her again as they approached the massive doors, the gravel crunching beneath their feet.

She expected a hunchbacked old man to be on the other side, just to complete the picture.

When a beautiful young woman easily swung open the doors before them, Emily almost giggled at the unexpectedness of it.

The woman's face was nearly angelic, framed by a river of blonde hair. Her eyes lit up with recognition as soon as they landed on Paoli.

"Paoli," the woman crooned with almost sickening sweetness. "It's been a long time."

"Many years, Mary," Paoli agreed with a friendly nod.

The girl stepped back and waved them into a massive antechamber.

It was magnificent.

White stonework surrounded them, nearly covered in old portraits and family crests. Some of them had to be at least five hundred years old. Marble floors gleamed beneath their feet, but much of the stone was covered in woven rugs in neutral colors, with dainty designs that popped in silver thread. Throughout the room, decorative pillars topped with cherub faces pushed into a ceiling at least ten feet high.

People stood around the massive room in small groups, while others walked by in pairs, whispering low. It dawned on her she was by far the youngest thing there, and the only fragile human.

Her heart began beating overtime.

William must have noticed, because he discretely put his comforting hand on the small of her back again.

"My goodness, William," Mary gasped, stepping toward William once she'd finally managed to tear her eyes from Paoli. "Look at you!" Her voice sounded almost awed. "I admit, I've never been able to picture you as an adult. The last time I saw you, I think you must have been just a teenager. But," she laughed a little ruefully, "in my mind, you've always been the child with a death sentence Paoli carried through these doors so many years ago."

William stiffened just enough for Emily to notice, but not enough anyone else would.

"That was centuries ago," William said stiffly.

Mary laughed, a high-pitched, musical sound.

"Yes, I suppose it was," she agreed easily.

Then her casual demeanor faded, and a new sparkle shimmered in her eyes.

It took Emily just a second to place the look.

Hunger.

Predatory hunger.

"And what have we here?" Mary asked, her attention riveted on Emily.

"Why, Paoli," she said, her eyes still on Emily. "In all your visits, you've never brought a hostess gift before."

Emily opened her mouth foolishly to tell the woman just what she thought of being equated to nothing more than a gift. Before she could utter a word, she was shoved behind William's back, and Paoli blocked them both.

"I still haven't," Paoli was quick to say.

His voice held a clear warning.

"You know how I feel about killing," he said.

Mary made a practiced and perfected pouty moue with her perfect lips and raised her hands in surrender to show she meant no harm.

"I always thought you'd outgrow that," she said.

Paoli broke the tense atmosphere with a teasing, boyish smile.

"Afraid not. Some of us are what we are, eh, Mary?" he said, throwing her a knowing wink.

Mary threw back her head and laughed carelessly. Her return smile was both overtly flirtatious and a little guilty.

"I suppose that's true," she said.

With a final pout in his direction, she turned toward the massive set of stairs in the center of the room.

"Follow me, and I'll get you guys settled in," she told them over her shoulder.

CHAPTER 11

Emily didn't feel remotely safe until the door to her room closed behind her and she was alone. She leaned against the door in relief and slid down to her butt right there on the floor.

With nervous fingers, she touched the silver cross in her front pocket, thankful Paoli had returned it.

A thousand panicked ideas flashed through her head.

At the top of the list was RUN.

But run where?

She was now in a strange country with no passport or even identification to prove who she was. Besides, the entire world of monsters was either already aware, or soon would be, that she knew about them.

There wasn't a place on earth she would be safe.

She silently cursed both Amber and her own stupidity. She should have refused to come here. Or even better, as soon as she learned her sister had gotten involved with actual werewolves, she should have left Amber to figure it out on her own and been done, once and for all.

Eventually, she pulled herself together and decided wishing she'd made different choices wouldn't fix her current situation.

With a huff, she made it back to her feet and went to explore her new surroundings.

A look around the room left her in disbelief.

She'd never seen such luxury.

The chamber was small and made of stone, as was the rest of the castle. A large fireplace graced one wall,

and wood had been laid in preparation for a fire but
sat cold and untouched. Along the opposite wall was
a tan sofa and a small table—complete with a basket
full of fruits and breads—boxed in by two plush chairs
that were just a few shades darker than the sofa and
accented it perfectly.

Against the other wall sat an antique highboy
right beside the ornate doorway that led to a spacious
bathroom. The center of the room boasted a large
sleigh bed, piled with pillows of all different colors
and textures. The space obviously reflected years of
many different cultures all coming together in this
one place. There were even matching Spanish night
tables on either side of the headboard.

It served to remind her there was no place on
earth immortals didn't grace.

She felt small and insignificant in the face of
splendor that spanned so many years into history.

She didn't belong among it.

A soft knock sounded on the door and startled
her.

Before she could even answer, William and Paoli
burst into the room with more noise and bustle than
two people should be capable of.

Emily was prepared for a horde of bloodthirsty
monsters to be following them, but they were alone.
Her relief was short lived when she noticed the look
on William's face. He didn't look happy, but Paoli's
eyes held an excited sparkle she didn't trust at all.

"What's going on?" she asked suspiciously.

Paoli closed the door behind them, crossed the
room, and sat in one of the chairs at the table without
answering. He motioned for her to sit across from

him, which she did with great hesitation and a questioning look in William's direction.

He gave her an affirmative nod.

"Do you trust me?" Paoli asked with all sincerity once she was seated.

She looked at him uncertainly.

"Somewhat," she answered slowly.

She didn't like how this conversation was starting. At all.

William moved to stand behind her.

If he was trying to make her feel protected, it had just the opposite effect and made her feel boxed in and trapped.

"You need to trust us now," Paoli said. His voice was level and serious. "Tomorrow we go before the Coven, and we need answers."

Something about his tone told her there was more, and she braced herself for whatever he was excited about.

"I'll tell you anything I can," she said.

He exchanged a cringing look with William over her head and gave her an apologetic smile.

"The answers we need are in your blood," he said with a hopeful yet questioning look.

She *really* didn't like the sound of that.

"What?" she asked, her voice already a resolute refusal.

Paoli winced slightly at her tone.

"I'm sorry to ask," he said quickly. "I know it sounds horrific to you," he went on, in an almost paternal tone. "We just need a few drops."

Emily stood slowly from her chair and moved to the side, keeping her eyes on Paoli.

She needed some space between herself and the two predators. Predators who suddenly wanted her blood. She absently fingered the cross in her pocket again.

"There's no way anyone in this godforsaken place is biting my neck to take *any* of my blood," she said.

Her tone was rigid and inflexible.

Emily tried to remember everything she knew about vampire folklore.

Weren't they known to play with their victims before they consumed them?

Her heart almost seemed to twist in her chest at the idea William could have lured her here as part of some sadistic game.

She looked at him. Wondering.

Something inside her said—screamed—no, but she was afraid to believe it. Why else would they want her blood?

"I told you I should have talked to her alone," William growled at Paoli before he turned his attention back to her. "Paoli's excited at a new idea. I'm sorry he was so . . ."

William shot a scathing look at Paoli.

"Blunt. Come back and sit down," he said in a commanding voice.

She looked at him like he'd just sprouted horns.

"I think not!" she cried.

A bubble of hysterical laughter escaped her.

"Emily, that's enough." William's voice became low and gentle. Persuasive. "You're upsetting yourself over nothing."

Nothing?

She shook her head hard enough to make her ears ring.

"My life's blood isn't nothing. Not to me," she said.

He held his hand out toward her and met her eyes.

His own were deep gold.

In their depths, she didn't see animal violence and death. Instead, she saw safety, honesty, and just a hint of raw pain.

Had her fear caused him pain?

She found herself catching a breath at the very thought.

"We would never hurt you. You can trust us," William whispered thickly.

She wasn't sure if he meant he and Paoli, or he and his wolf.

"I'm not talking about biting your neck," Paoli chimed in. "I don't drink from the source."

At her surprised expression, he laughed.

"It's true. I've never actually bitten a human. It's allowed me to keep a spotless record of zero vampire kills. Avoiding temptation is the best way to ensure everyone's safety," he said.

He gave a little nod, as if confirming what he'd just said to himself.

"Then how do you plan to get my blood?" she demanded.

"I'm talking about a pinprick to your finger. It'll help us find out what's really going on. If we go before the Coven with less than the whole story, we may get ourselves killed," Paoli said calmly.

"A pinprick?" she echoed, her panic seeping away to be replaced by embarrassment.

Paoli really should have started there, she decided quickly.

It was far less scary than the pictures in her head.

"Yes, a pinprick," William confirmed. "If it makes you feel better, you can even pick the finger."

She looked at him, trying to decide if he was making fun of her or not. She decided he was and fought the urge to give *him* the finger.

Now she felt really stupid.

"Why are you so determined to get my blood all of the sudden?" she asked Paoli, ignoring William.

Paoli nodded absently.

"That's a fair question. Mary pointed out it isn't possible for a human to be mated to a wolf," he said.

She gave him a confused look.

"Mated?" she asked.

What the hell did that mean?

"It's something we'll have to discuss another time," William said by way of explanation, but she noticed him throw Paoli a dark glare.

"So," Paoli went on, redirecting her attention back to him. "I realized there might be a clue in your blood."

"You can find clues in my blood?" she asked, intrigued.

She couldn't hide her surprise. It was interesting to consider and made sense once she stopped panicking and thought about it.

"Possibly," Paoli shrugged. "It's worth a try."

Emily slowly stepped toward the table and paused to pull the cross from her pocket.

"OK," she agreed slowly. "But I'm going to hold this in my other hand in case you get . . . I don't know . . . *hungry* at me," she warned.

Paoli quickly smothered a grin.

"All right," he agreed seriously. "But I promise not to get *hungry* at you."

She slid back into the chair and held her hand out across the table. In her other hand, she gripped the cross so tightly her knuckles were white.

She was very aware of William's presence behind her, now supportive instead of entrapping.

Paoli gave her an encouraging smile, then produced a small hairpin and hesitated. He glanced at William.

"Are you sure it's a good idea for you to stay?" he asked.

A few seconds passed in silence.

"I'm fine," William said.

"Hold very still, and please trust me," Paoli said to Emily in a serious, slightly pleading voice. "I can't promise not to look scary, but I won't hurt you. I've never killed a human."

He paused, seeming to consider his own words.

"Not as a vampire, anyway," he amended. "You're not going to be my first."

Emily nodded and took a deep breath to steady her nerves for the pain.

It was over almost immediately.

One sharp poke and it was done.

After that, she *really* felt foolish for making such a scene.

Until the blood drops welled on her finger and Paoli suddenly had fangs.

Big fangs, and his eyes glowed with a ruby red light.

She couldn't quite stifle a gasp of horror as he swiped the drops from her hand and turned his face away.

Seconds stretched into minutes, and she continued to stare at the back of his head, afraid to even blink.

She would never get used to his vampire appearance.

"This goes much deeper than we know," he announced finally with a touch of awe in his voice.

He turned back to her and stared.

His face was, thankfully, back to normal.

She waited for him to say more, but he just continue to stare at her.

"What are you talking about?" she asked a little impatiently.

"Mary was right," he said.

His gaze fell to William, then back to her.

"You're not human. Not completely, at least," he said.

"What?" she breathed, now in disbelief herself.

"What else?" William asked, having apparently noticed something in Paoli's face.

Paoli hesitated.

He looked back and forth between her and William, as if debating something.

"She will see her father tomorrow," he declared finally.

"My father?" Emily questioned skeptically.

She'd never even heard her father's name.

She doubted her mother even knew the truth of her paternity.

"Her father?" William echoed, his voice sounding as lost as she felt.

"I don't know who my father is," Emily interjected. "He doesn't even know I exist."

Paoli nodded, but it was more of a thoughtful gesture than an agreement.

"Who is her father?" William asked.

Paoli looked at him for a long, heavy moment.

"Lycaon," he said finally.

An uncomfortable silence stretched out.

"Are you sure?" William asked, his voice sounding very concerned. "I mean absolutely sure?"

Paoli nodded solemnly, this time in answer.

"Who is Lycaon?" Emily asked, allowing their heated reactions to infect her.

"He's king of the werewolves," Paoli said.

"What?" she gasped.

Surely, she'd misunderstood.

"Lycaon is your father," Paoli said with a slight shake of his head. "I don't know what's going on any more than you do, but we'll soon find out."

She barely heard him.

She was in shock. Her father was the king of the werewolves? How was that even possible?

"What's going on here?" William wondered aloud.

Paoli shrugged, clearly as lost as everyone else.

"Your guess is as good as mine," he said.

"I don't like this." William said. "It's unsettling. There's something happening we don't know about. Something a lot bigger than our failing to execute one woman."

"Why would Lycaon have children with a human just to leave them?" Emily questioned quietly, her mind reeling. "Did my mother know he was a . . . you know?"

She couldn't even bring herself to say the word.

Her father was a werewolf.

Not just *a* werewolf, but the *king* of werewolves.

"I don't know," Paoli answered. "But Lilith—the queen of vampires—isn't going to be happy when this comes out tomorrow. I doubt she's aware Lycaon has done this."

"The queen of the vampires?" Emily said in a slightly mocking tone. "She's going to be angry with me?"

That sounded just about right, considering everything else that had happened.

Why not?

Paoli gave her an apologetic look.

"Not with you, exactly. But she'll be angry when she learns the truth. This hints at betrayal. The best thing you can do is try to appear meek and stay behind William and me. We'll shield you as much as possible."

"Meek?" William snorted.

Emily rewarded him with a glare and he gave her a mock-contrite look, though his eyes glittered with humor.

"We'd better prepare you for tomorrow," Paoli said a while later. "It could get ugly. Coven members aren't human."

"Neither are the two of you," Emily pointed out reasonably. "Neither am I, apparently."

Her voice was full of self-mockery.

William smiled at that.

"True enough," he said.

"Are you at all familiar with mythology?" Paoli asked.

Mythology?

She remembered bits and pieces from high school, but not enough to mention. Something about a woman with snakes for hair and a kid who flew too close to the sun.

She doubted either of those stories would be helpful.

She shook her head.

"Sorry," she said.

"It doesn't matter. It would just make things easier on you if you knew what to expect," William said.

What to expect?

Great, she thought with a heavy sigh—that sounded reassuring.

"So, I'm going to see a werewolf who happens to be my father, and a very old female vampire?" she asked.

Simple enough.

Right.

Happens all the time.

"Lilith isn't a vampire," William corrected.

Emily frowned.

"But I thought she was the queen of vampires," she said.

Paoli nodded.

"She is. But she, herself, is not a vampire. At least not in the sense you might expect," he said.

She looked at Paoli for a moment. He wasn't exactly what she would have thought of as a vampire, either.

"So, no pale skin and fangs?" she asked.

"I'm afraid not. She's a succubi. Vampires were created when she lay with a human and gave birth to a child. That child was Lillu, the first daughter of Lilith. Lillu went on a spree through the world biting males during—" He broke off and gave William a beseeching look.

"Mating," William supplied helpfully.

"Thank you," Paoli muttered, then turned his attention back to Emily.

"Anyway, Lilith is unearthly beautiful, but her very essence is that of a seductress. She doesn't like women much. Sees them as competition, I suppose. She has wings—" he said.

"And a tail," William interrupted to add.

Wings and a tail?

What had she gotten herself into?

"Oh, God," Emily groaned.

If she survived this ordeal, she was killing Amber herself.

"Basically, you're saying I'm going to be the only human in a room with a monster straight from horror movies and nightmares, and the other one is my dear old dad?" she asked sarcastically.

William looked at her for a moment, as if trying to puzzle her out.

"Remember, you're not alone. Or human, for that matter," he reminded her reassuringly.

"I'm not human," she said, a weird, hollow note to her voice. "Then what am I?"

"You're a cambion," Paoli said.

She scowled at him, unfamiliar with the term.

"A cambion," he explained, "is what Lillu is. A mixture of human and demon blood. They're like snowflakes, with no two alike."

He said it like it should be a source of pride.

"You're saying I'm half demon?" she asked incredulously.

Both Paoli and William laughed slightly at her reaction.

"Please don't take offense," Paoli said after a moment. "I didn't mean it in a negative way."

Emily gave him a dubious look.

"You tell me one way being half demon could be a positive thing," she demanded.

Paoli sobered slightly, a small smile still playing around the edges of his mouth.

"The world of immortals is full of demons," he informed her patiently, as though he were speaking to a small child. "We aren't exactly the way it's recorded religiously. Here, being at least part demon is commonplace."

She wasn't appeased by his response.

He gave her a slight shrug, as if to say, "It is what it is."

"We'll find out more tomorrow," he said. "In the meantime, you need to eat."

He slid the basket of fruits and breads toward her.

She looked at the food and slid it away.

"I don't really feel like eating. Do you know where they took Amber? I'm sure she'd be interested to know about our father," Emily said.

Paoli frowned and looked thoughtful for a moment.

"Stay here. I'll go see what I can find out," he said.

He left the room much more quietly than he'd entered.

As soon as the door closed behind him, William slid the basket toward her again.

"You need to eat. You haven't had so much as a drop of water since yesterday," he said in his authoritative voice, and she wasn't up to battling him about something so trivial.

With a dramatic flourish, she selected a fat peach and held it up for his inspection before biting into it.

William grunted his approval and draped himself across the chair Paoli had vacated.

A knock sounded on the door just a few minutes later.

William moved to open it but paused halfway across the room and sniffed the air.

He stepped silently against the wall on the hinge side of the door and motioned for Emily to open it, instead.

She gave him a questioning look but did as he bid without comment.

She opened the door just a crack and saw a man who looked impossible in his perfection, like a statue of an ancient god come to life.

In his hands, a dinner tray gave off the most delicious scent and made her rethink her earlier stance about not being hungry.

"I'm Marcus," the man introduced himself, his voice low and heavy.

"Hello," she responded warily.

Marcus cocked his head expectantly.

"I brought you something to eat and a robe to wear tomorrow for your meeting with the Coven," he said.

He held out the robe and tray with a heart-stopping smile.

"May I come in, please? I'd like a few moments with you to discuss things," he said, but something about his tone made her uneasy.

His voice was perfect in pitch and cadence, and almost musical to listen to, but she couldn't help feeling there was more meaning in his words than she understood.

"Thank you," she mumbled.

She took the robe and food gratefully and threw a covert glance at William.

He gave a slight nod.

"OK," she agreed to Marcus.

She stepped back to allow him entrance.

As soon as he cleared the door, William grabbed him by the throat and slammed him into the wall without warning.

Emily gasped in surprise and horror and moved quickly toward the other side of the room without even closing the door.

She practically threw the robe and tray onto the table and found a spot she hoped was out of the way.

"Hear this now," William hissed at the man, Marcus, dangerously. "Tell all of your kind that Emily is my mate. If any of you come near her again, I will tear them limb from limb."

William was intimidating even when he smiled, but he was downright terrifying when he felt the need.

Emily swallowed hard.

Absently, she realized there was that word again.

Mate.

She needed to ask him about the term when he didn't look like he was about to break someone in half.

Marcus' face began to turn a deep shade of purple, and his eyes bulged. Blind and desperate fingers clawed at William's strong hand, trying to break his grasp to no avail.

"Do you understand me?" William asked, his voice gravelly with his wolf's power.

Marcus couldn't speak with William's hand squeezing his throat closed, so he gave a frantic nod instead.

"Good," William snapped and dragged Marcus toward the open door. "Then pass the word."

With that, he shoved the other man through the door and slammed it behind him.

"Incubi," William grumbled in clear disgust with a shake of his head. "Nasty creatures. Ruled entirely by their loins and incapable of any other thought," he said, apparently still mumbling to himself.

He turned back toward Emily, whose face must have shown the shock she felt.

He stopped and gave her an apologetic, slightly guilty smile.

"Sorry about that," he said hesitantly.

"Sorry about that?" she asked incredulously.

He had almost squeezed the life out of someone for bringing her dinner, and all he could think to say was "sorry about that"?

She stared at him expectantly.

He stared back for a moment, as if he couldn't figure out why she was alarmed.

"Marcus is an incubi," he explained, as if it should make sense.

Her eyes flashed with impatience.

William gave a slight gasp of understanding.

"A seducer," he said. "Incubi seduce young women while they sleep. We need the others to know you aren't here for sport."

As if tomorrow wasn't already going to be bad enough, now she had to worry about creatures seducing her in her sleep?

Where was a good, sturdy chastity belt when she needed one?

"Others? How many others are there?" she asked.

"How many other incubi are here?" William tried to clarify her question.

"How many kinds of immortals are there?" Emily asked.

Bigfoot, Loch Ness monster—were they all wandering around these halls, just waiting to snap her up for a midnight snack?

"Many," he said with a careless shrug. "I'm not sure of the exact number, but the Coven is the court for our world. There are hundreds here at any time."

"Of course," she mumbled bitterly.

It only made sense for her to land in the Grand Central Station of the immortal world.

Fabulous.

"Paoli is a vampire, I'm apparently half-demon, and you claim you're 'complicated,'" she counted them off.

She put finger quotes around the word "complicated," a testament to how infuriated she felt since she *never* air quoted.

"I *am* complicated," he insisted.

"Wait a second," she said abruptly.

Mary's greeting words suddenly floated into her head.

"Mary said you were a child with a death sentence when you first arrived here," she said.

Her mind raced as pieces started to fall into place.

William gave her a guarded look, his face carefully blank.

He didn't respond.

"You told me the Coven only reversed one order for execution. It was *yours*, wasn't it?" she gasped.

CHAPTER 12

Yes," William admitted quietly. "And like Paoli said, it came with a very high price."

Her brows knit together in confusion.

"You were condemned as a kid? But how did you continue to age if you were an immortal child?" she asked.

"It's—" he began.

"Don't even say it's complicated," she interrupted shortly. "This looks like a good time for explanations."

She crossed the room to sit down at the table, made an elaborate point of settling back in her chair, then gestured to the other chair.

While she was waiting for him to join her, she lifted the lid on the tray and found a delightful dinner of roast beef and carrots.

She didn't hesitate to start eating.

The food was surprisingly delicious. A sweet glaze on the carrots made them melt in her mouth.

William took the chair across from her and leaned back, watching her in a thoughtful silence. Only once she'd finished eating and pushed her plate away did he take a deep, resigned breath.

"Are you sure you want to know this?" he asked. "Knowledge is like Pandora's box. Once it's opened, there's no going back."

She looked at him.

Something about his carefully neutral features made her wonder if it made him uncomfortable to talk about the subject.

"I have a feeling I need to know," she said at last.

He considered her for another moment, then gave an almost imperceptible nod.

"If anyone needs to know my story, it's you, I guess," he said, and another silence stretched out.

"My mother was a werewolf," he told her finally, his voice flat and distant. "She interrupted a group of vampires when they attacked my father. Somehow— and I don't know the details—she managed to fight them off and save my father's life. At least, she *thought* she'd saved his life. She took him back to the small house she had in the mountains and proceeded to nurse him back to health."

He paused and looked at her before he continued.

"As it turned out, she hadn't arrived in time to save him, after all. He died and rose again as the undead. She was forced to kill him to protect the villagers, just as she'd tried to protect him," he said.

Emily's mouth fell open in horror.

William gave her a hard smile of agreement and continued.

"But before that happened, she'd already conceived a son," he told her.

"You," Emily whispered.

"Me," William agreed. "It wasn't long after my birth before she realized that while I could become a wolf—like her—I still had the need for human blood, as well. It fell to her to provide it for me."

Emily stared at him.

"So, after everything she'd done to keep humans safe, she . . ." Emily let the words trail off, as if the thought was too much to put into words.

She shook her head slowly, unable to imagine a mother put in such a position.

William nodded at her unspoken words.

"She didn't kill the way she should have. And rumors began that eventually reached the Coven. Because of her failure to remain discreet and undetected, an order for execution was issued against her. She saw them coming one night and sent me alone into the village," he said.

"How old were you?" Emily asked in a hushed tone, as if speaking too loudly might somehow dispel or disrespect the past.

William swallowed hard and turned his head away for a moment.

"Five," he answered finally. "Somehow, the executioner learned of my existence," he continued, turning back to face her. "But I'd been taken in by a local human couple, and he wasn't able to find me. He returned to the Coven, where it was determined I was an abomination. A new order for execution was issued against me. They sent someone else to track me down."

He chuckled slightly, though Emily couldn't see anything funny about it.

"It was meant to be his own punishment, as well," he said.

"Who did they send?" Emily asked, leaning forward slightly.

William held her gaze a moment.

"Paoli," he answered.

She gasped.

"They sent Paoli to kill you?" she asked, stunned.

She waited for him to nod, then asked, "But why was *he* being punished?"

"Back in those days, there was no set executioner. Whoever resided in an area was given the order to execute, and it was expected they would follow through with the Coven's dictates. Paoli had failed to carry out his orders multiple times. He hates death," William explained. "Instead, he brought most condemned people here, to beg for their lives. The last time he did so, the Coven killed the person right in front of him, then demanded he carry out the new order against me, instead. He was informed that if he failed, they would find a fitting punishment for him."

William's face hardened.

"And the Coven is known for some horrible punishments," he added bitterly.

"Wow," Emily breathed.

In her mind's eye, she could picture the scene perfectly.

"But when he found me, he couldn't do it," William went on. "Instead, he brought me here to beg for my life, at great risk to his own."

"And obviously, he was successful," Emily said, gesturing to him.

"Depends on how you look at it," William corrected gently. "They were afraid of me. There's never been an immortal with blood from both species, and they were afraid I'd be unstoppable if I attacked them. Paoli pointed out I could be useful if raised to follow their orders."

"Like a trained animal?" she gasped in outrage.

William nodded curtly.

"But they wanted insurance of my compliance. So, as his punishment, Paoli was forced to raise me. It was agreed that if I refuse to follow their orders, *his* life will be the one that is forfeit," he said.

"That's barbaric!" Emily said with heat.

"And thus," William concluded. "I've been enslaved as the Coven's executioner my entire life. I'm a slave, Emily. The Coven's property."

"No," she disagreed. "You're no one's property. You're just William, making the best of the hand you were dealt."

He gave her a smile that didn't reach his eyes, and they fell into silence for awhile, each lost in their own thoughts.

She was thinking about his story, imagining Paoli and the little boy that would grow up to be the executioner.

A new question occurred to her.

"What did you mean when you said I'm your mate?" she asked.

William seemed startled by the question and just stared at her silently until she squirmed.

"Sorry," he mumbled, then shook his head slightly, as if to clear it.

His eyes darted toward the door, then back to her. He shifted uncomfortably in his chair, then stood and began to pace around a small distance from the table.

She remained silent and waited for an explanation.

"I was raised by a vampire," he said carefully. "And there's a lot of bad blood between wolves and vampires. They've been at war since—" He stopped and gave a humorless chuckle. "The dawn of time, I think. I haven't spent much time with werewolves. All I know is what we read in Paoli's book."

Emily waited, not really following his thoughts.

"Anything is more than I know now," she said reasonably.

He made a noncommittal noise and resumed pacing.

"Werewolves are like regular wolves in a lot of ways," he said. "Wolves mate for life."

He eyed her for a second, clearly gauging her reaction to this news.

Emily just sat still, watching him and waiting for him to make sense.

She had a suspicion about where he was going with this and found her chest growing tight.

"Werewolves are the same," he went on. "Mates know each other instinctively."

His gaze grew heavy and meaningful, and he once again stopped pacing.

"Once they find each other, they can't be separated. There's only one mate for a werewolf."

He hesitated again, then plunged on.

"You're mine," he announced.

Silence stretched out as Emily just stared at him.

"I beg your pardon?" she said finally, her voice dangerous.

She pushed to her feet very slowly.

She was angry.

More than angry.

Just who did he think he was, to make an outlandish claim like that? And they could never be separated? She snorted aloud at the very idea. Well, that wasn't going to happen. She may be in crazy-land right now, but she was going back to normal-world as soon as this was over.

She stalked over to stand in front of him, drawing herself up to the extent of her five and a half feet, practically vibrating with rage.

"You can't just come into my life and claim me like undiscovered land. I have a life of my own to live. Once I get out of this mess, I intend to go back to it," she declared.

Even as she said the words, she could feel the pain rise from her stomach at the idea of going back to her lonely apartment and never seeing him again.

It made her even angrier.

What the hell was happening to her?

William stood still, watching her silently until she was done. Then he gave her a patient smile, laced with male superiority that made her want to slap him.

"You're not going back to your old life," he said gently.

"Oh-ho!" she scoffed. "Yes, I am. You just watch me," she proclaimed, her voice getting just a little louder and more forceful.

Unexpected tears gathered in her eyes. A silent denial screamed through her head, and it scared her. She had to get out of here, away from him before it was too late. She was so busy fighting with herself, she didn't even realize he'd moved until he was standing directly in front of her, crowding her with his . . . his . . . *maleness.*

When she met his eyes, she noticed his were gold and flashing.

"You're mine," he said in a dark, possessive tone.

Before she could open her mouth to deny it, he pulled her roughly into his arms and claimed her mouth with his.

Emily tried not to respond.

She really did.

But if ever there was a man who knew how to kiss, it was William. He didn't gently coax her but forced her to feel every bit of his desire, his need, and she was lost from the very start under an onslaught of sensation.

With a slight moan of surrender, she gave up the battle. There was no fighting it, anyway. His lips, teeth, and tongue all teased and thrilled, and his hands cupped the underside of her chin possessively. She responded to his passion with an equal measure of her own and kissed him back as though her very life depended on it.

William hadn't meant to kiss her. When she started talking about leaving, his wolf rose up and demanded their mate. He fed the wolf with her scent, her taste, her touch, and felt it settle down again.

His mate.

She was *his*.

Paoli was right. He never had a choice.

Once his wolf recognized her, there was no escape for either of them. She wasn't going anywhere, whatever she thought.

Her place was at his side, and he was going to keep her there, selfish or no. And the consequences be damned. It was time to claim her properly, so she'd never be able to think of leaving him again.

William gave a deep, throaty groan and pushed his throbbing erection against her. He needed her to feel the effect she had on him; to know how badly he wanted to be inside of her.

She rubbed against him just the slightest bit, which drove him even closer to the breaking point of his control. The powerful scent of her arousal reached his nose, and he continued to feed her need, moving one hand slowly up her side to catch the heavy weight of her perfect breast in his palm.

A knock sounded at the door, and William responded with a vicious warning growl that was all wolf.

Paoli entered the room in his usual high-energy manner.

Before William could stop her, Emily let out a small shriek and leapt from his arms to put the distance of the entire room between them, much to his frustration. He scowled after her, but since she was facing the wall, it didn't do him much good.

For a moment, he seriously considered chucking Paoli back through the door but grudgingly reconsidered. He settled for glaring at Paoli, instead.

The man had horrible timing.

"Sorry," Paoli grumbled under his breath, stopping just inside the door with a distinctively uncomfortable look on his face. "I didn't realize—"

He broke off after a warning look from William.

"It's not like you didn't know I was coming back," he hissed defensively.

Then, shrugging off the awkward moment, he announced cheerily, "I have some news."

William swallowed hard and cleared his throat before speaking.

"What did you find out?" he asked.

His voice sounded almost normal, if a little strained.

"They took Amber to Lycaon as soon as we arrived. She's been with him in his private quarters ever since," Paoli said.

Emily turned back to face the room with a frown.

"But we've been here for hours," she pointed out. "What could they have been doing all this time?"

Paoli flopped carelessly onto the couch and dangled his leg over the arm.

"Maybe something terrible, or maybe just catching up. I'm sure we'll find out soon enough," he said nonchalantly. "Dawn is breaking soon and we need to get some rest. Tomorrow night will be here before we know it, and who knows what it may bring?" he said.

He eyed William questioningly and—with his face turned away from Emily—waggled his eyebrows suggestively.

"I would prefer if we all stay together until tomorrow," Emily announced. "With Marcus and who knows what else out there waiting to prey on me."

She motioned to the door and the hall beyond, but William noticed her eyes never left *him*.

Paoli nodded absently.

"I agree. At least until after we meet with the Coven," he added when William gave him a dark glare.

CHAPTER 13

The following evening came far too soon. It seemed they had all just settled in their respective places to rest—Emily in the bed, Paoli on the couch, and William on one of the chairs—when it was time to start getting ready for their meeting.

William shook Emily awake.

She sat up, grumbling complaints, and looked at him bleary eyed. Her hair, which was normally bouncing in rich, dark waves around her, stood out in all directions, as if she'd tossed and turned all night.

"You should put this on. It's almost time," William said, holding up the white robe.

She groaned and swung her legs over the side of the bed, stifling a wide yawn.

When Paoli looked up at her, he jumped back in overly dramatic horror, grabbing at his chest as though the look of her had given him a real fright.

Emily made a face at him, then turned her attention to the robe in William's hand.

She took it and eyed it with doubt. The garment was a white robe with an unadorned gold braided belt.

Her face crinkled in distaste.

"Why should I have to go looking like a virgin sacrifice?" she asked.

"It's required for all mortals going before the Coven," Paoli said by way of explanation.

She laid it on the bed with a grimace.

"What are you guys wearing?" she asked suspiciously.

"Don't worry. We have to wear robes, too," William said placatingly. "It's just standard procedure."

"Do your robes look like *this*?" she asked, gesturing toward the offending garment.

William glanced at it.

"Immortals tend to be very symbolic and hold to ancient customs, especially here," he said.

"Then what symbol is this supposed to be?" she asked. "Because if I'm going into a room full of monsters who view me as a steak dinner, I'd rather not go in looking like an offering."

Paoli chuckled.

"Does the meaning really matter?" he asked.

"It does to me," she said stubbornly.

"All right, then," Paoli surrendered with a sigh. "Mortals wear white to signify they are pure. Vampires wear red to signify the blood, and werewolves wear black to signify the night."

She looked at William with the slightest teasing sparkle in her eyes.

"Do you wear stripes, then?" she asked with a smirk.

William chuckled slightly.

"I wear gray," he said.

She nodded as if she found his answer acceptable.

"How many times have you been before the Coven?" she asked.

"A few, but it's been many years," William said.

He didn't bother to tell her the last time was during his teenaged rebellion years.

He'd left yet another body for Paoli to help him dispose of. As Mary mentioned when they arrived, Paoli brought him before the Coven in the hopes they could find better control of his appetites.

Instead of helping, however, they simply pointed out that William was a natural-born predator. They said the best Paoli could do was keep disposing of the bodies in a way the humans would have no reason to question. They had also pointed out how poetic it was that Paoli's refusal to take a life had landed him the job of being responsible for the kills of such a predator.

William hadn't returned since.

Until now.

Emily looked at Paoli.

"And you?" she asked.

"I've been before the Coven many more times than William," he said.

She sighed, grabbed the robe from the bed, and disappeared into the bathroom.

While she was gone, both William and Paoli got into their own robes.

When she finally opened the bathroom door again, her hair was back to normal, and she was wearing her white robe. She paused in the doorway, looking apprehensive, as if she'd lost some courage while she was alone.

"How scared should I be?" she asked with just the slightest break in her voice.

Silence stretched across the room.

There was no way to put her mind at ease since they didn't know what to expect, either. Many words swirled through William's head, but he refused to give her false hope.

Instead, the three of them stood there in the silence, looking at one another until a knock sounded at the door.

Emily's gaze flew toward the sound.

She looked at William, her eyes wide and shimmering with alarm.

Her heart rate jumped up, and William could hear the rapid rhythm from where he stood.

He crossed the room and pulled her safely against his side to comfort her and remind her she wasn't alone.

It took a moment to recognize the new emotion in his own chest as nervousness.

It was a foreign feeling.

Since he'd found Emily, he had a whole new range of emotions to manage.

For so many years, he'd become utterly numb to the world around him. Not really living, but just going through the motions robotically.

She'd turned his carefully controlled world upside down.

He placed a kiss on the top of her head in gratitude.

"It's time," a voice said when Paoli opened the door.

William recognized the speaker. It was the werewolf Empusa.

He exchanged a look with Paoli, then William, and William could have sworn he saw concern in Empusa's eyes.

Not a good sign.

Empusa led them out of the room to meet up with the rest of their procession.

Waiting for them was one other guard William knew—a vampire name Sekhmet—and two he didn't recognize.

The trio followed the group of four Coven guards through the halls of the immense castle, walking down one corridor after another. Their footfalls echoed along the cold of the marble beneath them. Emily's breathing came in short bursts and William cold smell the adrenaline emitting from her pores.

"Try to calm yourself," he whispered lowly.

She nodded quickly without looking at him. Her eyes didn't stray from Empusa's back.

"Don't let them see your fear," William instructed quietly.

"Right," she whispered tightly. "I'll have to work on that one."

They paused in front of a pair of massive mahogany doors that boasted two family crests. On the left was a bird with a snake wrapped around its body—the crest of the vampire. On the right was a wolf with a lightning bolt behind it—the crest of the werewolf, signifying the curse of Zeus, which first transformed Lycaon nearly two thousand years ago.

"Let me do the talking," Paoli whispered as the doors cracked open.

When the room inside came into view, William found himself holding Emily up as her knees gave out and she almost sank to the floor. He practically dragged her inside with Paoli blissfully unaware on her other side.

The room was set in a half circle with two thrones on the far side, set into the curve.

The thrones sat on a raised dais, which dominated the area.

The floors were the same marble as the rest of the castle, and the walls were gray stone with banners and family crests adorning every corner. Below the dais stood six guards, three on either side of the thrones above them, garbed in purple robes, as was the norm for all members of the Coven guard.

The trio stopped just a few feet away from the dais and stood shoulder to shoulder to face what this day would bring, Emily—as always—placed between the two men.

Lilith sat on her throne, her bat-like wings wrapped forward toward her arms. Her blonde curls were long and draped down her back with an occasional stray tendril bouncing around her shoulders in a deliberately careless style. She wore tight black pants that looked like leather and a white shirt with a ruffled front and flowing sleeves, giving her the appearance of a winged pirate. Her face was pale white and almost painfully beautiful, but—as always—void of any emotion.

To William, her face always looked like a mask hiding something else; covering for something sinister. He'd never cared much for Lilith. She was cold and cruel with a complete lack of respect for life and a flair for torture.

Soulless.

That was the word that came to mind in her presence. It was her heartlessness—her lack of conscience and thrill of inflicting pain on others—that made most vampires believe their own souls were lost. One look at Lilith and a person knew there was no soul left within her. It was hard to believe she started with one in the first place.

Lycaon sat on her left; her polar opposite. He was a large man with a short-cropped beard. He appeared to be in his fifties, with crow's feet at the corners of his eyes and deep laugh lines. His hair was short and mostly black, but a silver streak ran down the middle of his head. His skin was always darkly tanned, and he dressed like he could leave the meeting and go right out into the mortal world for a round of golf, sporting black slacks and a polo shirt. Still, while it didn't show outwardly, he was known for his treachery and was not to be trusted.

After all, he bore the curse of lycanthropy from Zeus himself; a punishment meted out when Lycaon killed and served his own son as a meal for the gods.

"Lilith, Lycaon," Paoli greeted the Coven heads and bowed formally once they were situated before the dais.

"Paoli, it's been a long time since you came before Us," Lilith purred, using the plural form to represent the entire entity of the Coven.

"It's been a busy century," Paoli said.

Lilith nodded slowly. "Indeed?"

He held her gaze for a moment before dropping his eyes in a show of respect.

"We have come before the Coven after years of faithful service to beg a boon," Paoli said.

Silence stretched out for a few moments that seemed like eternity.

"What is it you beg Us for this time?" Lilith asked with a trace of mockery.

"As I have done before, I beg the Coven to lift an order of execution," Paoli said, his voice carefully level.

A heavy silence stretched out, in which Lilith watched Paoli unblinkingly.

"Have you come to question a decision of the Coven?" she asked finally, her lips thinning dangerously.

"I have come to present new information regarding the condemned," Paoli returned with the greatest diplomacy.

"I believe you refer to the two women you *stole* from the wolf den," Lilith said.

There was no mistaking the accusation in her voice. William stiffened.

Paoli needed to tread carefully.

Every conversation with Lilith was like a game of chess, and one wrong word could cost them all.

"Humans are sentient beings and therefore cannot be owned or stolen," Paoli said.

Lilith smiled maliciously and raised one mocking brow.

"Anyone can be owned, Paoli," she said with a meaningful look. "Including the two of you."

Paoli ignored the barb.

"One woman was already condemned, and the other *chose* to leave with us," he explained.

He put heavy emphasis on the word *chose*, clearly trying to remind Lilith humans were capable of making decisions.

"Ah, yes," Lilith said sardonically. "The condemned you failed to execute. She's been in Lycaon's company since she arrived. Where is the other one?" she asked, as though she couldn't see Emily perfectly well.

Emily gripped William's robe.

He clasped her shaking hand in silent support, running his thumb gently across her knuckles.

"She's here," William announced to Lilith's question.

Lilith's cold eyes landed on William for a long moment.

He stared back at her insolently, refusing to be cowed.

"Bring her to me," Lilith said finally, and her dark gaze slid to Emily.

It wasn't a request, but a clear command.

William's hesitation didn't last more than a split second, but it didn't go unnoticed.

"Would you dare defy yet another order from this Coven, even as you are here to explain such an action?" Lilith hissed dangerously.

Her anger was apparent and rising.

"I apologize. I mean no disrespect, but I'm quite—" He paused, looking for the right word. "Attached to this girl," he finished.

He didn't want to announce her as his mate and risk angering Lilith further.

It was a wolf thing, and Lilith was vampire through and through.

Lilith's eyes narrowed to slits even as Lycaon beamed with satisfaction.

"Attached in what way?" she demanded.

Lycaon saved William from having to stumble around for a more satisfying answer.

"She's clearly his mate," he announced, his voice just as cheery as it could be.

Silence fell across the room again.

William never took his eyes from Lilith, who looked like she was ready to explode.

"What are you talking about?" she finally asked Lycaon, her voice cold and hard and dangerously calm.

"Do you remember the old prophesy that was made regarding the executioner's mate?" Lycaon asked, his voice sounding utterly unconcerned.

Understanding replaced the confusion in Lilith's gaze, and her eyes grew wide.

"I was to father a mate for him. This girl and her sister are my daughters," Lycaon said, sounding quite pleased with himself.

Silence fell again.

It was a heavy silence, and the tension in the room rose further.

Energy began to build, and William moved closer to Emily in preparation.

"What did you do?" Lilith bit out each word, her voice low and menacing.

"I did what needed to be done," Lycaon said, waving his hand dismissively in her direction.

When Lilith continued to stare at him malevolently, he gave a heavy, impatient sigh.

"Without a mate, the death count will eventually weigh on him. He could be lost to the darkness," Lycaon said in a bored voice. "The only way to prevent it was for him to have a mate. The prophesy foretold I would be the one to father his mate. Therefore, I procreated through the years to fulfill the prophesy."

Lilith hissed, the sound vaguely feline.

"You took it upon yourself to make a decision such as this?" she demanded.

"We all knew it would happen eventually," Lycaon pointed out, his voice still quite calm. "It was foretold in the prophesy centuries ago. Besides, I don't see how my personal activities concern anyone except me."

Lilith pulled back her lip, exposing her fangs.

The others in the room were apparently forgotten for the moment.

"The executioner is owned by the Coven. Such a decision should have been made by Us all. You had no right—" she began but was cut short.

"To bed a human?" Lycaon interrupted with clear sarcasm. "It's hardly as though you refrain from doing the same."

Lilith stood from her throne so abruptly not even William's eyes detected her movement.

Her tail slashed toward Lycaon with enough force to sound like the lash of a whip when it struck him across the face and lay open a bloody strip.

Lycaon covered the area with one hand and growled at her dangerously, his body shaking with rage.

The atmosphere of the room was charged with the need to phase, and William had to concentrate to hold his shape, lest he be caught up in the force of Lycaon's anger.

The other wolves in the room started to shift, their faces contorting right before everyone's eyes. They clearly weren't able to fight off the release of Lycaon's power as well as William could.

Emily stepped close enough to William that she was plastered to his side.

Her eyes darted everywhere. William could smell the fear wafting from her in waves. That amount of fear would be like an invitation to the wolves if they shifted fully.

A moment later—as quickly as it had come—the power cleared.

It was as though a fresh breeze blew through the room and carried it away.

All shifting stopped, and within a few minutes, everyone was back in control of their human forms.

"Are you quite finished?" Lycaon bit out angrily at Lilith.

He pulled his hand away to look at the damage.

The sweet smell of blood tinged the air, putting all vampires present on edge this time.

Except Paoli—of course—who stood apparently unaffected, watching the power display from both sides with a look of concern.

The Coven had always been a strained partnership, everyone knew.

Both species had been at war for the better part of a thousand years when the Coven heads were forced to work together. At the time the Coven was formed, both vampires and werewolves had been at risk of being wiped out completely by the constant fighting.

Eventually, Lilith and Lycaon agreed that only together could they bring order and a sense of cooperation among the two species. They passed laws to stop the bloodshed. Since the formation of the Coven, things had greatly improved between the two factions.

Now it seemed something had changed, and William doubted it boded well for anyone.

"This will be discussed with the committee!" Lilith proclaimed loudly. "Your actions will have consequences."

"The committee?" Emily breathed to William.

He nodded almost imperceptibly.

"It's a group that acts kind of like the senate. If the Coven heads can't agree on something, it goes to the committee," he whispered under his breath.

"So be it," Lycaon growled.

He turned his attention back to the matter at hand.

"Bring her before me," he said directly to William in a much calmer tone. "I assure you no harm will come to her."

William's gaze met Paoli's for a brief second before William moved Emily forward toward the dais. Paoli gave the slightest smile of comradery, which gave William the extra strength he needed to drag Emily up those steps.

Paoli's look had promised he would stand with them, no matter what.

William didn't like Emily so close to either of the Coven heads, but to refuse would have been disastrous.

He and Emily stood together—presented almost like a mating pair of livestock—mere inches from Lycaon's intent gaze.

Lycaon stared at Emily in silence for many long moments, which put William's wolf on edge and made Emily fidget.

"You look a lot like your mother," Lycaon said finally. "She, too, was beautiful."

"Thank you," Emily said levelly, and in a surprise move, she met Lycaon's heavy stare.

"You're welcome," Lycaon returned with a thoughtful smile William didn't trust at all. "You will be a true asset to us all."

Emily clung almost painfully to William's arm but otherwise seemed outwardly calm.

William knew better, and so would Lycaon, since her fear gave off such a strong scent.

But she stood her ground and literally faced down the original werewolf with her shoulders squared and her head held high.

William felt a swell of pride.

Emily looked away from Lycaon and turned her attention to Lilith, who sat mere inches away.

Lilith's simmering rage was evident with every blink of her eyes.

"Boo," Lilith said quietly, holding Emily's gaze.

Emily swallowed hard and cleared her throat nervously.

"Hello," she said politely and averted her own gaze.

"Get off my dais," Lilith hissed dangerously.

William led Emily quickly back to where Paoli stood, careful not to move too fast and give the impression they were fleeing.

Emily was once again positioned in the middle, where the two men could better protect her, if the need arose.

"All else aside, the fact remains the executioner broke the law by taking the females from the den and killing the pack alpha without sanction. Further, he disobeyed a command from this Coven by failing to execute on an order. Worse than that, he introduced a *mortal* into our world," Lilith spat the word as if it disgusted her.

"What you refer to as a 'pack' was a group of wolves created without my approval. As such, I would have issued an order for execution when I discovered it. Therefore, the alpha's death is irrelevant," Lycaon interrupted reasonably to say. "And the original execution is a moot point, now, anyway."

"It is not," Lilith snapped furiously.

Lycaon gave a challenging growl.

"She's no longer a danger. She was repaired, and the order can now be removed," he said, his voice growing low and challenging.

Lilith stared at him with venomous eyes.

"That is not up to you alone, Lycaon," she said.

But Lycaon wasn't backing down.

"She has a place in our world," he insisted. "No harm has been done, so the execution is no longer an issue."

Lilith screeched in rage.

It was so loud everyone in the room had to cover their ears against the sound, including Lycaon.

Lilith then turned her fury back to the group before her.

"I want her ended," she snarled, her deadly stare fixed on Emily.

CHAPTER 14

Emily couldn't stifle her gasp of horror.

William's arm tightened on her side, almost to the point of pain. His eyes glittered gold, and she felt the low rumble of a dangerous growl.

"It would be a waste, don't you think?" Paoli said quickly, his voice flat and matter of fact.

He sounded calm, almost conversational.

After her initial gasp, Emily held a blank expression and refused to show fear in the face of someone obviously accustomed to intimidating others. If she was to die, she wouldn't go to her death humiliating herself by begging. She would face her fate with dignity, just as she'd been prepared to do with the werewolves. No one needed to know it took all of her will to keep her knees from giving out.

"Lycaon knows—as do I—if you push this issue, Emily will not be the only life lost here today. William and I will die with her. It's doubtful we'll be the only ones," Paoli said.

It was a subtle threat, but a threat nonetheless.

"If you would die for a worthless mortal, you deserve no better," Lilith hissed bitingly.

"No life is worthless. Certainly not Emily's," Paoli argued smoothly, as if he had all the time in the world. "Lycaon was right. William was becoming lost and dark before he found her. Now, he has a renewed purpose. Surely even you can see the value in such a thing."

Lilith sat back in her throne and shook her head at him condescendingly.

"Ah, Paoli," she said in a patronizing tone. "Ever the bleeding heart, eh?"

He wisely said nothing.

"How many times have you stood before Us now, begging for the life of someone or another?" Lilith went on in the same caustic manner.

"I find the unnecessary death of anyone a waste," Paoli returned without remorse.

"Some deaths are required by the law," Lilith pointed out sharply.

"But some lives can be spared," he insisted.

Emily had to bite back her desire to wholeheartedly agree with Paoli.

"We are not here to allow second chances. The law exists for the good of all and must be upheld," Lilith said.

"This is not a question of the law," Lycaon interjected. "The law states a mortal made aware needs to be ended or changed. Another option is available here, and it's one I think the committee will be pleased with, all things considered."

"Fine," Lilith ground out between clenched teeth.

Her wings beat angrily, causing a soft breeze to flow through the room.

"I want her either ended or changed before she leaves this castle," Lilith said.

"No," Emily gasped.

She may have been ready to face death with dignity, but certainly not being changed into a monster who lived on the death of others. Or like Amber ended up, trapped in an eternal phase.

"That's unnecessary—" William began, but a look from Lilith stopped him cold.

"Only two options are available," Lilith snarled at William. "She either dies here and now or is changed here. Name your option."

"She will be changed here," Paoli said immediately.

He pinned William with a look that begged him for silence.

"No," Emily repeated with more force, pushing against the wall of William's restraining arm.

She took a step forward. She wasn't about to just stand here while this group decided to alter her life so dramatically without even including her in the conversation.

"Fine," Lilith snapped, as if Emily hadn't spoken at all. She pointed to one of the guards who stood near her feet. "Change her."

Emily watched in disbelief as the guard stepped toward her.

William spun around behind her with his arms out, and Paoli stepped in front of her protectively, his arms also extended.

The backs of William's and Paoli's hands touched as they faced opposite sides of the room with their arms out and Emily sandwiched neatly between them.

"If she is to be changed," Paoli said in a rush, "we beg of you, let William be the one to do it. They need a blood exchange for the mating, anyway."

"Wait a minute, wait a minute," Emily cried, but her words went unheeded.

Lilith observed the group for a long moment, as if considering Paoli's words.

"She does not leave this castle alive, one way or another. Do you understand me?" she demanded finally.

"We do," Paoli agreed quickly.

"Make the change happen soon. I am an impatient hostess," Lilith warned.

Paoli nodded, his arms still out to box Emily behind him, though she was actively searching for a way out from between the two men.

She needed to be heard before it was too late.

"Understood," Paoli said to Lilith. "But when they tried to change her sister, it was a disaster."

"That is not Our concern," Lilith said coldly, just a hint of cruel smile showing.

"Brian wasn't strong enough to override the curse she carries in her blood," Lycaon announced soothingly. "William is plenty strong enough."

Emily opened her mouth to object to the decisions being made, but Paoli gave her an almost panicked look of warning over his shoulder, and she hesitated.

A moment later, William's imprisoning arms dropped away, and he slowly moved back to her other side, also shooting her a dire look.

She closed her mouth on all the things she wanted to say, her mind racing with panic.

This couldn't be happening. It just couldn't. She couldn't become . . .

She cast a look at Paoli and considered the irony that she now stood beside a bloodsucking vampire, and he was her ally.

She looked to William and remembered him exploding into a nearly car-sized wolf.

She couldn't become like them.

She wasn't mystical and legendary, she was just . . . Emily.

But her other option was death. Lilith had made that quite clear. Was she willing to scream her arguments and die?

Today . . . now?

Her tongue seemed frozen to the roof of her mouth.

"As for insubordination," Lilith announced with far too much pleasure in her tone, bringing Emily's attention back to the dais. "That does not go unpunished. No matter your reasons, orders from this Coven will not be ignored," Lilith said.

She was watching William like a spider might observe a fly. Then, her face split into a malicious smile.

"We shall have a bleeding, executioner. For two days. Then perhaps you will take your orders more seriously," she said.

Her eyes sparkled with an almost mad gleam.

"Take him below," she ordered the guards, but her eyes never left William.

William froze and watched as all six Coven guards started toward him. At first, the situation seemed unreal, like they all moved in slow motion; a sea of people closing in. He stood his ground and watched them with a carefully expressionless face.

Paoli grabbed his shoulders and shook him to command his attention.

Paoli's eyes were wide and questioning.

"Do we fight?" he asked earnestly.

William considered the options quickly, his mind running through every possible scenario.

Their chances of battling the Coven and escaping with a mortal still living were next to nothing. He wasn't even sure if Lilith and Lycaon *could* die. His gaze swept the room, mapping out the lay of their surroundings, then landed on Emily.

His Emily.

Beautiful and perfect, with her bright purple eyes now wide with confusion and fear. She was so fragile. No matter the cost, he could never risk her in such a way. Not simply to save himself.

"I can withstand," he answered Paoli's question, tearing his eyes from Emily to look at Paoli.

He gripped Paoli's forearms in a warrior's embrace and met his eyes with determination.

He *had* to withstand.

"What's happening?" Emily cried as the group pushed past her toward William. "What does she mean by bleeding?" she cried, shoving against the guards.

Two of the guards grabbed William's arms roughly and forced him onto his knees on the cold, marble floor.

He didn't resist.

His eyes were locked with Paoli's.

In Paoli's gaze shone years of loyalty and companionship and the love of both a brother and a father.

William braced himself and refused to react.

They should have expected something like this.

After all, they'd known there would be repercussions for the situation.

Still, in the end—despite his punishment—they were victorious.

He allowed the knowledge to bolster him. They'd won. They'd gotten the execution rescinded, and Emily was given a pass.

Sort of.

She wasn't dead, anyway.

They'd met their goal.

Silver cuffs were snapped onto his wrists, and William steeled himself against the burn. He locked his jaw, lest he cry out or give Lilith any sign of pain. He wouldn't give her the satisfaction.

Her love for torture was well known, and he wasn't about to give her a thrill.

This show of power was nothing more than a reminder she was in charge, and he was determined to see it as such.

"Stop it!" Emily screamed when his flesh hissed against the silver.

Human though she was, she was trying to fight off the guards around him.

To save him.

His mate, determined to defend him, even while denying what she was. He nearly smiled, but his concern for her stopped him.

"Emily, please," he warned quietly, a pleading note in his tone.

If they killed her now, all bets were off.

"Don't draw attention to yourself," he said. "Stay near Paoli until I return. Don't go near anyone else, and trust no one."

His eyes were a little desperate, begging her to listen and understand.

Paoli fell to his knees in front of William and met his eyes intently.

"I will protect her with my life, I swear it. Lean on your wolf," he said quickly as the guards pulled William to his feet.

Paoli rose with him.

"Your vampire side will cripple you on this. Get Emily's face in your mind and keep it there," he said.

He hesitated and swallowed hard when the guards pushed William forward.

"Come back to us whole. She'll always have a guardian in me, but she needs the mate in you," Paoli said.

William focused on breathing slowly as the guards led him toward a small door he'd never noticed before. He looked over his shoulder and caught one last glimpse of Paoli.

His face was set in lines of fury, and William hoped he didn't lose his head and do something drastic.

They *had* won, after all.

Now, they just had to ride out Lilith's revenge.

If Paoli made a rash judgement, it could undo everything they'd accomplished.

Emily stood at Paoli's side, looking terrified.

William wished he had time to offer her comfort, but he simply had to trust that Paoli would take care of her.

Her eyes met his for the briefest of seconds before William was pushed through the small doorway.

The group headed down a flight of circular stairs that seemed to go on forever.

Unlike the rest of the castle, this area had never been updated, and the darkness loomed around them like a cloak.

Sekhmet carried an old-fashioned torch he pulled from a hole in the wall to light the way.

It was a bit theatric and unnecessary, considering vampires and werewolves alike could see in the dark. But it set the mood for torture nicely, causing shadows to dance across the walls.

A bleeding.

William tried hard not to think of what was coming, but the word kept rolling around in his head.

As far as he knew, the Coven had stopped bleedings more than a century ago.

Most vampires subjected to the torture lost their minds and had to be destroyed afterward, so it was really a pointless punishment and had, therefore, been abandoned.

Clearly Lilith wanted to make a statement.

In the archaic practice of bleeding a vampire, all the blood the vampire contained was drained into a hole in the floor. They were then left in a room made of brick and stone, ten feet thick and underground to prevent them from being able to knock their way out.

Of the hundreds of vampires bled over the years, only a handful emerged with their mind intact. The others had to be destroyed because they were no longer capable of higher level thought, having been ravaged by madness during their incarceration.

It was a sorry state to be in, so the executions were merciful.

If William went mad, he hoped he could get to Lilith before they killed him.

The group made their way from the last step into a narrow hallway and turned a corner down a different passage. No one spoke. The only sound was their footfalls, echoed from the stone of their surroundings.

William watched the light dance around them and decided if ever a place would be haunted, this was it.

They passed a room that clearly served as the holding cell. It stood empty and stale with disuse. It reeked of impending madness, the opening yawning before him like an omen.

William stared in as the group walked by it on their way to the next room over.

Inside this one was a solid silver slab with chains hanging from the edges where the arms and legs of the victim—him, in this case—would lie. Under the slab was a metal funnel to drain the bloodshed.

His bloodshed.

Above the slab was a huge grate of metal spikes. The spikes were approximately two feet in length, which guaranteed they pierced all the way through the body from the front to the back.

William swallowed against a lump in his throat and closed his eyes, unwilling to face the reality of what was to come.

Sekhmet uncuffed his hands and allowed the silver to drop to the floor with a clang. He pulled the robe from William's shoulders, leaving his torso bare.

William began to calculate the odds he could kill the six guards with him and get out of the castle with Paoli and Emily in tow. He was unarmed, but his wolf was vicious, and he could be in wolf form far quicker than any of the others.

It was tempting.

So very tempting.

William's eyes snapped open and met Sekhmet's steady stare. There was such torment and guilt in Sekhmet's eyes, William almost pitied him.

He knew Sekhmet, though not well. What he did know of him, he'd always liked. Paoli knew him far better and even considered him a friend. It was clear to William that Sekhmet didn't want to do what had been ordered.

But Lilith's word could not be ignored.

Clearly.

"Shackle him," came Sekhmet's hesitant command.

William tried to keep himself steady and relaxed, his mind centered.

He could kill the guards with him.

After all, he was the executioner; the Coven's own assassin.

Death was his specialty.

But if he did, then what?

Lilith would win.

She'd have no trouble explaining his, Paoli's, and Emily's deaths after that.

The guards headed toward him with reluctance.

With *fear*, William's nose informed him.

They obviously knew how much danger they were all in.

William focused on the mechanics of breathing.

In and out.

He willed himself to be calm.

These men were not his enemy, regardless of the situation. They didn't want to be here much more than he did.

William fixed Emily's face firmly in his mind.

He was determined to hold it there and think of nothing but her through the ordeal. Just the thought of her gave him an echo of calm, and it was enough.

It would have to be enough.

Two days.

He could do anything for two days.

He closed his eyes again, forced out all sensation, and focused on the image in his head. Hands grabbed his arms and legs and lifted him. He remained relaxed.

When he was lain on the table, the silver burned his flesh, causing smoke to rise from his back and limbs. The pain tore through his entire body as his skin bubbled and hissed. He hadn't been prepared for it. For an instant, he lost the picture in his head and began to fight.

He'd knocked two of the guards across the room and reached for the third when Empusa grabbed his arm and—with the help of the others—affixed each of his limbs to the table until he was strapped down completely, the length of his body hissing in protest as he was scorched, his flesh burning away. The chains on his wrists and ankles only added to the agony. He bit back a scream, determined not to make a sound.

It was then the strap across his chest was pulled taut, which held him firm against the table and increased the pain even further. Every nerve in his skin screamed in protest as it was destroyed.

"I'm so sorry," Empusa's impassioned voice whispered in his ear just before William heard the creak of the old lever, which caused the spikes to fall.

He focused all the energy he possessed on relaxing his muscles to minimize the resistance as the spikes came down. They drove home with a sickening thud, the weight of the grate resting fully on top of him.

He felt the pop of his lungs deflating as they were impaled and found himself listening to the sound it made.

Something like air leaking from a tire.

His body was torn through from shoulders to thighs, and he was pinned to the table completely.

At least the spikes distracted him from the burn.

They added a new sensation of pain so great his mind wasn't even capable of comprehending it. He wondered vaguely if he'd gone into shock; if it were even possible for one such as he.

He opened his eyes to slits and saw six faces watching with horrified fascination as his blood—his strength, as it were—flowed from his body and through the drain. They all looked exactly as he would have expected; both hungry and disgusted.

With each drop of blood that flowed from him and ran down the stakes, his energy waned. It wasn't long until he was too limp with weakness to move at all, aware of nothing but the warm wetness of his life's blood flowing and the burn of his skin.

He lay there, helpless, his back growing tighter and tighter as the burn continued into bone. He had no idea how much time passed, but it seemed an eternity to him.

"All right, get him up," a voice finally said—he thought he recognized it as Sekhmet—though he couldn't be sure. It sounded like it came from far away and he couldn't make himself focus well enough to place it.

Chains rattled a moment later, and there was a slight sucking sound as the stakes were raised.

William noticed it only distantly.

The shackles holding him were lifted, and the guards rolled him from the table. His head flopped to the side, but Empusa was there, cushioning it with his hand.

The guards carried William to the first room they'd passed. It would serve as his prison for the next two days.

They laid him gently on the stone floor.

He heard footsteps but couldn't open his eyes to watch them leave.

A hand touched his head and pulled his face up.

William lacked the strength to even open his eyes.

"William." It was definitely Sekhmet this time. "Listen to me carefully. Find strength in something, and hold on to it. It's only for two days. Much is changing in the Coven, and we all need you to come through this. Do you hear me?" Sekhmet added urgently when William failed to respond.

"Mm," was all William could manage to say through his dry, cracked lips.

"In two days, we will return and replenish you. Hold on to that. Just keep your mind intact," Sekhmet urged. "Your body will fix itself as soon as your blood is replaced."

William fully lost consciousness then.

His body seized with emptiness, and he fell into the blissfully unaware. He had no memory of Sekhmet leaving or of anything else for a while.

There was no way to know how long he drifted in and out of unconsciousness, but every time he opened his eyes, he was aware of the cold stone beneath him and the gaping holes covering his body and happily succumbed again and again to unawareness.

CHAPTER 15

Emily was in a daze when Paoli guided her through the castle and back to her room in silence. A thousand questions swirled in her head, but the foremost on her mind was simple.

Were they killing William?

She held herself together until the door to her room clicked behind them. Then she turned to Paoli and grabbed his shoulders.

"OK, we're safe. Now tell me. What is a bleeding?" she asked.

She could hear the desperation in her own voice, but she didn't care.

Paoli met her eyes with a hooded look. He took a deep breath and let it out slowly.

"It's an ancient form of torture," he said, his voice barely more steady than hers.

Emily felt something in her gut tighten painfully.

Torture?

"Are they going to kill him?" she whispered.

She wasn't sure she could stand the answer.

"No," Paoli said.

His voice was soft and flat.

Almost an echo.

A wave of relief washed over her but was quickly dampened by Paoli's unusually serious countenance.

"They're not?" she asked hesitantly, afraid to hope. "They're really not?"

He remained rigid, which stole her relief. She crossed the room and sat on the edge of the bed, a new feeling of dread in her gut.

"What's happening?" she asked.

Paoli closed his eyes as though praying. Then he took a slightly shaky breath and followed her.

Apparently, he was too distressed to act human. Instead, he glided in traditional vampire fashion. He didn't even seem to notice Emily's surprise when he was suddenly standing in front of her.

"They're draining his blood," he said heavily, sitting on the couch to face her. "And I couldn't do anything to stop them from taking him."

A small furrow of confusion marred her brow.

"Why are they draining his blood?" she asked.

Paoli's sigh sounded a little irritated.

"Because nothing is worse to a vampire than not having enough blood. The hunger . . ." He gave a small shudder. "It's indescribable. But to have none—" He broke off, apparently unable to finish the thought.

"Oh, God," Emily whispered, understanding dawning. "It would be unbearable."

"Worse than that," Paoli said grimly.

He lay back on the couch and turned his face away.

"It would be hell," he said heavily.

William's strong face flashed through her mind.

"Will he be all right?" she asked, sounding like a child desperate for reassurance.

"I don't know," Paoli said. "Most vampires weren't."

She wasn't sure she wanted to know any more.

"What happened to them?" she asked, unable to stop herself.

He turned to look at her.

"They went mad," he said.

The words hung heavy in the air.

Emily couldn't even allow herself to consider the possibility.

She shook her head.

"Not William," she denied.

He couldn't go mad. Could he?

The very idea of it made her sick to her stomach.

"I hope you're right." Paoli's voice was thick.

His face looked pained and drawn.

"But William's always struggled with control, even under the best of circumstances," he said.

"I don't care," Emily said bitingly. "He's stronger than anything they can do to him. You, of all people, should know that. Don't you have any faith in him at all?" she snapped.

She needed him to tell her William would be fine, but instead he was scaring her even worse.

William could come through this.

She had to believe that.

"I have *hope* in him, Emily," Paoli ground out between clenched teeth. "But I choose to be honest with myself. I buried many people when William rebelled as a young man. I continue to help him dispose of bodies when he slips up, even now. His hunting instincts are strong. Stronger than any other immortal because they were born into him. If he claims you, like—he—should—have—done—immediately—" He bit out the last bit angrily, word by word. "It may give him the control he's always lacked. But first, he has to survive this. Being drained of blood will leave him in agony, and his instincts will be in full force. I don't know if he can get control back," Paoli said.

For the first time, Paoli looked old to her.

Ancient, in fact.

His eyes usually sparkled with life and humor. But now, they were creased with years of worry and far too much pain for any one person to bear.

Emily felt like she was watching his jolly façade crumble to give her just a glimpse of something else. Something he usually kept hidden.

"How old are you, Paoli?" she asked suddenly, her voice calm and quiet.

Her question gave him pause.

"Old," he said finally.

"I'm sorry if I'm prying," she said quickly.

That's just what she needed to do; offend the one person who might keep her safe in this place.

Paoli threw an arm over his face and leaned back into the couch again.

"I haven't fed tonight. It starts to take a toll. I'm sorry. To answer your question, I was born in 1562 in a little village in Hungary," he said.

"You're over four hundred years old?" she asked, a touch of awe in her voice.

Paoli chuckled just a little from behind his arm.

"I suppose I am," he agreed. "After the first century, I stopped counting."

"Is it rude of me to ask you questions?" she wanted to know.

Paoli uncovered one eyeball and looked at her.

"I don't know what other people would consider rude, but you can ask me anything you want," he said.

"Can I ask how you became a vampire? You told me it wasn't your choice." Emily said hesitantly.

Paoli nodded absently, turning his face into his arm again.

"It wasn't," he confirmed.

He was quiet long enough she started to think he may not say more.

"My village was near the castle of a countess. My family was poor, as were most back then. My sister was offered a chance to go to the castle as a finishing school for young women."

He stopped again for a breath of time before continuing.

"At that time, the chance to improve yourself was very rare, especially for a woman. So, my mother sent my younger sister, Anne," he said.

He took another deep breath before he went on.

"She never returned. We were informed she'd run away with a man, but we knew better," he said with a bitter scoff.

He hesitated again, and Emily waited silently for him to continue.

"Eventually, rumors began to reach us about the countess. I went to investigate," he said, his voice hollow. "I can still picture that castle like it just happened. On the outside, it had ivy growing all along one side. It looked like a normal castle. Nothing hinted at the horrors within those walls."

"Did you find out what happened to your sister?" Emily asked, her mind on Amber and how far she'd gone to save her.

Mostly, from herself.

"Yes and no. I snuck into the castle and found—" He stopped speaking, and Emily noticed the small crack in his voice.

She realized she'd asked him to remember things better left in the past.

"I'm sorry. I didn't mean to bring up painful memories," she said.

He gave a loud huff and shook his head.

"It's OK," he said.

He sounded like he meant it.

"I just haven't thought about that castle for many years. Anyway, I found many young women being tortured and killed in unspeakable ways. Let's leave it at that," he said firmly.

Emily nodded in agreement, then realized he couldn't see her with his arm over his face.

"OK," she said.

"Back then, a peasant couldn't make an accusation against the nobility without serious consequences. I made camp nearby and spent the next several weeks smuggling women out of that house of horrors. Those women were in terrible shape. They told me unbelievable stories about monsters and blood. I really didn't believe a word of it until the countess got wise and attacked me. I don't have a lot of memory of it, except for teeth that seemed to tear me apart. When I woke up, I knew I was changed," he said.

He paused and gave a shudder.

"Nothing could have prepared me for the hunger. Luckily, I'd made a reputation for myself. Some of her servants were helping me save the women. They risked their lives at the hands of a newly made vampire to have cups of blood ready when I woke up," he went on.

"Which is how you learned to get blood without killing," Emily guessed.

"Exactly," he agreed. "It was a different world then. Even though I was only twenty-seven, I'd already spent years on the battlefield. There was enough death and pain there to last a lifetime. Several lifetimes," he amended quietly. "I decided she may have taken my mortality, but she couldn't take my humanity."

Emily fought the urge to hug him.

She could tell he was hungry, and she didn't want to make it worse by getting too close. Plus—if she was fully honest with herself—she didn't like the idea of being in the embrace of a hungry vampire.

It went against all survival instincts.

Instead, she gave him a caring smile from a somewhat-safe distance when he moved his arm and looked at her again.

"And the Coven knows how you feel about death," she said.

"Yes," he answered, though it wasn't really a question.

Respect bloomed in her. She saw Paoli in a whole new light. He wasn't a monster at all. Just a man trying to make the most of the hand he was dealt.

"William was lucky it was you who found him," she said softly.

Paoli moved his arm and looked at her intently.

"No," he disagreed. "*I* was lucky it was me who found him."

CHAPTER 16

Emily was sleepwalking.

She *had* to be.

One minute, she was sleeping fitfully in the bed in her room. The next thing she knew, she was padding silently on bare feet past Paoli, who was sleeping on the couch. She wanted to cry out for help. But, as with many dreams, she couldn't seem to get her body to work quite right.

She walked through the door and around the castle. Her mind screamed at her to stop and get back to the safety of Paoli and her room, but her feet continued on.

She was convinced her certain death would step out from any corner in the castle halls, but still she kept moving, despite her fear. Her body seemed to be under someone else's control, and she was powerless to stop herself.

It was daytime, and the castle was thankfully empty this time of day. Room after room she went, through the halls, past the crested doors, and into the throne room where the Coven heads held court, until she found herself in an ancient hallway. It seemed the further she walked, the closer she came.

To *something*.

Walls and rooms made from stone surrounded her, and the only light was from a flickering torch set into a small recess high in the stone.

Shadows danced all around.

She felt, more than saw, a figure.

With certain dread, she became aware of who else was in the creepy stone hall.

———————

William woke with a start, which smacked his head sharply on the stones beneath him and sent little flashes of light dancing in his vision. A sound akin to a sigh escaped his ruptured lungs.

He'd come to hate consciousness.

The pain was so great in his entire body, he just wanted to remain unknowing. Each time his heart tried to beat, he could feel more dry tissue tear apart with the effort.

Worse yet was the thirst. It was the most horrible thirst he'd ever suffered, and it caused his body to seize again and again, taking what little strength remained. His mind seemed to exist in a haze of feeding frenzy, pushing out all other consciousness. His insides felt as though they were on fire and stuck together with dehydration. His tongue attached itself to the side of his mouth and required great effort to free, and he shook continually like a heroin addict.

He tried again and again to phase to wolf form to escape the thirst, but he simply didn't have the strength it took.

He growled in frustration and felt his sanity slip with the all-encompassing need.

He was so thirsty.

It was no wonder most vampires lost their mind with nothing to focus on but the torching drive for blood. His hope that his wolf could save him began to slip.

Just a sip.

Even a tiny sip could take some of the edge from his need.

Somewhere in the back of his mind was a nagging thought, demanding attention. He frowned in the dark and tried to recall what it was as sleep crept up again and threatened to pull him back under. He fought against it with all his pitiful strength left—that of a newborn kitten—and searched for the thought to make it solidify. It was important. *So* important. But what was it?

Emily.

The answer came at last.

He focused hard and tried to bring her image into view in his mind's eye. Dark hair, purple eyes, strength of character, and stubborn to a fault.

Ah, he thought when her face came to him. *There she is.*

He held the thought of her tightly, like a drowning man to a life raft. She could keep him sane. He was sure of it. After all, she was his mate. He had to hold himself together for her. She was waiting for him somewhere.

But where? Where was she? He couldn't remember. She should be with him, but she wasn't. Why wasn't she with him?

A scratching sound from the other side of the wall pulled him from his reverie, followed by low voices. He listened closely and tried to make out what was being said, but with no luck.

Was someone else being brought down here?

Stone scraping against stone signaled someone opening his prison door. He struggled to pull himself into an upright position in case he needed to face a foe. He didn't want to be found lying on his face like a dried piece of jerky.

His body was too weak to obey the command, so he settled for rolling halfway to his side. Not that it was much of an improvement. He fixed his gaze in the direction of the sound.

"Keep the torch. I want you to see what's coming for you."

William recognized Lilith's nasty voice just before the blinding light from a single torch illuminated the dark space.

William had to squint against the brightness of the light after so long in total darkness. It dazzled his vision and made him dizzy as it bounced around.

More scraping sounded, signaling his cell had been resealed. It made no difference. He tried to focus on the torch in the room and the person holding it. Then the scent hit him.

Human.

What strength he had multiplied tenfold.

He never stopped to consider why a human would have been brought to his torture chamber. He struggled to his feet like an animated corpse, totally mindless. Instinctively, his feet carried him toward the salvation that flowed in the veins of the unfortunate person brought to be a sacrifice.

He never considered resisting.

He was far too desperately in need of blood to think of anything except the warm, sweet relief right in front of him.

"William?" said a timid voice in a hushed tone.

It didn't penetrate the fog in his mind.

He was beyond even noticing a word had been uttered. His only thought was blood. Inside the human was the end of his torture. It was nothing personal. Just bad timing.

The torch backed away, and he pursued it to the wall. He trapped the light—and the person behind it—between him and the stone.

"William, stop," came a frantic cry, then the torch's fire was right in his face as the person tried to use it as a weapon. But there was no way a mere human could stop him.

He growled and knocked the torch aside. It fell to the ground with a clank and continued to burn behind him. A pair of hands braced against his bare shoulders.

"Listen to me, please," cried the voice.

He gripped a handful of hair roughly and pulled it to the side to bare the delicious, fragile skin of a slender throat.

His fangs made a little popping sound as they pierced the skin over the jugular vein, and blood flowed freely into his mouth. It was like nothing he'd tasted before.

Honey or nectar in its sweetness, hot and pulsing, it came to him in a torrent. He suckled wildly, relishing every delicious drop as it passed his tongue. He paused only long enough to lap the stray bits like a dog, unwilling to lose any of the feast. Then he returned to the puncture marks to slide his fangs back in for more.

The feeble struggle of the human was meaningless.

It wasn't long before the legs holding his victim buckled, and they slid to the floor together. He moaned in pure ecstasy. The burn inside him dimmed, and part of his strength returned. There was a slight tickle sensation as his wounds were healed.

"William, it's all right," came a ragged, throaty whisper.

He finally recognized the voice.

Emily.

Her words pierced the fog in his mind. He jumped away, both horrified and stunned.

Shock settled in.

What had he done?

Blind panic replaced everything else in his world. Even the thirst evaporated and left his mind clear.

Emily seemed to crumple in on herself like a wilting flower. A single tear slid down her cheek to fall onto the cold stone floor, and she fell utterly still.

William was at her side instantly, his anxious eyes searching her unconscious form.

She was so pale.

How much blood had he taken from her?

Far more than she could stand to lose, obviously.

With shaking arms, he gathered her and pulled her into his lap. Frantic fingers searched her throat and located her pulse.

He felt like a band was loosened around his chest. Relief flooded in, and he could breathe again.

She was alive.

Her pulse was weak, and her breathing was ragged.

But she was alive.

He hesitated, his mind racing.

She wouldn't survive without blood.

Her change was inevitable, anyway.

Lilith had ordered it, and he wouldn't risk losing Emily, no matter what it took.

He tore his wrist open with his teeth and held the wound to her mouth, forcing her to take what little blood he had. Hopefully it would be enough.

She may never forgive him for forcing it on her.

But at least she'd be alive to hate him.

Once she swallowed enough blood for him to be confident she'd survive, he stepped away and used his remaining strength to shift into his wolf form. In the wolf's body, she was safe with him.

The vampire side of him focused on nothing but bloodlust.

But the wolf saw his mate, wounded and in need of protection.

He returned to her cautiously and stood at her side, watching her chest rise and fall with each breath.

As gently as possible, he nudged her head to the side and sank his wolf's teeth into her shoulder. He didn't bite with enough force to remove tissue, but just enough to make sure he addressed both sides of his nature.

She gave a small whimper and tried to turn away when his teeth scraped the fragile bone, but she didn't wake up.

Once he was satisfied, he released his hold and examined the wound. It was deep enough to be effective, and not deep enough to inflict further damage.

He licked the opening clean.

Then he lay down, curling his heavy body around her to cushion her from the stones and keep her warm.

After a few minutes, she turned toward him and buried her face and hands in his thick fur.

He gave a sigh of contentment and closed his eyes.

When they left his prison, he knew there would be hell to pay for the events of the night. But he couldn't bring himself to regret what had been done. In time, she'd come to see he'd made the only choice he could have. For now, he decided to simply enjoy having her against him, safe and whole.

And changing, whether she knew it or not.

CHAPTER 17

I don't know." Paoli's worried voice carried loudly through the stone. "But his time is up, and he can find her anywhere."

The heavy door slid open and torchlight spilled in.

"William?" Paoli's voice sounded uncertain and wary.

He peered into the small cell.

"Emily," he gasped in surprise and rushed to her side. "How did you get in here?"

Emily tried to open her eyes at the familiar voice.

"Paoli?" she asked, too confused and weak to be sure it was him.

"What happened? How did you get in here?" Paoli repeated.

He took her hands and pulled her to her feet, then gasped when her knees gave way and she nearly crumpled.

"You're so pale," he murmured, catching her around the waist to steady her. "Are you all right?"

William's emaciated-looking wolf stood and growled a warning. His heavy side pressed against Emily's hip, and he bared his teeth warningly at Paoli.

Paoli didn't remove his hand from Emily's waist, but he watched William closely.

"She needs help," he said to the wolf. "And you're in no shape to provide it. She's your mate, and it's your duty to keep her safe." He both acknowledged William's claim and reminded him of his responsibility. "I would never hurt her. Allow me to help you both."

After a tense moment, William stopped growling and settled slightly, but his eyes were trained uneasily on Paoli.

Emily's fingers ran absently through the ruff at the wolf's neck. The movement seemed to settle him further. He relaxed against her, though his gaze remained on Paoli.

"He fed from me," Emily told the room at large.

Her voice was weak and dry.

"I don't think he even recognized me. What if—" Her words trailed off, and she was unable to finish the thought.

Her gaze skittered back to the wolf that was William.

He had to be whole.

He just *had* to be.

Paoli shushed her gently and gave her a brief squeeze of encouragement.

"He's anxious right now because he can't properly protect his mate. It's a good sign. It means the wolf is still intact. It doesn't guarantee the rest of him," he admitted with a grimace. "But it's a good sign."

Another man stepped into the small space, and Paoli quickly introduced Sekhmet.

Emily recognized him as one of the guards responsible for what had been done to William. Rage swept through her like an inferno. If she hadn't been struggling to remain upright, she'd have hit him. Not some weak little feminine slap, but a good, closed-fisted punch.

"You need to leave so we can get him replenished when he resumes his shape. We don't want this to be any more difficult for him," Sekhmet told her, his voice low and kind.

She stared at him in incredulous disbelief. How dare he act as though he cared what happened to William?

"Hey now," Paoli said haltingly to Emily. "You can't hate them for carrying out orders. They didn't have a choice unless they wanted to share his fate."

Emily continued to glare at Sekhmet, but she gave Paoli a tight nod. She knew there was truth in his words, but it didn't change how she viewed the situation.

William was in the shape he was because of the actions of *that* man. Just because Paoli could forgive didn't mean she was about to. Knowing Paoli was right didn't mean she had to like the man.

She mustered her strength and straightened her spine with every intention of walking past Sekhmet with the bearing of a queen. But when she stepped away from Paoli, her strength belied her intention, and her legs refused to hold her.

It was Sekhmet who caught her before she sank to the ground this time.

It was a mistake.

Sekhmet's sudden movement set off William's instincts, and he lunged viciously forward, his long teeth bared and clearly intent on the kill. William hit Sekhmet square in the chest, knocking him flat on his back against the stone floor with a thud.

Sekhmet managed to raise his arm just in time to block his throat, but the sound of bone giving way made Emily cringe.

"William, no!" she cried sharply.

To the surprise of everyone in the room, the attack stopped immediately.

Wolf-gold eyes met her gaze.

Emily held her hand out to him in silent entreaty.

William abandoned the attack and moved to her side.

She again buried her hand in his fur comfortingly.

"Paoli, can you help Emily?" a third man asked from the doorway.

Paoli quickly introduced him as Empusa.

Emily recognized him, as well, and again took a moment to glare at him.

He didn't seem to notice.

"As unsettled as William is, I'm not coming in there. Another male presence is the last thing he needs right now," Empusa said. "Sekhmet, come out here with me and give him some space."

"What's he planning to do?" Emily asked Paoli, watching as Sekhmet moved slowly through the doorway, careful to avoid looking like fleeing, wounded prey.

He cradled the obviously broken arm but hadn't made a sound.

"I'm not sure," Paoli said.

"Slowly get her settled somewhere in there. Then come out here with us," Empusa instructed Paoli.

Paoli shook his head.

"I'm not leaving her alone with William like this," he said.

Empusa kept his voice low and level, his tone calm and placating.

"We're not dealing with William right now. We're dealing with his wolf. *Just* his wolf. I suspect the rest of him is too weak from the blood loss to control the beast. We need to keep him calm. That's easiest with no other males close to his unclaimed mate. He won't hurt her. She's the safest person down here right now," Empusa said patiently.

Paoli eyed the wolf dubiously.

"I was alone with him a long time. He hasn't killed me yet," Emily said with a weak smile. "Help me get to the wall again, and go do whatever you're doing."

She pushed weakly away from him and motioned to the wall a few feet away.

Paoli moved very slowly and supported her until she reached the stone.

The wolf paced unhappily beside them, a low, warning growl in his chest.

As soon as she was close enough, Emily reached out and put one hand on the wall and the other on William to keep her steady.

"We've got it from here," she said to Paoli. "Get out of the room before he eats you."

A small smile tugged at the corner of Paoli's mouth. His gaze slid questioningly from her to William. He stepped away from them and into the center of the room.

"Are you sure about this?" he asked Emily.

Emily slid all the way to the floor.

William lay down beside her. He lay his massive head in her lap.

She stroked his ears and gave a slight nod to Paoli.

"He won't hurt me," she said with absolute certainty.

Once Paoli stepped out with the other men, William visibly relaxed.

"We brought enough blood to replenish you," Paoli said to William. "But you need to get back to human form."

When nothing happened, Sekhmet took one step into the room. He slid a glass vial across the hard floor as far as he could manage without spilling the contents.

"It's a decanter of blood," he explained. "We have three more out here."

Emily continued to stroke William's head calmly, as if nothing at all was happening around them. She spoke softly to him, reassuring him they were both all right.

"It's time to be human again," she murmured finally. "Then we can get out of this cold place. I need something to drink and a warm bed to recover in."

William raised his head and met her eyes for a long moment. His breath was warm on her face, and she gave him a weak laugh.

"Stop breathing on me with your dog breath," she chided.

He lay his head back down on her lap. A few heartbeats later, he gave a deep sigh and began to change.

She continued to stroke his fur until it was human hair beneath her hand.

Then both Sekhmet and Paoli descended into the room, both bearing additional decanters full of dark liquid to replace what had been taken from him.

Emily got her first good look at his human form and gasped in horror.

While his wolf was emaciated to the point of being little more than skin and bone, his human form was far worse. The bones of his shoulders and back pressed through the skin, clearly visible. His skin was dark and leathery, like the images of exhumed mummies she'd seen years ago in a documentary. His lips had receded from his mouth so far his gums and teeth were exposed grotesquely. His eyes sparkled with almost wild hunger when they landed on her.

It lasted for only an instant before Paoli pressed a decanter into his hands, and Empusa drew a robe around him. Empusa motioned Emily aside and scooted in behind William to prop him up.

"There now, William," Empusa said encouragingly. "Drink up."

Emily's attention was riveted on William's shriveled form.

Both Sekhmet and Empusa gave apologies for all that had happened, but she simply nodded distractedly and gave polite acknowledgement to their words, too afraid for William to hate them.

As William drank the decanter, his features slowly filled out before her eyes. It was an amazing transformation to watch. Almost like a stop-motion film. With each swallow, he grew more and more whole again. Before long, he was nearly recognizable, though clearly still extremely weak. By the time he finished off the second decanter, the wild glimmer had faded from his gaze, and the gray eyes that met hers were clear and intelligent once more.

And pained with guilt.

"I'm so sorry," he rasped.

"Are you . . . you again?" she asked earnestly.

The smile he gave, or *tried* to give her looked awful—like something out of an old horror movie with bad special effects—since his face hadn't completely filled back out and still looked skeletal.

"I will be," he promised, his voice a weak thread of sound.

To which Paoli grabbed him in a sudden embrace.

"You made it," he said, his voice thick with emotion he didn't quite manage to hide.

"Let's get them out of here," Sekhmet announced, reaching down to pull one of William's arms across his shoulder to hoist him to his feet.

Standing—somewhat, at least—William looked even worse, Emily noticed with a sick knot in her stomach. It killed her to see him in such a state. He looked ravaged and dead. Decayed, even.

She couldn't tear her eyes away from his damaged form and didn't even realize she was crying until the tears dripped onto her hand.

Without a word, Paoli lifted her into his arms like she was nothing more than a child, despite her protests. She was too weak to put up much of a fight and had fallen asleep before they even made it back to the circular steps that led out of the man-made hell.

CHAPTER 18

For the next two days, William stayed with Paoli while Emily recovered from their ordeal in her own room. William spent more time asleep than awake to allow his body to fully heal. Every time he woke, he went directly to Emily's side, only to find her asleep and still pale.

Her breathing was deep and even, and he allowed it to reassure him. Still, each time he saw her like that, he was gripped with another wave of guilt.

He'd done that to her.

Paoli's attempts to bolster him only managed to make him feel worse.

"You're looking at it all wrong," Paoli informed him when he returned from Emily's bedside on the second evening.

William gave him a questioning look, one brow raised quizzically.

"You've never left a victim alive, before," Paoli pointed out with a nod of approval. "That's a huge accomplishment for you, especially under the circumstances."

William felt the word all the way to his soul.

Victim.

He'd made Emily his victim.

"What if she can't forgive me?" he asked aloud, giving voice to his worries. "What if she's afraid of me?"

"Forgive you for what?" Empusa interjected from across the room.

He and Sekhmet had practically moved into Paoli's room since William was pulled from his cell, apparently determined to make amends for their part in the event.

While William held them blameless—after all, they'd really had no choice—they seemed determined to take his recovery as their personal responsibility.

"You called her to you, and she came." Empusa shrugged. "You needed blood, and she provided it. That's what mates are all about. It's about having someone to lean on. If you were properly bound together, it would have been much easier to call her."

William frowned at that. Had he called her to be hurt? To be food? The idea sickened him. He didn't remember calling her. All he remembered was thinking about her and trying to figure out where she was. He growled a silent growl. He must have been calling her then without realizing it. The knowledge did nothing to ease his conscience.

"And she's always been afraid of you," Paoli point- ed out. "How did she even get into the room?" he asked.

It wasn't a topic William had been cognizant enough to discuss before.

"It took two of us to open the damned door, and we have immortal strength. Emily's just a human, and a woman, at that," Paoli went on.

"It was Lilith," William answered, a harsh note of bitterness to his voice.

A strange silence fell over the room at his declaration.

"Are you sure?" Sekhmet asked.

There was something in his voice William couldn't quite pinpoint. Eagerness, maybe?

"What's going on around here?" William asked, looking back and forth between Empusa and Sekhmet, who seemed to know more than they were saying.

"Trouble brews between Lycaon and Lilith." Empusa spoke first.

William scoffed and rolled his eyes dramatically.

"That's nothing new. Their alliance has always been rocky," he said.

"Yes," Sekhmet agreed. "But it's getting more serious. So far, it's just a bunch of small stuff. But the discord between them is unmistakable. Think about your own meeting," he urged. "Previously, if they disagreed with one another, it was done privately. Now, they seem on the verge of violence anytime they're together. We don't know what's happened, but something clearly has. Most of us believe a restart of the war is inevitable. It's just a matter of time."

William looked at him in surprise.

While he and Paoli normally stayed isolated from the other immortals, he couldn't believe they hadn't been informed things had grown so tense. Tense enough the Coven itself was in jeopardy.

If nothing else, the committee should have told them. A change in the Coven would affect them in a profound way.

"Another war between the species could wipe us off the planet," William said.

He frowned as Empusa and Sekhmet shared a glance.

"What am I not getting?" he asked suspiciously.

"Even if the Coven itself breaks into civil war, it wouldn't have to spread," Paoli said cryptically, apparently having no trouble following the thoughts of the others.

William had been through too much and was too tired to interpret what they were getting at.

"I don't understand," he said.

The Coven had been the only way to bring peace. Granted, it was an unsettled peace, but it was still a vast improvement. Without it, the war was sure to resume.

"There's no longer a black-and-white line separating the immortals. Things have changed in the last couple of centuries," Empusa said carefully.

"What's changed?" William asked.

He sat on the arm of the couch and regarded the other three men, who were all looking at him.

"We now have proof the two species can coexist and be the better for it. We even know they can both exist in the same person and make that person more powerful than either side alone," Sekhmet said pointedly.

William finally understood.

Things were different because of *him*. Because there was now a hybrid of the two factions, where there had never been one such as he before. It meant they didn't have to stand as "us vs. them."

Together they could stand as *we*.

"Lycaon tires of Lilith's cruelty and tyranny. Everyone knows that. He's been waiting for you to find your mate in the hope you'd be moved to join his cause," Empusa said, looking at William expectantly.

"Why would I join his cause when I found my mate?" William asked with an exasperated groan. "I'm tired of death. I have no interest in anything bound to cause more."

Which was true.

Especially now, with Emily at his side, he wanted to be away from anything to do with death as much as possible.

"Besides, Lycaon's own sickness got him cursed in the first place. Lest we forget," William reminded the room at large. "He served his own son for dinner. That hardly makes him a gentle and just leader. Certainly not someone to be trusted."

"But Lycaon is Emily's father," Paoli reminded him. "What if she wants to join his cause?"

"I can't answer that," William said after a moment's thought. "All I can guarantee is that no matter what happens, I will protect her with my life and follow her anywhere she needs to go."

"If war's inevitable, there's no way not to be touched by it," Paoli said.

"I disagree. Just because our kind may battle one another doesn't mean we have to join the fight," William said.

He shot Paoli a questioning look.

"Since when have you been worried about politics, anyway?" he asked.

Paoli gave him a humorless smile.

"Since the politics came knocking on our door," he answered.

William's thoughtful gaze lingered on Paoli while he considered all that had happened.

Then he turned to meet Empusa's intent stare.

"If you're asking me to lead an attack on random immortals, the answer is no. However, if they threaten those close to me, I will destroy them. I don't care which side they're on. But I remain neutral," he said.

"What if your mate makes a choice?" Empusa asked.

Sekhmet cleared his throat uncomfortably.

"Amber joined Lycaon," he confided.

William nodded, processing the new information.

He wasn't sure how it would affect Emily, considering the state of the relationship between the two women. While Emily obviously had some kind of hope for her sister, a lot had happened in the last few days.

William didn't trust Lycaon.

He didn't like Lilith. Not at all. And the feeling was clearly mutual. But at least Lilith was direct in her dislike.

Lycaon was more likely to double cross and betray those who trusted him. Like he'd done to his son.

"Amber agreed to act as a general in Lycaon's cause," Empusa said.

William noticed he didn't sound thrilled about it, which meant the other wolves wouldn't be, either.

Amber would not long hold a position of power.

William looked from Empusa to Paoli.

"If Amber feels the need to stand with her father, that's her choice. I take no sides in this matter. It isn't my fight," he said.

He paused, then pinned Paoli with a heavy, meaningful look.

"It isn't *our* fight," he said. "This struggle for power has gone on way before any of us."

He turned to the others and looked at them all in turn.

"It will likely continue forever, and I refuse to get in the middle of it," he said.

He had enough battles of his own to worry about.

"And you all realize, this very conversation constitutes treason," he felt the need to point out.

Empusa ignored his last.

"You may not be left with a choice. If the war restarts, everyone will have to decide where they stand," he said.

William knew he was right. If the war were to resume, they'd all be forced to choose a side or be targeted by all involved.

"I'll worry about that when the time comes. Right now, I have my own house to get in order," he said.

Empusa watched him for a long moment.

"I understand," he acquiesced. "When the time comes, however, I do hope you and I find ourselves on the same side. You have more power than you realize and more respect from everyone than you know."

William didn't reply to that. He wasn't sure how to respond.

"Anyway," Sekhmet broke into the deep conversation with a light tone, signaling a shift in topics. "We're all excited you found your mate at last."

He reached into his pocket and brought out a small piece of paper.

"Both mine and Empusa's numbers are on this," he said, holding the paper out to William. "If you need anything, don't hesitate to call. Allies are always good to have."

William took the paper from him with a sound of agreement.

Then he considered the strangeness of the two of them working together.

Especially if they expected a war between the species to begin again.

When he thought about it, he realized they'd always been together when he saw them, as far back as he could remember.

"How do a wolf and a vampire remain friendly with this going on?" he asked.

Sekhmet gave him a sly grin.

"It's a different time we live in. Sometimes, the real strength lies in diversity," he said.

William returned the smile in spite of himself. It was a good point.

He bid Sekhmet and Empusa goodbye, then stubbornly refused to discuss the situation with Paoli until Paoli gave up and left the room in frustration.

William thought about going after him but decided against it.

They both needed time to think about what had been said and what it meant to them before they'd be able to have a calm discussion about it.

And anyway, William's thoughts were more on Emily than anything else.

Until he got things situated with her, he couldn't focus his attention on other matters, no matter how important they seemed to everyone else.

CHAPTER 19

Emily eased the heavy wooden door to her room open slowly and peered down the hall in both directions. She breathed a sigh of relief at finding it empty.

With her heart in her throat, she slipped from the relative safety of her room and into the empty corridor.

She'd awakened feeling almost back to normal, but one look in the mirror made her realize the gravity of her situation and spurred her into action.

Her reflection showed her skin was nearly gray.

Her eyes were sunken, as if she hadn't slept in days.

But what really scared her wasn't any of that, or even the two puncture marks left behind by William's fangs. It was the bite mark that covered her shoulder, as if a huge dog had tried to take a chunk of her.

She knew perfectly well what those marks were from, and it had brought Lilith's decree to her mind, crystal clear. If she didn't escape this castle now, she wouldn't leave it at all.

Not alive, anyway.

No matter how connected she felt to William, she had no intention of sitting around, waiting for her life to be ripped from her.

William would simply have to understand.

She couldn't be like him.

Like Paoli.

A mental image flashed through her head and she shuddered slightly.

Or like Amber had been.

She couldn't take the chance.

The idea of feeding on other people was revolting. She simply couldn't do it.

Her plan was shaky at best. After all, she had no passport with her to get home. No money, or even identification. But she was sure if she could just get out of the castle, she'd think of something. She was nothing if not resourceful. And once she got back home and back to reality, she'd feel better. More like herself again.

Under no circumstances could she allow herself to think of William.

Just the thought of never seeing him again made her chest feel tight and her stomach clench. But she wasn't that kind of woman, and no man was going to make her into someone who was afraid to stand alone. In her mind's eye, she saw his deep gray eyes and pushed the image away angrily. She had to think of herself now.

The castle halls seemed to stretch on forever. She passed a few people on her way and felt her heart nearly stop with fear. But no one seemed to notice her at all.

It was almost disconcerting. She watched them out of the corner of her eye as she drew close to them, but they didn't even stop their conversation.

After Mary's response to her when they arrived, she'd been sure the first immortal she came across would drain her dry. Not that she wanted to be someone's victim, but the sudden difference made her uneasy.

Were they just too enthralled in conversation to take notice, or had something else caused the change? Absently, she rubbed the tender bite on her shoulder, and a horrible worry began to bloom.

She arrived at the staircase that led down into the main hall and paused. Her nerves seemed to get worse with each step she took. Her hands were shaking so hard she clasped them in front of her to still the trembling.

The steps seemed far steeper than the last time she'd descended them. For one horrible instant, her vision seemed to tunnel in, and she thought for sure she was going to faint and fall down the stairs. She stopped moving and clutched the railing, pressing her eyes tightly closed.

When she opened them again, her vision was back to normal, and she gave a sigh of relief, trying to convince herself it was fear. Just fear. A few more rooms, and she would make her escape.

It had been far easier to navigate the castle than she'd expected. With her iffy sense of direction, she'd half expected to end up on the wrong end of the castle, blundering along lost. But she'd made it without taking a single wrong turn.

Everything was going more smoothly than she'd anticipated, in fact.

Until she stepped off the stairs onto the tile and found herself facing a large, familiar chest.

She froze and allowed her gaze to climb up slowly until she was looking at his face.

William did *not* look amused.

His jaw was set in an angry line, and a small muscle ticked in his cheek.

Emily opened her mouth to say something—maybe make a clever excuse of some sort—but nothing came out.

William didn't say a word. He simply spun her around so her back was to him, then wrapped his arm around her middle and hoisted her up like a sack of potatoes, heading right back up the stairs she'd just come down.

"William, that might not be the best way—" came Paoli's voice from behind them.

William paused and looked back, and Paoli fell silent.

Emily searched Paoli's face beseechingly, but he simply gave her an encouraging, though apologetic, look before William turned back and she lost sight of the only person who might help her.

Back in her room, William set her down as he kicked the door shut behind them. He made no move away from the wall, while she practically leapt the distance of the room. Once she had put as much space as possible between them, she turned back to face him.

He watched her with a hooded look.

Her fear was nearly choking her.

William took a deep breath and let it out slowly, clearly struggling to control his anger, and—his amber eyes told her—his wolf.

"You can calm down," he said, his voice tight. "I'm not going to hurt you."

With a heavy-booted foot, he took a step forward.

Emily held up her hands as if to warn him off.

"Not going to hurt me, huh?" she asked, her voice dripping with sarcasm. "Just kill me and turn me into an undead monster?"

William stopped and flinched as though she'd struck him. He said nothing but continued to watch her.

"I'm sorry," she said in a rush. "But I can't be like you. I'm human, and I intend to remain that way."

The little muscle ticked in his cheek again as he clenched his teeth.

"It's too late. That's not an option," he said, his voice very gentle and conflicting with his body language.

"It is if you help me escape," she returned, a tiny glimmer of hope in her voice.

"No," he said and took another step toward her.

She backed up to keep the distance between them.

"You're not even listening to me," she accused, unable to keep an edge of panic from her voice.

William gestured to the table across the room.

"Let's sit down and talk, then," he offered.

Emily faltered, looking at him suspiciously.

"Talk?" she asked, as though confused.

He crossed to the table and sat in one of the chairs, then pushed another one out for her with his toe.

"Talk," he agreed finally, leaning back casually in his seat while he waited for her to join him.

After a couple of long minutes of consideration, she reluctantly crossed the room and slid into the chair.

"I know you think what's happening here is normal," she said quickly, sitting on the very edge of her seat, as if ready to spring and run if necessary. "But it's not. Not to me, anyway. To humans, I mean," she clarified.

He nodded slightly, acknowledging her words.

"And I have no desire to become . . . different than I am. I just want to be me. Trying to help my sister has gotten me into a lot of trouble over the years," she said, then scoffed a little at the understatement. "But I've officially learned my lesson. I just need to go home. It's not like I'd ever tell anyone about all of this. Who'd believe me anyway?" she pointed out reasonably.

"Are those all of the concerns you have?" he asked slowly.

His voice sounded completely calm, if a little deeper than normal.

"I've always been an independent woman," she said in answer. "A real loner. I don't think all of this," she waved her arm to encompass the Coven, the immortal world, and *him*, "is for me. It's just not my thing. It's nothing against you," she added quickly with a small smile to soften the blow. "You and Paoli have been amazing. But this life isn't for me."

When his eyes met hers again, she saw they were still liquid gold.

But there was a trace of what she was sure was amusement, and something else. Pity, maybe?

Her spine stiffened at the thought. Was he secretly laughing at her or looking on her like some pathetic little mortal?

"Very few people have chosen this existence," he said.

His voice was soft and reassuring, without a trace of amusement, but she believed what she saw in his eyes over anything else. His wolf was still very close to the surface, and something had amused him.

Something she didn't understand.

"You're no different from everyone else in that respect. You don't get a choice in whether or not you're changed."

He held up a hand when she opened her mouth to argue.

"The fact is you *will* be changed. Not even *I* have enough arrogance to ignore a direct order from Lilith. However, you're like me in that you were born into this world, whether you like it or not."

His eyes darkened and took on a slightly predatory heat.

"As for our relationship," he held her gaze and gave her a tight smile. "I couldn't give you up even if Lilith hadn't made it an order. You are my mate."

Without moving as far as Emily could see, he was kneeling front of her.

She gasped and jumped back in surprise, but his hands were suddenly cupping her face, forcing her to meet his eyes.

"And I'm your mate. You can't escape it. There's no running away from this," he said softly.

Emily couldn't look away. There was no pull to his gaze, no preternatural power of any kind that she could feel. But she still couldn't look away. There was nothing but stark honesty in his gaze. As much as she wanted to deny his words, she saw the truth right there in his eyes.

There was no going back.

A silent tear slid down her cheek, unnoticed as the realization washed over her. From the time she'd first fallen into this world, there had never been any escape.

William's rough finger wiped away the moisture.

"Let me show you what it means to be mates," he murmured softly, seductively.

Their gazes met and locked.

In his was the dark heat of desire.

Her own must have showed her surrender, because he moved closer.

It didn't matter anymore.

There was no use fighting what was between them.

She was tired of fighting.

Tired of being afraid.

He was offering her a place to belong and be sheltered. Protected.

Nothing else mattered but this moment. There was no future. There was nothing else but him and her, alone with the night stretching before them.

His lips found hers softly, almost tentatively. His mouth moved gently at first, coaxing her to respond. It wasn't a demand, but a gentle request for her to give in. His large, rough hands caressed the sides of her face, and the heat built quickly between them.

The kiss deepened, and Emily found herself returning his kiss, his heat, his passion with her own. Her lips parted easily, allowing his seeking tongue to explore the recesses of her mouth.

When she shyly brushed against his tongue with her own, William moaned low and dragged her down into his lap.

She didn't protest.

Instead, she wrapped her arms around his neck and continued kissing him as though her very life depended on it. The kiss had gone to an almost frenzy of lips, tongues, and teeth, guiding, sliding, and nipping at one another.

His hands moved from her face and roved over her back, gliding lower to cup the globes of her buttocks and pull her against his hardened member more fully.

His mouth continued to build the heat within her, even as his hands cupped and kneaded her rump.

He tore his mouth away and stood, lifting her into his arms as though she were light as a feather. Two strides took them to the side of the bed, and he didn't so much lay her down as fall onto it with her still in his arms, his mouth searching hers out once more as his hand slid beneath her shirt and across her ribcage.

She gave a groan of sheer pleasure when his thumb stroked across her hardened nipple through the lace of her bra, and she pressed into his palm, needing more.

Needing so much more.

He broke the kiss and leaned back to pull her shirt over her head with jerking movements. Her bra followed immediately, leaving her torso bare to his examination.

And examine he did.

His eyes glided slowly over her creamy expanse of exposed flesh, and the heat in his gaze intensified further.

"You are so beautiful," he said, his voice rough and husky with desire.

Emily squirmed a little under the intensity of his gaze.

He slid his hands up either side of her ribcage. With slightly trembling fingers, he cupped her heavy breasts. His thumbs gently slid over the stiffened peaks until she couldn't keep from crying out.

He jerked his own shirt off and threw it carelessly aside before he lowered his head to her breast and flicked that expert tongue across her nipple. The heat from his mouth nearly sent her up in flames.

Such tension built inside of her, she felt sure she may explode with need. She cupped his head and urged his mouth toward her breast.

"Don't ever think of running from me again. You are mine. Do you understand me?" he hesitated to murmur thickly.

There was a possessive bite to his words.

She panted with desperate need and nodded, arching toward him.

"Answer me," he commanded. "You are my mate, and I claim you as my own. Do you understand?"

"Yes," she whispered breathlessly.

"Yes what?" he demanded savagely.

"I'm your mate," she gasped, her body throbbing with need.

He gave a groan of triumph and finally closed his hot, wet mouth on her aching breast.

Emily gave a cry of ecstasy, holding his head to her while he suckled, licked, and teased her aching nipple. His other hand continued to caress her remaining breast, his roughened skin across her sensitive flesh driving her almost past the point of endurance.

She gasped and panted, her hips pushing toward him helplessly.

He pulled away and his mouth closed on hers once more.

She clung to him in desperation, her fingers dragging across the heavy muscles in his arms and shoulders.

His hands slid down her body, then her jeans and sensible boy shorts slid away.

She just had time to wonder that he was as gloriously naked as she, though she hadn't noticed him remove his remaining clothes.

His body was as beautiful as she'd imagined. There wasn't an inch on him that was soft. He was all hard muscle and heavy sinew. His arms and chest she'd seen before and already knew they were like something from a fitness ad. His legs were thick, heavy columns, leading up to his perfectly sculpted hip bones. And his heavy erection thrust proudly forward, thick and full.

He returned to her and captured her lips once more.

His fingers bit into her hips as he pulled her into position without lifting his weight from her.

She felt the heat from the tip of his heavy manhood slide through her folds, separating her.

Opening her like a flower.

He moved forward and buried himself deep into her wet sheath.

Emily gasped at the delicious friction of having him inside of her.

Then he began to move within her slowly, allowing her body to relax and adjust to his invasion.

She moved with him, following his lead in a dance as old as time itself.

He moved slowly at first but gradually built speed and force until he was thrusting wildly, dragging sounds of aching pleasure from her with each movement, pushing her higher and higher.

Then the building tension finally broke, crashing over her in wild, pulsing waves of pleasure. She cried out, his name escaping her lips as though torn from her.

Within seconds, William's throaty moan joined the chorus of hers as his seed spilled deeply into her slick body and he practically collapsed on top of her.

For a long moment, they lay very still.

Entwined together, both breathless and spent, neither of them moved.

Then William rolled to his side, adjusted the blankets over them, and pulled Emily against him. With his arm across her protectively and the feel of his hard chest against her back, she fell into a blissful, contented sleep.

CHAPTER 20

William woke the next evening to find Emily coated in a fine film of sweat.

Confusion set in momentarily, and he sat up to notice there was enough sweat to soak the sheets around them.

His heart began to hammer almost violently when the realization took hold of him.

She was beginning the change.

Guilt seized him like a physical thing.

He should have told her.

He'd intended to explain it all last night and clear the air between them, but he'd gotten distracted.

He had no regrets about sealing his claim on her, but something nagged at his conscience just the same.

By not telling her what he'd done, he hadn't properly prepared her for what was happening now. It was his job as her mate to keep her safe and protected.

Another twist clenched in his gut.

If he'd told her last night, would she have rejected him?

He pushed the idea away.

It didn't matter.

She couldn't reject him now.

Not with the bond fully sealed.

He wasn't proud of how he'd handled the situation, but it was too late to change it.

"Are you OK?" he whispered softly, reaching out to touch her bare shoulder, which was peeking out above the heavy blanket.

Her skin was cold and clammy to his touch.

Emily rolled onto her back and looked at him.

There was no accusation in her gaze, as there should have been. Instead, her beautiful eyes looked dull and sunken. There were deep, bruised circles under her eyes. Her face looked gray and waxy.

"Something's wrong," she whispered, a note of fear in her voice.

William swallowed hard, his stomach a knot of dread. He watched her chest rise and fall rapidly. She was breathing far too fast. Almost a pant. It was nearly a physical pain to watch her struggle for breath.

"I'll be right back," he said.

He strode to the bathroom and got a wet cloth. He returned to the bedside and wiped her face. Once he wiped the worst of the sweat away, he folded the cool fabric and lay it across her forehead.

"I'm so sorry," he said.

She frowned without opening her eyes and ran her tongue across dry, cracked lips.

"For what?" she asked weakly.

Silence stretched out.

He'd never hated what he was more than he did in that moment.

How could he tell her what he'd done? He'd stolen her life without her consent.

Against her will.

But he owed her the truth.

"This is my fault," he admitted. "The night you came into my cell, I took more blood than you had to lose."

Emily's eyes snapped open. The accusation he completely deserved was shining out at him.

"What did you do?" she demanded.

"Lilith had ordered your change anyway," he defended himself. "So, I replaced the blood I took."

Understanding dawned in her eyes.

"Did you," she stopped and gasped for breath, "feed me your blood?" she asked.

She sounded absolutely disgusted, horrified.

William tried not to take offense at her tone. He reminded himself humans all found the consumption of blood repulsive.

"Yes," he said quietly.

"Get out," she hissed.

"It was the only way to save your life," he insisted.

"You had no right—" she began but had to stop and pant for breath again.

"I had every right," he argued. "But I should have told you immediately."

"Get out," she repeated furiously.

William hesitated. He didn't want to fight with her. Not now. Not when she was so weak and clearly in need of care. But he didn't want to leave her alone, either.

"I mean it, William," she said. "Get away from me."

He rose from the bed and crossed to the door with the greatest reluctance. When she came through the change, he was going to have one hell of a fight on his hands, he knew. But for now, all that mattered was getting her through it.

He'd worry about her anger later.

He stepped from the room and pulled the door closed behind him. Then he practically flew down the hall and banged insistently on Paoli's door.

Paoli didn't answer as fast as William would have liked, so he banged again and considered tearing the damned thing from the wall.

"What the hell?" Paoli demanded as he jerked it open, clad only in his lose pajama pants. "What's wrong?" he asked in a completely different tone when he saw William's face.

"Emily needs help," William said. "And she doesn't want me near her."

Paoli froze and searched William's face for a long moment.

"Did you complete the mating last night?" he asked, a bit hesitantly.

"Yes," William said.

Paoli continued to watch him closely.

"Was she a . . . ah . . . willing participant?"

William frowned in confusion for a second, then a look of complete rage came across his normally blank features as he understood what Paoli meant.

He launched himself into Paoli and sent them both crashing to the floor.

Paoli had been caught by surprise by the attack, but he recovered quickly and used his feet to push William up with his own momentum.

William flew over Paoli's head and landed on his back above him.

William sprang to his feet and spun to face Paoli, who was already standing again as well.

"William, calm down," Paoli said, his voice quiet and full of authority.

"I didn't rape my mate," William snarled. "You should know me better than that."

"You're right," Paoli agreed simply, taking much of the anger from William. "I apologize. When the two of you left the corridor yesterday, I was worried about your control with all that's happened. Forgive me."

William's anger didn't dissipate entirely, but it lessened enough for the guilt to return. He stared at Paoli for a long moment, then offered his hand in a grudging apology.

Paoli took his proffered hand and used his arm to pull him into a hug.

"I'm sorry," William said, clapping Paoli on the back before he stepped away.

"I gather you haven't handled things—" Paoli paused for just a fraction. "Perfectly?"

William snorted at the understatement.

"You might say that," he said.

Paoli nodded in understanding and didn't ask any more about it.

Good man.

"What type of help does she need?" he asked instead.

"The change has started, but she won't let me help her," William said, and he couldn't keep the edge of resentment from his words.

Paoli was still for a second, carefully studying William's face.

"Can I ask why she's angry with you?" he asked tactfully.

William looked away, unable to meet Paoli's gaze.

He fought the urge to inform Paoli it was none of his damned business.

William *really* didn't want to discuss it.

Not with anyone.

But Paoli was excellent with women and might be able to help.

"I didn't get a chance to explain what happened in my cell," William said.

Paoli gave him a look of puzzlement.

"She remembers the attack," he said slowly.

"But not the extent of what happened afterward," William replied.

Paoli's gasped with comprehension, then gave a low groan.

"You performed the exchange while she was unconscious," he guessed.

It wasn't a question, but William answered anyway. "Yes."

"Then you, my friend, have a long trek back into her good graces," Paoli said.

He turned toward Emily's room and clapped William on the shoulder.

"Come on. I'll sit with her for a while," he said, heading off toward the other end of the hall.

William spent the majority of the day in a chair beside the door to Emily's room. Whenever he tried to return to her bedside, she ordered him out again. Sekhmet and Empusa had joined the vigil, and Paoli was keeping William informed.

It killed him that she was dying on the other side of the door and she wouldn't let him be there. His anxiousness and isolation gave him far too much time to consider all that had happened.

While he wished he would have handled her transition a bit differently, he couldn't bring himself to regret it, even now. Eternity was a long time. Surely even Emily couldn't stay mad that long.

Finally, with dawn nearing, Paoli stepped out of the room. He looked extremely solemn.

"She's stopped breathing," he said.

William swallowed hard.

It was normal and expected. He knew that. But it didn't make it any easier to hear. If anything went wrong and she didn't rise with the moon—

He couldn't allow himself to even consider the possibility.

She *would* rise.

He nodded silently to Paoli and went to Emily's side.

She lay in the bed, propped up on pillows. Her eyes were closed. Someone had pulled the blankets up to her chin.

Probably Paoli.

She looked like she was sleeping. Her raven hair spilled around her like a dark halo. Her skin was pale. So pale.

William sat on the edge of the bed and ran a finger down her cheek. If anything went wrong, it was his fault.

All his fault.

"I know you wanted to be with her," Paoli said. "But she was adamant all the way to the end."

William almost smiled, imagining her defiant little face.

"Stubborn," he said.

Paoli did chuckle then, just a little.

"Very," he agreed. "I think you've found a good match in her."

"If she ever forgives what I've done," William said absently, his eyes on Emily's still form.

"She'll forgive you," Paoli said, then paused. "Eventually," he added with a small chuckle.

He crossed the room and sat down on the couch.

"I was planning to stay in here until she rises, if that's all right with you. The first rise might be difficult."

William hadn't given any thought to that.

He'd always heard the initial hunger was unbearable.

That certainly wasn't going to soften her to him any.

"That's a good idea," he agreed without looking toward Paoli. "I want this to be as easy on her as possible."

Paoli gave a humorless scoff.

"It's never easy. Not for anyone. And you're not exactly standard," he said.

William raised thoughtful gray eyes to Paoli, considering his words.

It was true.

There was no way to know what they could expect when she rose.

Paoli was simple. He was a vampire. Undead. If he changed a human, they would follow an expected pattern, and they could be prepared.

But William wasn't undead. Not technically.

There was no way to know what they could expect when Emily rose. And she *would* rise. There was no other option he could even allow himself to consider. She would rise.

"She wouldn't be your mate if she couldn't make the transition," Paoli said, as if reading his thoughts. "Get some rest. I have a feeling we're going to need it," he said.

With those cryptic words, he slid down on the couch to sleep.

CHAPTER 21

Emily opened her eyes and immediately closed them again with a slight groan. Light seemed to be everywhere, and it was far too bright, though it wasn't sunlight. The bedrooms in the castle were all blocked against sunlight, Paoli had told her.

She lay there a moment, taking in her surroundings without opening her eyes again. Sounds were everywhere, and she found if she focused on too many of them, they became a dull roar in her head that seemed to press against her mind. It didn't take much effort to block them out, though.

Eyes still closed, she took stock of her own body. Everything seemed to be in working order, she decided after having wiggled her toes, legs, and arms. A smell wafted across her nose and slowly seemed to saturate her. It was vaguely familiar and comforting somehow. Warm and slightly musky, with a just a hint of something—

Her eyes snapped open and she turned her head to find William sitting beside her bed. She opened her mouth to tell him to get lost, but the words froze in her throat when she looked at him.

The face that was normally so confident—bordering on arrogant—looked strained and unsure. Deep gouge marks marred his cheek and disappeared into the collar of his shirt, like something had clawed him.

"How are you feeling?" he asked, his voice very serious.

All the things—the hateful words, the nasty insults she'd intended to fling at him—died away with the sound of his voice.

Her anger fled.

It left behind a quiet understanding. All that had been done had taken a toll on him, as well.

She might not agree with, or like, the choices he'd made, but once she let go of her own blind rage, she could at least understand them.

Emily cleared her dry throat and considered the question.

Other than her senses being heightened a bit, she felt pretty normal. She didn't seem to have a desire to eat small children or tear the heads off virgins to bathe in their blood. While it sounded too stupid to say aloud, it really was what she'd expected. Maybe she'd seen too many Dracula movies.

"OK, I think," she answered finally.

William nodded.

"You seem better," he said.

Emily gave him a look of confusion.

"What do you mean?" she asked.

"I mean you seem like you're just about back to normal," he answered.

She continued to frown at him, still not understanding.

"When was I not normal?" she asked, thinking of when she demanded he leave her alone.

William was silent for a minute.

"What's the last thing you remember?" he asked.

She looked at him suspiciously and thought about it.

"I remember Paoli saying my heart was slowing down and that it was almost over," she said.

William looked at her, his face impassive.

"That was a week ago," he said quietly.

"What?" she gasped and sat up slightly.

She'd lost an entire week?

"I've been asleep for a week?" she asked in disbelief.

William hesitated again.

"What?" she asked.

"Your heart didn't start again until the fourth day. Normally, a person rises on the second night after their change," he said.

He swallowed, and his voice became thick.

"I thought we'd lost you. That I'd done something wrong," he said.

Emily could hear the worry in his voice.

"I'm all right," she told him soothingly.

She'd never seen him looking so raw and vulnerable. She didn't like it.

"When you finally rose, you weren't yourself," he went on.

"You mean I've been awake before now?" she asked.

He nodded.

"But you weren't normal. I'd begun to think your mind wasn't going to come through the change," he said.

She looked at the gouges on his face. There were four of them, she noticed. Perfectly spaced to be fingernail marks. A dawning suspicion crept into her head.

"Did I leave those marks on you?" she asked in a small voice.

William's finger traced the lines almost absently.

"You got me pretty good that time," he said with a shrug. "I deserved it. I should have handled things better. I'm not used to being so lost."

Emily stared at him. She tried to look at the situation through his eyes. She did understand why he'd done what he had.

But it didn't change the end result for her.

She wasn't up to having the discussion. Thinking too much about all that had happened made her temper spark, so she put it out of her mind. She'd dwell on it later.

With more effort than expected, she sat up and looked around the room. There was destruction as far as the eye could see.

Chunks of antique wood lay in broken splinters all across the floor like Lincoln logs. The table had been knocked onto its side, the chairs across the room from it, also lying on their sides.

Had she done all that?

She looked at William and decided not to ask. Something in his face told her she didn't want to know.

"Are you all right?" she asked.

He looked so tired and worn down, like he'd aged decades since they arrived at the Coven. It made her stop and consider all he'd been through here, as well.

William gave a short, humorless laugh. He reached out and stroked aside the pesky lock of hair that always seemed to fall into her face.

"Only you could come through this insanity and worry about me," he told her, humor now shining in his eyes.

All the starch seemed to leak from her spine at the touch of his fingers.

"I don't feel much different," she said, more to distract herself than anything else. "Are you sure it worked?"

His humor faded, and his eyes took on a shadowed look.

"This is the first day you've been lucid. Trust me. It worked," he said.

"From all the movies I've watched, I thought I'd wake up and be a starving, ravening beast," she admitted.

Her eyes skimmed across the room again, and suddenly what William wasn't saying became clear.

She *had* been a monster.

That's what he was trying not to say.

Her eyes returned to him, and she allowed her gaze to linger again on the gouges marring his cheek.

She took a deep breath.

"Then again, maybe it's good I don't remember the last few days," she ventured.

"All that matters is you've come through the transition intact," he said.

There was no doubting he meant it. The relief was clear in his voice.

A long, meaningful silence stretched out.

"What happens now?" she asked, her voice sounding a little lost.

Another quiet moment passed.

"We take it one day at a time," was his answer. "You have a lot of adjustments to make. We have a very long time to worry about it all, though. For now, I say let's sleep and worry about it later."

Emily held his gaze, taking in his exhausted appearance.

She nodded slowly.

He obviously needed to sleep, and something told her he wasn't about to rest unless she did. She gave him a smile to break the tension and scooted over to make a space for him in the bed.

He slid from the chair without a word and stretched out beside her.

"I can't tell you how worried I was," he said, pulling her against his large frame.

He buried his face in her hair and took a deep breath.

"I'm fine," she said again reassuringly, slowly relaxing against the heat of his body. "I'm sorry for whatever I did before. But I'm fine now."

And safely wrapped in each other's arms, they slept.

Emily woke first.

She lay in William's embrace and cherished the feeling of being surrounded by him. It was strange, since she'd thought of running away from him and had been convinced she never wanted to see him again when she learned what he'd done. But still, it just felt right.

Her mate.

She had so much to learn about what that meant.

Hell, about who and what she was now. Questions and uncertainty swirled in her head until she needed to distract herself or scream in panic.

Her back was against William's chest, so she couldn't see his face to know if he was awake. His right arm was across her ribs. She examined it, following the white lines of so many scars that ran from the side of his hand all the way to his shoulder.

So many wounds. So many times something had hurt him.

To her surprise, the idea of something hurting him filled her with rage. She wanted to kiss each and every mark that touched his skin and take away all the pain he'd ever suffered. She wanted to tear the Coven itself apart for making him do what he did and putting him in harm's way.

"Whatever you're thinking about, stop it," William's deep voice whispered in her ear.

His breath sent a delicious shiver down her spine.

She snuggled against him and let him pull her from her thoughts.

"How did you know I was thinking about anything?" she teased.

His nose nuzzled the sensitive spot just behind her ear, sending another thrill through her.

"Because, now that we have a blood bond, I can feel your emotions," he said.

She thought about that.

"What do you mean, 'blood bond'?" she asked.

"When a vampire exchanges blood, it forges a bond between the people involved," he explained, his nose still nuzzling into the sensitive area of her neck and ear.

"What does the bond do?" she asked, not sure if she liked the sound of that.

"Lots of things," he answered distractedly.

She let out a sigh of annoyance, but some of the heat was stolen by the soft meowing sound that escaped her when his tongue touched her earlobe.

"Like what?" she asked, refusing to be distracted.

"For most people it's some limited telepathy, phantom images—" he said.

"Phantom images?" she cut him off.

"The projection of thoughts or images," he answered the question, then continued as if she hadn't interrupted. "Feeling each other's emotions, and a vampire can always track down someone they've given blood to."

He chuckled just a little bit.

"Well, usually," he amended.

"What's funny?" she wanted to know, but his hand was slowly sliding up her thigh, and she wasn't sure it was really all that important anymore.

"You're the first person I ever exchanged blood with," he said. "Paoli's first blood exchange was with a girl a few years ago. It was to seal a pact he made with her. Now that it's time to collect on their deal, he can't track her, for some reason."

His hand slid up her ribcage and cupped the underside of her breast.

"Why would that be?" she asked, her voice husky and low as her interest in the conversation quickly waned.

"I have no idea," he said, but his mind was clearly on other things, as well. "But watching him get frustrated in his struggle to track her has been entertaining."

His thumb slid gently across Emily's nipple, hardening it into a taut peak, and she had no further questions that couldn't wait. With a sigh of surrender, she pressed against him.

William needed no further prompting.

He turned her face toward him and covered her mouth with his own hungrily. He made no attempt to control himself. He no longer had any fear of hurting her. She'd shown him her passions were as wild as his own, and there was no reason to hide his need. But this time, he stripped her leisurely and took his time.

He kissed each beautiful, rounded curve of skin as he exposed it and explored her body with his mouth and hands until neither of them could bear it any longer.

Then he covered her body with his own and entered her quickly.

She gasped in pure pleasure and gripped his back to pull him closer.

Suddenly, she went rigid and shoved him away with a horrified shriek.

He stopped moving and propped himself on his elbows to look at her with concern.

"What's wrong?" he asked.

Had he hurt her?

She had one hand clamped firmly over her mouth and shook her head silently, her eyes wide.

His gaze lit with understanding, and he had to fight back a grin. He had a strong suspicion what was wrong, and she wouldn't appreciate his humor in the least.

"Did you find your fangs?" he asked gently.

Emily could feel the tears burning her eyes. She nodded just once, a quick up and down of her head.

She was mortified.

But also hungry.

So hungry.

His blood pounded in his veins, sweet with their lovemaking. It called to her so much, with such promise of fulfillment. Her eyes were glued to the strong pulse in his neck, the heat, the hypnotic beat.

"Let me see," he said patiently.

She shook her head almost violently without taking her eyes from his pulse.

His strong, masculine pulse.

"Let me up, please," she begged from behind her hand.

Her voice sounded weird, her words being formed around the sharp teeth that suddenly felt huge.

Panic started to set in.

She couldn't stop watching each small beat in his neck, and it was pulling her in.

He wasn't safe.

"Let me show you how to use them," he said, his voice seductive and low.

Her eyes flew to his and locked in the intensity of his gaze. She saw no fear. If anything, the raw desire was even stronger than before.

"Come to me and let me feed you. You're so hungry," he murmured.

His voice was rough and thick, his most persuasive.

"Come and take what you need," he urged.

He moved in her again, thrusting gently, rhythmically, with each beat of his heart. He scooped one hand beneath her head and guided her to his throat.

"I don't want to hurt you," she whispered desperately, but she was lost.

His pulse beat strong against her lips, and she didn't have the will to resist.

"You won't hurt me," he said, still moving inside her in time to his own heartbeat. "Stop fighting it," he ordered. "This is what we are. Let me show you how to feed."

She couldn't stop herself.

Her body moved with his, feeling each amazing thrust push her higher and higher toward ecstasy. She sank her fangs into the side of his neck with a gentle pop as the skin covering the vein gave way. A flood of hot, pulsing blood filled her mouth with the most wonderful of tastes.

William's head fell forward in absolute pleasure. His erection swelled almost to the point of pain. He held her to him and continued to move inside her, building speed and power with each thrust.

Control be damned! It was pure bliss, perfection. Better by far than he'd ever dared dream.

He was suddenly slamming himself into her, using her hips to pull her onto him for more force.

She continued to feed with equal abandon, suckling his blood right into her own body. She arched backward with a cry, allowing his blood to flow across her face. Her muscles tightened around him, pulling and pulsing as her climax gripped her. He leaned forward and found the magic spot on her throat.

Without a thought, he sank his fangs to take what he needed as his seed spilled.

For hours, they lay naked in one another's arms, their limbs intertwined, together as immortal equals. William was happy—truly happy—for the first time he could ever remember. He'd finally found the place he belonged. It was right there, in Emily's arms. So many whispered words were spoken, promises of the future before them. Of eternity.

CHAPTER 22

The following evening went just as well. The committee was well pleased with Emily's transformation, and permission was granted for them to leave. William couldn't wait to have the island and the Coven with all its problems behind him.

Mere hours before they were to depart for home, he and Paoli returned from making flight arrangements to find Emily missing. On the table was a simple note which read:

Gone with Amber to meet Lycaon.
Back soon,
Emily

William froze in place, his mind running to the meeting with Sekhmet and Empusa.

Amber.

Amber had taken sides.

She'd come while he was gone and taken Emily right to Lycaon, into the hands of the man who was running a secret agenda.

"Oh no," Paoli whispered as he read the note.

"How are we on weapons?" William's voice was low and menacing. He felt for Emily through their blood bond and found wariness growing in her.

Something wasn't right.

He pushed strength at her through their mating bond and tried to control his own fury.

"Just a couple of daggers," Paoli answered.

"Are they silver?" William asked, trying to keep his voice steady.

"Of course," Paoli said.

He dashed from the chamber and returned mere seconds later, carrying four silver daggers by their rubber handles.

William stuffed them into the pockets of his jeans and tore through the castle with Paoli close on his heels. An icy cold hand stole across his heart at the thought of her—alone and unprotected—with Lycaon.

What was she thinking?

"What are you going to do?" Paoli asked urgently.

"I'm going to tear this whole place to the ground to find her. So help me, if they hurt her in any way—" He left the sentence unfinished and moved with all the speed in him through the long corridors as he fought back the wolf, who wanted to take control and find their mate.

Two guards were posted outside the door to Lycaon's private chambers. It confirmed what William had already surmised.

Lycaon was inside.

At their approach, the guards stepped together to bar the way. One guard held his hand out toward William aggressively.

"You can't go in there. King Lycaon gave orders he is not to be disturbed," said the guard.

He appeared to be in his early thirties.

William knew that meant nothing since he himself looked like he was in his late twenties, and Paoli looked younger yet.

The guard was wolf and dominant. Though not nearly dominant enough.

William knocked the guard's hand away.

"Step out of my path," he ordered darkly.

William bared his teeth and growled in warning. He could feel Emily go from wariness to fear, and it fueled his rage.

"I-I'm sorry," the guard stammered, suddenly uncertain. "But, as I said—"

William was in no mood to negotiate. He threw a dagger that hit the guard in the shoulder and pinned him to the door. The man howled in surprise and pain as the silver burned. With his free hand, the guard tentatively touched the blade, as if he thought to pull it out.

William pulled a second dagger and looked at the other guard, whose eyes were popping in shock.

"Step aside," William said, his voice deceptively calm.

The guard dropped his head and moved out of the way, his eyes trained on the floor as they passed.

William entered the extravagantly decorated room like an enraged bull. His eyes flashed around the garishly expensive items; the crystal chandelier that occupied more than half of the recessed ceiling, three—he counted them—*three* life-sized marble sculptures of Lycaon himself, and various paintings and furniture that dated all the way to ancient Rome.

William found Emily against the far wall, locked in Lycaon's grasp.

Lycaon held her arms tightly, her body pulled backward against his. He peered over the relative safety of her shoulder at William and Paoli.

"Let her go," William hissed.

"I'm just trying to answer a question," Lycaon said conversationally.

He twisted Emily's arm until she cried out.

"Lycaon, stop this at once!" Paoli demanded. "It won't go well if the committee learns of this."

Lycaon laughed.

"Let them learn. I have the two most powerful immortals in the world right here. One of them is my own daughter. With them by my side, the wolves can rule over all. I just want to find out if she can shift. I can force a shift to human form, but not animal," he said.

Emily's eyes were wide and frightened, but it wasn't pain William sensed from her most strongly.

It was hate.

Cold, hard hate.

Her sister had betrayed her.

Again.

Amber sat across the room on a lounging chair, calmly watching Emily be tortured at their father's hands.

William wondered how much of her moral rot was related to her change and how much had always been there.

He gripped a dagger and weighed his options quickly. At the rate he was going, Lycaon would break Emily's arms before they could get help. Waiting was not an option.

He watched Lycaon for a few seconds and made a decision. Using every bit of speed and strength he possessed, he threw the blade right into the arm Lycaon used to hold Emily.

It was a calculated risk for sure, but William didn't have a lot of other options on such short notice.

He was the executioner.

The bringer of death.

His dagger's aim was true.

Lycaon yelped in pain and stepped back when the knife embedded in his arm. He looked in complete shock at the handle protruding from him. A second later, his rage rolled through the room like a wave, but William's own anger was too high to be affected by it.

Quick as a flash, William pulled Emily away from Lycaon and pushed her to Paoli.

Paoli moved her behind him and through the open doorway as William launched himself at Lycaon.

William knocked into the old king with enough force to put him off balance and landed them both on the floor in a heap, William on top. With a jerk, William pulled the blade from Lycaon's arm and pressed it to his throat. William bared his teeth and growled directly into Lycaon's face in pure satisfaction at the smell of seared flesh.

"If you ever come near her again, Lilith won't get the chance to end you." William made the dark promise very quietly.

"William, this is not the time!" Paoli called urgently. "We need to be gone, and soon, before the guards send reinforcements after us. An attack on a Coven head would result in death, no matter the reason."

"You side with Lilith?" Lycaon's voice was strained, yet incredulous.

"I side with no one," William said flatly.

"And my own daughter?" Lycaon demanded through clenched teeth.

William caught movement from the corner of his eye. He realized Amber had taken the opportunity to slip into the corridor where Emily was. All he could do was call a warning since he was still holding Lycaon.

Paoli turned to intercept. Before he could go to her rescue, Amber backed back into the room with her hands up in surrender.

Her eyes were the size of saucers, and she shook her head slowly from side to side, her mouth open in a soundless scream. She was followed closely by a giant wolf.

Sort of a wolf.

It was similar to a red wolf in appearance but nearly as large as William's own wolf form. Huge black wings were held out on either side.

William recognized her scent immediately. Even in the midst of absolute chaos, he couldn't stop the surge of pride.

Emily.

His mate.

His very *big* mate.

Lycaon's energy surge must have forced her first phase. Now her impressive form filled the entire room.

"Emily, please." Amber continued to retreat until she hit the wall in the far corner with nowhere else to go.

A tremendous howl sounded that hurt William's ears so much he dropped the dagger from Lycaon's throat and pressed his hands against his head instead, as did everyone else in the room.

Even Lilith's screech didn't have the power of Emily's new howl.

Amber just stared in horror.

Emily stood over her, anger emanating so heavily, it was nearly palpable. Everyone in the room held their breath, unsure how this would end. Emily stomped her feet one at a time and flapped her wings angrily, then turned and moved toward the door.

Paoli and William leaped from their positions and followed.

"I want her." Lycaon's booming voice trailed down the corridor.

CHAPTER 23

They went straight for the plane at full speed ahead. They needed to get as far away from the Coven as possible.

Immediately.

If Lycaon had time to gather his guards, they wouldn't get away at all.

A few miles separated them from the runway, but they never slowed.

They hit the front door of the castle and just kept running.

Emily was worn out enough when they neared the plane that she stumbled and almost went head over tail when her body began to regain human form of its own volition.

William looked behind them and saw no one in pursuit, so he motioned for Paoli to halt.

A quick glance told Paoli what was happening. He stood with his back to them, clearly on the lookout for enemies while one of their party was so vulnerable in the midst of a shift.

It took just a few minutes for the wolf to basically melt away, and Emily was left too exhausted to stand.

William pulled his shirt off and threw it around her naked form. He swung her into his arms, and he and Paoli walked the remainder of the way at a close-to-normal pace, so as not to cause alarm.

They boarded the plane silently and Paoli gave the pilot the order to leave.

Tension ran high; nerves were stretched to the breaking point. None of them took an easy breath

until their plane lifted from the runway and made it
into the air.

"Well," Paoli finally broke the silence a while later.
"That went well."

William looked at him with sudden indulgent
humor at the ridiculousness of his statement.

"Only *you* could come up with that," he said.

Paoli ignored him and turned his attention to
Emily.

"And you!" he exclaimed. "You are the most amazing thing I've ever seen, and boy, am I proud to know
you!"

Emily's mouth turned up just slightly at the corners in the face of Paoli's excitement.

"Did you see her?" Paoli demanded rhetorically
from William.

William chuckled slightly and nodded.

"I saw her, all right," he agreed.

"She turned into a giant wolf. And when I say
giant, I really mean *giant*. She's nearly as big as you
are," Paoli went on.

His eyes sparkled.

"And she had wings," he continued, as if they
hadn't *all* been there.

He hesitated, his brow furrowed.

"I wonder how long it will take her to learn how
to fly," he said.

Emily's cheeks flushed as Paoli spoke. She looked
at William, and her face grew concerned.

"What?" she asked.

"What were you thinking?" William burst out,
breaking into Paoli's excited chatter. "Do you realize
you could have been killed?"

"Amber came for me," Emily said, clearly taken aback. "I just wanted to talk to her and meet my father—"

"Your father?" William scoffed. "Lycaon may have donated to your DNA, but that's the extent of how much father is in him. You and Amber are pawns in his drive for control, that's all."

"But Amber—" Emily started to say hotly.

"Is now in Lycaon's power," William cut her off. "That was her choice to make. Whatever remained of the sister you loved is gone. I hope you learned that today."

Her face fell in the most forlorn expression he'd ever seen.

His anger was gone, just like that. He shouldn't have snapped at her, but she had to see the truth before her blind faith in Amber got her killed.

"I'm sorry," he tried to apologize.

His anger was fueled by his fear of how easily he could have lost her. He reached for her hand, and she snatched it back and turned away.

"Emily," he said gently. "Look at me."

"I need to sleep," she said stiffly, her back to him.

William's beseeching gaze sought out Paoli's.

Paoli gave him a look that clearly said he needed to give her some space.

Reluctantly, William moved away toward the front of the plane and took a seat next to the window, where he could look out and get himself under better control. He shouldn't have yelled at her. But she had to realize the position she'd put herself in.

"You OK?" Paoli took a seat next to him almost an hour later.

"Nope," William answered, still looking through the window at the ground below.

"Want to talk about it?" Paoli asked lightly.

"Nope," William said, still not looking at him.

"Well, that's too bad," Paoli said in that same casual voice.

He turned in his seat to face William.

"What is wrong with you? Your mate came through the transition intact. She has an amazing wolf, and we escaped the Coven, together and unharmed. What's your problem?" he asked.

William turned to face Paoli at last, his temper flaring again.

"Didn't you hear what Lycaon said when we left? He wants her, especially now," he said.

He looked at Paoli intently, willing him to understand.

"Do you really think this is over?" he demanded.

"Oh," Paoli said.

That one word weighed heavily in the air.

"Some things cannot be avoided," Paoli said after a moment. "Besides, you saw her today. It's not like she's a helpless mortal anymore. They'll think twice about grabbing hold of her when they realize they can't let go."

"He thinks to control us," William said.

He looked across the plane's cabin to where Emily slept off the effects of her first shift.

"Do you honestly think he's above using us against one another?" he asked.

Paoli sat for a moment, seemingly considering the question.

"The committee's aware problems are brewing. I'm sure they already have a plan in place to stop this before it gets too out of hand," he said.

"Where was the committee today when he tried to break her arms just to see what would happen?" William asked pointedly.

"Do you think it's going to turn into another war?" Paoli asked.

"I don't know," William sighed. "All I know for sure is Lycaon wants me and Emily under his control. We're walking targets now."

He would do anything to keep her safe.

Blood would flow like rivers if Lycaon declared war on them.

"All right," Paoli said, as if coming to a decision. "This is what we do."

He held his hand out and ticked off the plan on his fingers.

"First, we get home and spend a few days resting. I'll make arrangements at the bookstore. Second, we train Emily. She's going to be very powerful once she learns to shift at will. Besides, you two need to work on the ins and outs of your mate bond. From what Empusa said, there's a lot to it. I'm not a good source of information, but you can always call him with questions. Third, we live our lives as usual until trouble comes looking for us, if it ever does. It's possible we're overthinking this," he said.

"Trouble always finds us," William retorted.

"Fair enough." Paoli had to concede the point. "So, when trouble *does* come looking, we go nomad again. It's nearly impossible to track someone with no place to begin. We can wait it out until the committee gets things back under control."

"I wonder if we should inform the committee of Lycaon's actions," William said.

Paoli nodded.

"We should. I'll make some calls. Maybe we can end this before it begins," he said enthusiastically.

CHAPTER 24

Paoli made several calls over the next few days, trying to reach anyone in the committee, but to no avail. The only thing remotely close to helpful he learned was the committee was aware of the situation and were actively taking steps to thwart the plan. The steps did not include removing Lycaon from the Coven, and things would continue as they always had. Which translated to mean everyone was too afraid of Lycaon to stand up and do anything to stop him. Ergo, no help could be found there.

William expected as much, but Paoli had really put his faith in them and was livid with their lack of action.

"I cannot believe," Paoli complained one day, "they intend to do nothing."

Emily rolled her eyes at William in an overly dramatic, exasperated expression.

They'd been cooped up in the house together for days—everyone in agreement she needed plenty of time to recuperate from her first transition—and they'd heard Paoli's "I can't believe it" rant about a thousand times.

William couldn't stop the laugh her expression caused. He tried to disguise it as a cough, which earned him a dirty look from Paoli, who made it clear he wasn't buying William's bad acting.

"I'm taking Emily out," William said, redirecting the conversation.

He'd been thinking about if for a few days and finally made up his mind.

It was time.

His wolf was going stir-crazy, and Emily's must be as well, though she never complained. Then again, she might not be able to identify the emotions of her wolf yet, being so new.

She really hadn't seemed to struggle at all with control.

If William hadn't seen her take wolf form, he'd have thought only the vampire side of him had carried to her.

Since her change, Emily had yet to be exposed to a single human.

William had begun to worry they might be overprotecting her, which was not a good thing. The hunting instinct was something she needed to learn to overcome. It was especially true if they had to go nomad sometime in the near future. He wanted her prepared so she didn't go after a human in front of witnesses and leave a mess to be cleaned up.

Although his wolf wouldn't mind hunting down human prey, Emily would never forgive herself, and Paoli would never forgive *him*.

"Do you really think she's ready for that?" Paoli asked, his earlier pique seemingly forgotten. "She's a little new to this life to have her around humans, don't you think?"

William considered his concerns and dismissed them with a nonchalant shrug as he held out his hand in invitation to Emily. She took it without hesitation, making it clear he'd been right in thinking she needed to get out, as well.

"I'm not taking her to a party. We're just going out in the slums," William said. "Don't worry," he went on with exaggerated calm. "If she gets out of control, there won't be anyone left alive to tell about it."

He was joking, but the look on Paoli's face said he took William seriously.

William regretted the jest immediately. He flashed Paoli a slight smile and tried not to take offense to Paoli's lack of faith in him.

He and Emily got into the car and headed out, exchanging the house that had begun to feel like it was closing in on them for the wide-open space of the world and clear night air.

"What was he worried about?" Emily asked on the drive.

William realized they'd spent very little time discussing the issues of her new immortality. He felt a twinge of guilt for neglecting something so important. Her transition had been so smooth after the first week—and so much was happening around them— that all three of them had sort of forgotten about it.

"Since you joined the immortal world, you haven't been exposed to humans at all," he said.

"So? I've been 'exposed' to humans all my life. What's the big deal?" She looked utterly confused.

"Things are different now because *you're* different. Humans don't smell the same to us as they do to one another," he said carefully.

She was silent for a moment.

"In what way?" she asked, a note of suspicion coloring her tone.

"They smell very . . . good to an immortal. Especially a hungry one," he paused, eying her reaction to his words.

"I just fed," she reminded him.

He nodded.

"It may be uncomfortable for you at first. It's hard to be prepared for it. Let me know right away if it's too much," he said.

He silently smiled to himself at the thought of her ever admitting a weakness.

Not Emily.

She'd stand there and burst into flames with thirst before she'd ever admit she couldn't handle it, especially since *he* could. Her strength was one thing he loved the most about her. Her stubbornness was a close second, though he'd never tell her that.

"I will," she promised, then set her hand on his thigh and rubbed it reassuringly.

He sucked in a breath and eyed her hand.

"If you want to try your strength with humans, I suggest you get that hand back to your own side of the car, or we won't ever get to town," he half teased.

She grinned unrepentantly but withdrew her hand just the same. It was already too late, though. His thoughts spun wildly in another direction, and he considered pulling the car over and enjoying the bounty of his mate. After all, the exercise in control could always wait another day.

"All right, I'll behave," she said with a broad smile. "I really want to see what this human thing is all about. But I do love that I can distract you so easily."

Just like that, he decided to hold off on his physical desires so he could fulfill her wishes. He wondered if it was a mate thing—his need to put her wants and needs ahead of his own—or if it was something else.

He looked at her and knew it didn't matter.

She was nervous.

He could see it in the way she fidgeted. But there was a new challenge ahead of her, and she was determined to meet it head on.

That was his Emily.

"I trust you not to let me hurt anyone," she said, her voice betraying her anxiousness.

"I won't let you do anything you'll regret tomorrow," he said. "Although I still struggle with humans myself," he admitted. "Don't let it bother you if you have trouble. This is your first time, and I've been at it for centuries. You're the only person I've ever fed from without killing. Most vampires can leave people alive after the first few years. But I can't."

It wasn't an easy thing to admit, but he felt it was important she be prepared for what was coming.

"Why not?" she asked.

Her voice seemed suddenly stiff.

William gave her a sidelong glimpse and considered the question.

"Because my wolf instinct is to hunt, and my vampire requires human blood, which makes them my natural prey. It's a dangerous combination. And one you now have, too. Since I was never human, I can't rely on my humanity the way Paoli can," he said.

She was quiet for a moment.

"That's why you guys always use the blood bags," she guessed.

"Exactly," he said. "You can't kill if the person isn't there when you drink the blood. It keeps everyone safe."

"Where do you get the blood?" she asked curiously.

"I don't. My control isn't good enough," he said with a touch of regret. "Paoli does all the hunting.

A few years ago, he decided to get in touch with the times and bought an old blood bus. You know, like the ones they use for the blood banks?"

Emily laughed out loud.

"You're kidding?" she said.

"Nope," he said simply. "At first, I thought it was ludicrous. But it's actually a genius idea. Every few weeks, he fires up the bus and posts notices at college campuses for donations at different schools. In a single day, he can usually get enough to last us a month or more."

Emily chuckled lightly.

"Modern-day vampires," she said, more to herself than him, he thought. "I'm surprised he doesn't run an add on Craigslist."

At that, it was William's turn to laugh.

"It's a whole lot safer than hunting," he said.

Emily shivered visibly at that, her humor fading.

"Hunting. It makes humans sound like . . . well . . . prey," she said.

William sobered.

"Humans *are* our prey," he said.

"Why not just use animal blood?" she asked. "Doesn't it make more sense?"

William gave her a slightly indulgent smile.

"That's like expecting a lion to enjoy a salad. We can't sustain on anything other than human blood," he said.

"What about your wolf side? It needs meat," she said, then gasped as soon as the words were spoken and looked at him in horror.

"Yes, but I don't eat human flesh," he said quickly and watched her visibly relax. "I hunt at least once during the full moon to keep my wolf satisfied and a day or two throughout the month if I get restless. Hunt animals, I mean," he clarified, just to make absolutely sure she understood he didn't eat people.

"Then you never kill humans," she said.

She sounded so relieved he almost didn't tell her. But then, an omission was as bad as a lie. He forged on with the truth.

"Paoli doesn't," he said very carefully. "He never has."

Silence.

He regarded her heavily with a sideways look but waited for her to digest his words.

"How often do you kill people?" she finally asked in a very small voice.

"I try very hard not to," he assured her in a rush.

It was the truth. More so than anyone could ever know, he fought his inner beast.

"But every few years, I can't fight the drive and I . . . well . . . I slip," he said.

It was like an alcoholic admitting to occasional trips to the bar. It made him feel uncomfortable to actually say it aloud, especially to Emily.

More silence stretched out. It was a heavy, uncomfortable silence.

"Does that mean I'll kill someone eventually? Since you made me, I mean. Doesn't that mean I'll be like you?" she asked, her voice haunted.

"Most people carry part of their human selves into this life. You won't necessarily be exactly like me. I'm the exception to the rule. You're an exception as well, because of your connection to Lycaon. I'm not sure why that makes your wolf have wings, though.

I've never heard of that before. You may prove to be different in other things, too. But, aside from Paoli, all of us have killed at some point," he said, hating that he couldn't reassure her.

He didn't want to give her no hope, but he wanted to be honest with her.

"It's an unfortunate part of what we are. That's why it's so important to learn control," he stressed.

Emily turned her attention to her window and watched the night go by.

William gave her time to mull over the new information and figure out what it meant to her.

"What's it like?" she asked, still gazing through the window.

Her voice had a strangely eerie sound to it.

"What?" he asked.

"Killing someone," she said with that same eerie, flat tone in her voice.

William groaned aloud and gripped the wheel, trying to block out all the memories of a past better off forgotten. He didn't want to consider how many times he'd knelt, cradling a drained body in his arms. How could he explain a thing like that to her? She'd never see him the same way again.

"It's like losing a part of who you are, of who you've fought to become," he confided softly, praying that would explain enough.

"Do you enjoy it?" she whispered.

The question took him aback, and he glanced to her in surprise.

"No," he said automatically.

Then, he thought about it. *Really* thought about it. The feeling of not having to fight for control, of letting the hunger take him where it would, and the taste and feel of fresh blood on his tongue.

"And yes," he admitted, ashamed. "But it always comes with a little loss of yourself."

"Then why do you do it?" she asked, turning to look at him, clearly trying to make sense of it. To understand. "I don't want to live with someone's death on my head."

He gave a self-deprecating smile.

As much as he didn't want to see it, there was condemnation in her eyes, and it cut deep.

"That question will be answered tonight," he said, his tone clipped and short. "This will be a good experience for you, since we may have to run soon. There will be little choice about human contact then, and it's better you be prepared."

She took a deep breath.

"That's what I'm afraid of, too. Lycaon terrifies me," she said. "Does he really believe he can rule everyone if he controls us?"

"He's never been particularly stable," William declared. "And he was after great power and world domination as a human."

She squared her shoulders after a moment and seemed to perk up before his very eyes, as though shedding her fears.

"What are we going to do about it?" she asked.

He met her eyes and took her hand in his. He brought it to his cheek and brushed her knuckles along his jawline.

"We're going to be prepared and protect each other, just like we were made to," he declared.

"Mates," she agreed.

There was no longer condemnation in her gaze, he was relieved to see.

"Exactly. We're mates, and together we're strong enough to withstand anything," he said.

Her touch warmed him.

She calmed the beast.

With her, he finally knew peace.

He needed her to make him whole, and she needed him just as much, in a different way.

He needed her for control, and she needed him for strength and protection. Her relationship with her own sister proved that.

She was so unselfish and giving. Without him by her side, the world would slowly take everything from her, and leave her an empty shell.

He wished her change could have been by her choice. But she didn't hate him like he'd been so afraid she would, so he decided not to dwell on it.

He prayed this night wouldn't change that.

Since she became immortal, he and Paoli had kept her far from humans and given her time to adjust to some of the changes in herself. They'd made it a little too easy on her, shielding her from the darker side of what she'd become.

But they couldn't keep her locked away from temptation and anything unpleasant forever. He could teach her to be an immortal. To be a *good* immortal. But only after she understood what it really meant, both the good and the bad. Lessons had to be learned. Then maybe she'd have a better understanding of him. Of herself.

CHAPTER 25

Brace yourself," William whispered, one hand on the car door's handle.

When she looked at him questioningly, he pointed through the windshield at a couple in the distance.

"You're about to get your first scent of a human. Be ready," he cautioned.

She rolled her eyes dramatically in response.

He didn't reply.

As soon as his door opened, the distant scent of humans wafted into the car and saturated them both with the sweet, siren scent of fresh blood. Even braced for it, William still had to work at blocking the instinct to feed.

"Emily," William said calmly, watching her reaction closely.

Her lip curled up to display fangs that were suddenly prominent, and her eyes became unfocused. His mind went back to the first few days after her change. Days she thankfully had no memory of. It had taken all four of them, he, Paoli, Sekhmet, and Empusa, to keep her under control. Could he restrain her alone if it became necessary?

"Are you sure you're ready for this?" He was suddenly unsure about this idea.

Maybe Paoli was right to say it was too soon.

William hesitated.

He didn't want to push her too far too fast. If she killed someone while caught in the throes of bloodlust, she'd be crushed.

He watched her, trying to decide what to do.

After a moment of fang baring, Emily took a deep breath and seemed to pull herself back together.

"I'm all right now," she announced, and her voice sounded close to normal. "It caught me off guard. I can handle it," she said, and there was no doubt about her determination.

William searched her face and saw the gold flecks in her eyes. It was a sure indicator her wolf was close, which was a good sign. It meant she was instinctively using the wolf as a shield from the blood. She was going to see this through, and he could do no other than help her.

"It can be overwhelming at first," he said soothingly.

He got out and walked around the car to open her door for her. While it was an old-fashioned and gentlemanly gesture, he did it mainly so he could hold tight to her arm.

She looked at his hand on her arm as they stood together beside the car, but she didn't say anything about it.

"The smell calls to me," she murmured longingly, turning her face toward the scent.

"It does," he agreed calmly.

"Do all humans smell like this?" she asked dreamily, her eyes sliding closed, like a wine connoisseur inhaling the fragrance.

"Yes," he said. "It's the scent of our natural prey. It triggers our hunting instinct, like the gazelle and the jaguar. But, unlike the animals, we have a higher level of thought. Our instincts are there for a reason, but we don't have to be controlled by them. You just have to expect it, so it doesn't take you by surprise."

"I hear the blood," she said, her voice thick and hungry. "It sings in their veins."

Her gaze remained glued to the couple until they disappeared around the corner, gone from sight but not scent. She continued to stare after them as she asked, "How do you block it out?"

"I don't," he said simply. "But it gets easier to ignore with time."

"How much time?" she asked, turning her face back to him. "I really want you to say it won't bother me for long. A week, for instance," she said with a slightly forced chuckle.

"It's different for everyone," he said with a hint of a smile. "This is your first exposure. Now you know what to expect. Next time, you'll be ready."

The scent of humans faded out with the distance, and Emily seemed to be deflating back to normal.

"I think that's enough for tonight. I don't feel very stable," she said.

Emily looked at him, and he could clearly see her wolf reflected in her eyes now.

William tried to subtly use his dominance to push her toward calm. It took a lot more effort than he expected. He frowned slightly at her in silent surprise and pushed harder. He was trying to be gentle enough not to alert her of what he was doing, but he found it took a lot of energy to influence her.

He hadn't considered the possibility of her wolf being so dominant, though he should have, he supposed. Dominance was part of personality, and Emily had a very strong personality.

He smiled to himself in pride.

His.

"You can't think of humans like you used to," he said bracingly. "That part of you died at the Coven.

You have new instincts now. You just need to learn to control them so they don't control you. The temptation is always there. Your resolve must be stronger," he said.

She nodded slightly, but her face looked distant, as if she was still deep in thought.

"I'm sorry if I seemed," she paused and searched for the right word, "judgmental earlier. I guess you really can't understand until you're there."

He refused to dwell on their earlier conversation.

He reached over and pulled her into the warm comfort of his arms for a reassuring squeeze. He held her for just a moment. Standing there, bathed in moonlight, he breathed her in.

She was such a miracle to him.

"Blood has always been my weakness," he admitted, guiding her back to the car to start the trip home while they could still call the experiment a success. "I've always pretty much stayed in harmony with the wolf in me. But the blood . . ." He shrugged. "It still triggers my vampire nature. Sometimes my instincts have more control than my head."

They drove in silence for a while, both lost in their own thoughts.

William was thinking about Emily's wolf. He hadn't expected it to be so dominant. Dominant enough he'd had trouble getting it to obey. He'd never encountered another wolf with such a powerful will.

His eyes traced the line of her face.

What a surprise his Emily was turning out to be.

lright," William said encouragingly a few days later.

He and Emily were in the woods surrounding the house. It was a beautiful evening, much warmer than it had been, though there was still a small bite to the air.

The pair didn't even notice.

They were working together in a small clearing, surrounded completely by the dense forest. The beautiful mixture of purple and gray across the sky signaled dusk, and long shadows were starting to form from the trees.

"Focus all your energy on reaching into the pit of your stomach, and make yourself stretch," William instructed.

"OK," Emily agreed enthusiastically.

She stood with her feet apart and knees bent like a miniature sumo wrestler.

"I can do this," she said, more to herself than him.

Her weight shifted back and forth in nervous excitement. Her face crinkled in concentration. She tried to focus on the way the wolf had felt at the Coven during her one and only shift. It was turning out to be a lot harder than she expected since William made it look so easy. Simply explode outward from within, and ta da!

Wolf.

She didn't allow herself to consider that William was born with a wolf half and had nearly four centuries of experience.

Nope.

None of it mattered as far as she was concerned. If he could do it, so could she.

She concentrated on stretching herself outward, on feeling her arms and legs stretch forward and . . .

For a second, she almost had it.

Almost.

Fur bloomed across her legs and face, only to vanish when she got excited about it.

"Oh!" she screamed in frustration as the fur faded back to skin.

William laughed aloud, unable to stop himself as her face turned red in anger.

"Would it help if I give your wolf a little 'push'?" he asked, serious, though still chuckling.

"It would help if you shut up," she grumbled, low enough it was plain she didn't intend for him to hear.

She'd neglected to consider the acuity of his hearing.

That just made him laugh harder.

"It isn't funny," she insisted angrily.

"All right, all right." William raised his hands in surrender and tried to subdue his chuckle, though he couldn't help the laughter in his eyes.

"You're supposed to be helping me, not making fun of me," she pointed out tartly.

"Yeah, William," came Paoli's voice through the trees an instant before he walked into view. "What kind of teacher are you?"

"I learned from the best," William returned, walking across the clearing to meet him halfway.

"That you did," Paoli agreed with his usual lack of humility.

The pair walked back to where William had been, facing Emily.

"Show me how it's going," Paoli said.

William nodded, took a deep breath, and looked at Emily. He gestured to her with a wave of his hand.

"All right," he said to Paoli. "Ready?" he asked Emily.

Emily nodded and resumed her ridiculous stance in preparation for another attempt.

"OK," Paoli interjected suddenly. "Watch this."

With that said, he produced a small kitchen knife and stabbed William right in the shoulder, burying the blade to the hilt.

William howled in both pain and surprise. His wide eyes dropped in disbelief to the protruding knife handle.

"What the hell are you doing?" he roared.

"Oh, stop whining, you big girl. Look." Paoli pointed across the space separating them from Emily.

Right before their eyes, she shifted in the span of no more than three heartbeats.

It was amazing to watch her stretch effortlessly. It seemed like a ripple of liquid fur poured across her body, and before it rolled to her feet, she was in wolf form.

She was so majestic.

William stood, mesmerized by the wild beauty of his mate. She was enormous and perfect in her luscious sable fur.

And angry, he noted almost too late.

Very angry.

Emily crouched low on her haunches, her hackles up, ready to pounce. Her mouth was pulled back in a silent snarl, and her fangs were bared. They had to be nearly eight inches long, razor sharp, and deadly. Her furious eyes were trained on Paoli, unblinking, and full of the promise of death.

The wound to his shoulder was forgotten.

William stepped forward, putting distance between himself and Paoli, hoping to calm her. He spoke gently, beseeching her to find her center, remember the wolf was all instinct, but *she* was the one in control.

His words didn't even seem to register. Her eyes never left Paoli. Not even to blink.

William pulled his wolf to the forefront. He'd intended just to use the heightened senses, but he immediately let the wolf form change his body. As soon as he'd felt her through the wolf's senses, he realized how much trouble they were in. Her dominant energy was like electricity, and she was far beyond reachable. She was poised for the attack, and there was no stopping it.

William needed their sizes more evenly matched if he was going to keep Paoli from harm.

William stood in his wolf form between Emily and Paoli and decided Paoli must have been insane to force a shift this way. It was stupid and dangerous, and oh so Paoli. And now—thanks to Paoli's brilliant and half-contrived plan—instead of a nervous new wolf to control, they had a raging, angry one instead.

The energy coming from her was very close to his own in power and said she intended to tear Paoli limb from limb.

Emily gave no warning before she attacked. She was just suddenly moving toward them at full speed.

Lucky for them, she hadn't practiced enough yet to use vampire speed in wolf form. If she'd had the ability, William wasn't sure he could have stopped her.

It was a very concerning realization.

William ran forward, teeth bared, to meet her short of her target and block the path. They collided against one another with bone-jarring force.

Emily continued to snarl and push against his massive form in her struggle to reach her prey.

William moved with her, step for step, and made sure to keep Paoli blocked as he growled in warning, trying to back her down.

He was determined to reach Emily within the wolf.

So many strong and unfamiliar instincts would be hard to control—and thanks to Paoli, rage was the driving one. It swallowed her and blotted out her rational side.

She eventually started to hesitate, as though unsure what to do.

William thought—with relief—she was fighting through the haze enough to get back in control.

"Not yet," Paoli declared from behind.

The sound of his footsteps moving with all the speed a vampire could muster heralded his approach. A second later, he jumped right onto William's back.

William was positive Paoli had lost his mind.

Paoli buried his hands in thick fur and bounced, screaming, "Yahoo!" like a crazed rodeo cowboy.

Emily snarled loudly in outrage and leaped forward. She attempted to swipe Paoli off with one massive swinging paw after another. Her claws raked through William's fur without making contact with his skin as she fought to free him from what she considered an attacker.

"Are you trying to get me killed here, or what?" Paoli cried, dancing around on William's back to avoid the claws. "Run, man. Run!"

It was then William finally realized what Paoli was doing. He was trying to give her more time in animal form to get comfortable with it. Familiar with it. Only with familiarity would she ever learn control, but damn!

This was a serious trial by fire.

William spun on his back leg and bolted through the forest with Emily quickly advancing on them. Fortunately for Paoli, he was more familiar with the area. William used this to his advantage since Emily was a touch faster than he was.

Her body was sleek and built for speed, while his was burly and built to fight and defend.

He weaved first one way, then another, bobbing in and out of the low brush and trees, ignoring Paoli's screaming complaints when he was repeatedly slapped with branches. The brush was helpful. It slowed Emily down.

A little.

Very little.

"Is this seriously top speed?" Paoli screamed nervously as Emily continued to close the gap between them.

William snarled for him to shut up and spun sideways. His feet kicked up dirt as he struggled to hold his footing in one of the soft spots of earth the recent rains had left behind. He changed directions and plowed past Emily with only a few feet separating them.

Her growl was loud and frustrated. She tried to change course, but her movements were slightly clumsy from the newness of her wolf form, and she slipped, which caused her to fall further behind.

"That's better," Paoli yelled approvingly when William was able to put some distance between them. It was followed immediately by a panicked, "Holy crap!"

The loud sound of beating wings signaled she'd managed to take flight.

There was no way he could outrun a giant, flying vampire wolf.

So—to Paoli's horror—William stopped and rolled over, knocked Paoli to the ground, and laid right on top of him like a hen with an egg.

Paoli squirmed beneath him as Emily hovered over them like the world's most terrifying humming-bird. She growled furiously, the same horrible sound she'd made at the Coven.

It made William's head feel like it was about to split open, but he clenched his jaws and endured it silently. When it ended, he slowly stood and met her eyes. He pushed at her with every bit of dominant energy he had, forcing her to be calm.

Her own energy fought him, and for a second, he felt the rage—*her* rage—as though it were his own.

Then it was gone, and Emily slowly came back to the ground. Her eyes, however, were not averted, as was the norm for a wolf forced to submission.

Her calm told him he was the more dominant of the two, but her eyes said not by much.

After a few minutes of lying flat to calm and catch her breath, Emily's wolf melted away, leaving Emily lying on the forest floor, panting and exhausted.

William took human form and rushed to her side. He shook her gently.

"Guys," Paoli said a moment later, then threw the pile of extra clothes toward them and nodded at Emily before pointedly turning his back. "If you don't mind."

William picked up the clothes and handed them to Emily, wincing as the movement tightened the muscle around the blade that was still stuck in his shoulder. He groaned in dread and took a deep breath, then gripped the handle and removed it with a quick tug.

At least it wasn't a serrated edge, because those hurt like sin to pull out.

"Are you insane?" William demanded of Paoli, throwing the unlikely weapon into the ground as he spun on him.

"Is she dressed?" Paoli asked calmly and waited for William to confirm it before he turned to face them, a giant smile on his face.

"Quit complaining," Paoli said in exasperation to William's scowl. Then, in a slightly accusatory tone, he said, "You *laid* on me! Damned near squashed me flat, so I think we're even. Besides," he pointed to the small wound in William's shoulder, "the wound is healing right now. In two minutes, it'll be gone completely, but think of what we learned."

"What did we learn?" Emily said contemptuously, sitting on the ground, unable to gather enough energy to make it to her feet. "Other than you have issues we aren't licensed to manage?"

Paoli rolled his eyes.

"We learned you can shift very rapidly if you think there's a need," he pointed out.

"Great. So she can only help if I'm losing a battle?" William asked sardonically.

"Of course not," Paoli said, waving a dismissive hand. "Don't be ridiculous. Her problem is just lack of experience. She's not comfortable in her other shape yet."

"That's true," Emily said slowly.

"Plus," Paoli went on. "This time you got to fly. You'll have to take me for a ride one of these days."

He added the last distractedly, as though he were already imagining flying around on the back of giant winged wolf.

"That could be very helpful if we ever need to escape a battle," William thought aloud, considering the current situation with the Coven.

Paoli clapped him on the back and said, "Glad to help. You kids spend some time playing animals. See if you can teach her to shift her clothes so she's not always naked. I'm going to open the bookstore tonight."

CHAPTER 27

Over the next few weeks, Emily and William spent days at a time in animal form while she became comfortable with her wolf. She spent much of her time flying just over his head as he loped lazily through the trees, going nowhere in particular.

It was amazing to watch her become more comfortable in her giant shape. On several occasions, they included Paoli in her training, having him hide in various places in the woods for her to track.

William took Paoli's advice, and they spent most of one hilarious afternoon on shifting natural fibers, so she could be dressed when she regained human form. It was hysterical to see a wolf in a blouse and jeans. She did eventually start to get the hang of it, though she panicked when she shifted her jeans over her face and had her head stuck in the pant leg.

William's levity with the situation was *not* appreciated.

Some days they went back into town for brief trips to give Emily more exposure to humans. She was growing more confident in her control.

Her life had changed dramatically in a short period of time, but Emily was determined to see the upside of things and be the best damned immortal she could be.

All the while, Paoli kept getting a vague sense of unease, which made them feel the need to train even more diligently. William wondered if it was because no new execution list was forthcoming. There had never been a lack of executions before, so either all immortals had suddenly become rule abiding, or something was wrong. Given the conditions they left the Coven under, it wasn't difficult to figure out which was the case.

Still, William enjoyed the break from being the deliverer of death—especially now—since he wasn't sure how Emily would take him going out night after night to risk his life. Not only was she his, but he was now *hers*, as well.

Besides, for the first time in a long time, William had no desire to risk his life. Now he had something to live for.

"Do you smell that?" Emily asked one day, pausing in the middle of a grappling session so quickly he nearly plowed her over.

He regained his balance with less than his usual grace to avoid laying her flat. His warning system kicked in full force. He smelled the area, but came up with nothing.

"I'm not sure what you're smelling," he said cautiously.

Emily closed her eyes, lifted her face to the air, and took a slow, deep breath.

"I smell something that . . . doesn't belong here," she said hesitantly, then opened her eyes to look at him. "It's familiar somehow, but I can't place it. I can't believe you don't smell it."

She inhaled deeply through her nose again and shook her head in bewilderment.

"It smells so strong," she said.

Alarms went off in William's head and he pulled her close to his side while he scanned the trees for any sign of movement, since he apparently couldn't rely on his nose.

"Can you tell which way it's coming from?" he asked, his eyes still on the trees and an arm in front of her protectively.

"It's coming from over here," a new voice said from behind them.

William spun and found Sekhmet standing just inside the line of trees. He noted that—for some reason—he still couldn't smell him, even though he stood only a hundred yards away.

It was unnerving.

His nose had never let him down before, and he should be able to smell him very clearly from such a close distance. He didn't trust his eyes nearly as much as he did his nose, which kept him uneasy.

"Sekhmet?" William said, his tone wary.

Could it be a trap of Lycaon's? He'd never heard of someone taking the shape of another person, but there were plenty of things he wasn't familiar with.

"That's where I know the smell from," Emily announced proudly, peering over William's shoulder, clearly oblivious to his discomfort.

"It's Sekhmet?" William asked her. "You're sure? This is very important. Are you sure?"

She gave him a puzzled look. With her eyebrows raised, she gave the air another small sniff to double-check her findings.

"It's him," she confirmed.

"I'd offer you a secret handshake or password if we had one," Sekhmet said lightly as he continued toward them with deliberate slowness, his arms held out to either side of him in a classic pose of surrender.

"But since we don't, you'll have to take my word for it. I'm me. Scout's honor. I know you can't smell me, but there's a reason for it," Sekhmet said.

If Emily was sure, William decided to trust her judgement. He dismissed the issue and headed forward for a manly hug and slap on the back from the older vampire.

Sekhmet greeted Emily with a smile and a brief hug that made William feel a little possessive of his mate, though he said nothing about it.

Only after the greetings were exchanged did he notice the worry in Sekhmet's eyes, which told him he had news from the Coven, and it wasn't good.

"I take it this isn't strictly a social call?" William queried in response to Sekhmet's tension.

"I'm afraid not. Much has happened, and we need to talk. Is Paoli at the house?" he asked, his tone heavy and solemn. Resigned.

William gave him a look of concern.

"Yes," he confirmed.

William indicated the direction with his arm, and they headed back through the trees, up the small path lined by old red bricks, and through the sliding glass doors at the back of the house.

They found Paoli in the study, organizing a new shipment of books for his new-age bookstore. Paoli glanced up when William entered, but when he saw Sekhmet behind him, he gave a heavy, resolved sigh and got to his feet.

"What's happened?" Paoli asked without so much as a greeting.

Sekhmet smiled. He looked around the room and spotted a black leather couch along one wall. He strode over and sat down, and with a wave of his hand asked everyone else to be seated, as well.

Paoli sat in his desk chair, and Emily sat on the couch opposite Sekhmet. William sat on the arm beside her.

"This information stays in this room," Sekhmet began.

He waited for everyone's solemn nod before he continued.

"The Coven is no longer intact. When word of what happened in Lycaon's chambers reached the committee, Lycaon was so enraged, he attacked Lilith," Sekhmet said.

"My goodness," Emily gasped. "Is she dead?"

Sekhmet shook his head. "Not exactly. Her physical body was destroyed, but she carries a curse from Gabriel himself. Eventually, she'll either find or grow a new body, but it may be centuries. There was virtually nothing left of her body after the attack."

Emily frowned. "You mean the archangel Gabriel, from the Bible?"

"Yes," Sekhmet confirmed.

"Wow," Emily whispered, leaning back against the couch in awe.

She had so much to learn.

"Where is Lycaon now?" William asked.

"He has disappeared," Sekhmet said grimly.

"Of course he has," Paoli said sardonically. "He's a wily old wolf. Keeping him backed into a corner would be nearly impossible. His immortality isn't as defined as Lilith's."

Paoli shook his head slowly, as if thinking about the situation.

"He hasn't survived almost two thousand years by being easy to catch," he said.

Silence stretched out while everyone considered the significance of this information.

Their government was no longer standing. As with any culture, with no clearly defined government in place, the result would be chaos.

Wolf pack alphas would have no one to answer to, which would allow them absolute power. Wolves with absolute power tended to slowly lose control of the instincts of the wolf and would become more and more animalistic. Eventually the humans would get involved when the attacks became more obvious, which would cause the vampires to get involved. The old war would start again, and none of them would be safe.

"Can the committee take power?" William asked.

Sekhmet shook his head doubtfully.

"They may be able to hold power for a little while, but there's too much going on in the background. They don't invoke the fear it takes to actually rule."

"So, we can expect the return of anarchy, and kill or be killed. If the humans get involved—" Paoli shook his head slowly, as though he couldn't even stomach the thought. "They're not the easy prey they were last time around. It may not end the way Lycaon expects."

Emily listened carefully to their words but found herself using her heightened wolf nose to detect the worry of the men in the room. It was a strange smell, and it put her on edge. She didn't grasp the full significance of the destruction of the Coven, but she knew when governments collapsed, it was never good.

William nodded agreement with Paoli's concern.

"All it would take is one video of an attack to hit the internet, and we'll all be hunted. The vampire hysteria in Europe did significant damage, but it would be nothing compared to what we'd see now," he said.

"I have someone in the human world," Paoli said. "Is it bad enough for her to need protection?"

Sekhmet seemed to consider the question for a moment, then shrugged slightly in a gesture of uncertainty.

"It may not be that bad yet, but it's not far away. Lycaon is organized and determined to have complete power. In his human life, he led many armies," he said.

Paoli let out a long breath slowly.

"He may be able to hold complete power with werewolves, but the vampires will create their own faction. They'd never blindly follow a wolf," he said.

Sekhmet sat silent for a moment, then looked at William and Emily with deep intensity.

"No," he agreed. "And many of the wolves won't follow him, either. Not after this dramatic break from the Coven. Which is why he's after the link."

William swore vehemently.

At Emily's questioning gaze, he gave her a tight smile.

"Us," he explained. "He's after us."

It took a moment for that information to sink in. Her heart dropped.

"An ancient king who led many armies?" she questioned in a constricted voice.

She gave an almost hysterical chuckle.

"Of course he's after us," she said sarcastically.

Why not?

"But why us?" she asked. "I mean, I know it has something to do with William's blood, but how would that help him?"

"Because." It was Paoli who answered. "You two are the only ones who can represent both species and bring them together as a single group, thus allowing them to fall under a single ruler."

"Oh," she whispered, finally understanding.

William reached out and put a hand on her arm to comfort her. His touch was warm and reassuring, and she allowed his closeness to give her some strength.

"He'll never take us without a fight," William vowed.

"Which is why I'm here," Sekhmet said. "I've been sent by the committee to help you."

William looked at him in surprise.

"You intend to join us?" he asked.

"Many intend to join you, William. Empusa will be here in a day, and we need to begin rallying forces and establishing allies. I know you don't want to be involved in this, but you already are. Lycaon's after you and Emily. He's bringing this war right to you," Sekhmet said.

Emily watched William tense. His jaw clenched, and his eyes darkened to amber. She could actually feel the wolf inside him, which made her own wolf stir inside her in response.

"Empusa's not going to make it in time, though," Sekhmet said reluctantly. "Lycaon has forces headed here as we speak. And Amber is leading them."

CHAPTER 28

A cool numbness spread over Emily at his words. She braced herself for the pain of her sister's hatred, but it never came. After so many years of dealing with the pain, it was almost alarming that it was simply gone.

She looked around the room, taking in William's carefully controlled expression, and to Paoli, who had a very animated face beneath his long, dark-blond hair that was almost always tied at the back of his neck, and even to Sekhmet.

It dawned on her at last. As dark and just strange as her life may have become, this was where she belonged. She was loved and protected and accepted, just as she was. Flawed and weak though she may be at times, these men would stand with her eternally. It was a humbling certainty.

Amber had long ago walked away from her, despising her ability to move on after their mother's death, she thought. Over the years, it had slowly become something stronger and more destructive. Hate. It wasn't until the day in Lycaon's chamber that she realized the truth at last. Amber didn't just dislike her. She truly hated her.

Emily had always held on to some small sliver of hope that Amber would one day come back to her and they could pick up like nothing had ever happened. But the day she sat with a smug look on her face as their long-lost father nearly twisted her arms off, Emily had been forced to face reality. Without even realizing it, she'd let Amber go. Miraculously, she felt empowered by it, like she'd carried a weight most of her adult life that she'd finally released.

"When will they arrive?" Paoli asked, his voice calm and level.

"In a matter of hours." There was no fear in Sekhmet's tone at all. His voice was flat and matter of fact.

Emily felt a knot of panic in her belly, but no one else in the room seemed overly concerned. They might as well have been discussing last night's sports scores instead of a legion of werewolves coming their way.

She looked at William, fear shining in her eyes.

He noticed her upset and gave a gentle smile. He lay one large hand at the nape of her neck.

"Don't worry," he said conspiratorially. "We grew up during raids and wars. This is nothing."

With his hand still on her nape, he spoke to Sekhmet.

"Do you know how many there are?" he asked.

"I estimate about twenty or so. Mostly new wolves, but there are a few older ones in the group, as well. Amber tried to get Lycaon to recruit the pack she was in initially, but he had them destroyed."

Sekhmet gave a pained look to the room's other occupants.

"I've been a spy for the committee for a long time. We've been watching the situation between Lilith and Lycaon with growing suspicion. That's how I knew what happened in Lycaon's chambers. Anyway, they gave Empusa and I a little magic to hide our scent, so I was able to get quite close on my way here," he explained.

William gave him a look of surprise, then nodded absently.

"Which is why I couldn't smell you," he concluded.

Sekhmet nodded.

"I'm not sure why Emily could, unless it's connected with her link to Lycaon," he said.

"Wait," Emily cut in. "He killed the entire pack?"

She couldn't believe someone could just go through and destroy so many wolves. Especially Lycaon, who was basically the father to all the wolves since the original curse started with him.

His punishment.

"You're still thinking in human terms," Sekhmet admonished gently, which earned him a low growl from William. "Those were unsanctioned wolves," he explained after a nervous look in William's direction. "They had no right to exist at all, and they were weak and out of control. So, they were destroyed. It wasn't a properly sanctioned elimination, but I do have to agree it was necessary."

"Our world is not as gentle as the human one, Emily. It has to be this way for the good of everyone, including humans. Imagine if that pack had torn through a town, out of control," Paoli said. "We're not as lenient as human courts. If someone does something mild, there are punishments in place to correct the situation. Otherwise, they're destroyed."

Emily glanced at William, thinking about the day Lilith ordered him bled. Yes, she had to admit. She was aware their punishments were a bit extreme.

"And," Paoli continued, "if someone is unable to blend with the human world for any reason, they're destroyed to protect us all. In Europe, it only took one vampire to spark the hysteria that nearly wiped us out over there."

"Do you know when Empusa will arrive?" William redirected the conversation.

"Tomorrow evening at the earliest," Sekhmet answered.

"Tonight, it's the four of us against all of them," Paoli said. "Luckily, William stays well stocked on weapons."

"The best weapon we have is the fact they don't want those two killed." Sekhmet gave Paoli a rueful smile and jerked his head toward William and Emily. "You and I, however, are another story."

"What's new?" Paoli asked dryly. "Let's hope they attack during the night. If they're all wolves, they could just as easily wait until morning. Then you and I would be worthless to help in the fight."

"If something happens during the day, we can wake you up," Emily offered.

She regretted her words as soon as they left her mouth. What was she thinking? They couldn't be in the sun without being killed.

Sekhmet gave her a smile that looked suspiciously patronizing.

"My dear Emily, you can't wake us during the day. We're not asleep. We're dead," he said.

A look of horror crossed her face before she was able to hide it.

She knew vampires couldn't be out during the day because the sun would kill them. She'd never considered they were actually *dead* during that time. Which meant while she was at the Coven, she was in a building with tons of dead people.

Her eyes moved to Paoli. During the day, he was dead? Just dead? She didn't want to think about it, but once the words were out there, she couldn't think of anything else.

It was horrifying.

Paoli laughed at her.

"You really need to work on your poker face," he said.

"I'm sorry. I just didn't realize you were . . ." she shrugged uncomfortably.

She didn't want to offend him.

"Dead?" he finished for her, running a finger across his throat and making a strangled sound.

Then he flicked his fingers to wave off her concern.

"I'm not dead right now, and I'd like to keep it that way. We need a plan," he said.

"I think we need to move Emily for tonight, just in case this doesn't go as smoothly as we expect," William said.

"I still have my gun with silver bullets," Emily objected immediately, pushing him away so he could see she was serious.

She turned to see his face and noted the resolve in the hard line of his jaw. She frowned at him. It was a little late to hide the truth from her now that she'd learned Paoli and Sekhmet would be dead in a couple of hours. What was the point in trying to shield her beyond that?

"I think William may be right," Sekhmet said. "You do need to learn to fight, especially now. You'll need to be something of a warrior to see this mess through. But battle should be learned a little slower than this."

After a lot more debate, Emily grudgingly agreed her presence would be a distraction and consented to be placed elsewhere for their safety. She wasn't thrilled about it, but if she continued to argue and one of them died, she'd always wonder if her presence had led to it. She didn't want to live with that kind of uncertainty.

She was scared for them.

They were only three men, ready to stand against a group of twenty, and if daylight hit before the attack came, only William would be alive to fight. His comrades, apparently, would be dead until nightfall.

CHAPTER 29

With Emily safely settled away from the house, the men prepared for battle, packed the bloodmobile, and made plans. Then they each took up a post to wait. Dawn was only a couple of hours away. If the attack came tonight, it needed to come before then. As Paoli said, it was possible they planned to wait until tomorrow during the day. If so, they'd be long gone because William wasn't waiting around after dawn. He was good in battle, but not take-on-twenty-werewolves-single-handed good.

While it hurt Paoli to leave his little bookstore again, he'd reopen in a new location when things got a little more back to normal.

For William, it was much more dangerous.

His wolf was a natural hunter. Even though he made sure to run at least once during the week of the full moon to chase rabbits and deer, it wasn't nearly as satisfying as tearing apart a humanoid creature. He had a long history of losing control and going on what Paoli referred to as "benders," though he hadn't slipped in a long time now.

He hoped tonight wouldn't change that.

With luck, his new link to Emily would give him the control he'd always lacked. Between his wolf's need to hunt and his vampire's requirement for human blood, control was a very delicate balance he and Paoli had learned through years of trial and error.

They were only about half an hour from dawn's arrival when a sound caught William's attention. It took only a few seconds before other sounds started to come to him, and he motioned to the others and pointed out the general direction.

Paoli indicated a spot outside where they could go to meet their attackers and shrugged in question.

William considered the idea and agreed it would allow for better movement, so he gave a curt nod and led the way outside.

They stood in the little clearing behind the house that acted as the backyard and watched eyes appear along the tree line. Wolf eyes, one and all, until they nearly lined the trees. There were far more wolves than the twenty they were expecting. It appeared Lycaon had been busy recruiting long before the attack at the Coven.

Paoli sighed, a resigned sound. He adjusted the bag full of weapons on his shoulder and spoke without taking his eyes off their foes.

"Well, this isn't good," he said conversationally. "Sekhmet, how many arrows do you have in your bag?"

Sekhmet snorted.

"Not nearly enough. Maybe fifteen at most. How about you?" he said.

Paoli shook his head slowly, still watching the trees.

"I'm with you. Not nearly enough," he said.

"Great," William said in a calm monotone.

"Got any ideas?" Paoli asked.

"Why are they all in wolf form," William wondered aloud as he got the first twinge of unease.

It seemed to grow stronger until it nearly robbed him of breath. He stood perfectly still, wondering at the strangeness of a feeling he couldn't quite name.

Just when the first wolf started forward, he realized it wasn't his emotion he was feeling.

It was Emily's.

"This is a diversion," he said with certainty. "We need to get to Emily."

Paoli loaded his crossbow with a silver-tipped arrow and let it fly. There was a thud, followed by a yelp that said he'd hit his target.

"We're running out of time to escape, and fast," Paoli announced as the ring of wolves moved to box them in.

Sekhmet glanced around a bit ruefully, as if it pained him to leave a battle unfought.

"They can have this place," he announced. "Let's go while we can."

While it went against William's nature to run away as well, getting to Emily was far more important.

His nose told him neither Lycaon nor Amber was among the wolves in the clearing, and that—coupled with Emily's emotions—gave him a sinking feeling he knew where they were.

He tamped down his own growing fear and backed into the house, decapitating one wolf who was apparently braver than the others and attempted to follow him through the door, muzzle first.

The head landed just inside the house with a thump, and he wiped his blade clean against the fur on the side of the body. Then he turned and tore through the house toward the bus they'd pulled into the driveway earlier.

He started the engine and threw his phone over his shoulder to Paoli as he and Sekhmet closed the door.

"Call Emily," William said, pulling the bus into gear with two wolves slamming against the door and another one on the hood.

Long teeth snapped furiously toward the windshield, and a large circular crack appeared and nearly obscured his view before he turned onto the street sharply enough to send the wolf flying.

He ran over two more without ever slowing down when they darted into his path.

He had to get to Emily.

Now.

He hoped he wasn't already too late even as he cursed his own foolish decision to leave her unprotected. If they hurt her, he would hunt Lycaon to the end of the earth.

"No answer," Paoli informed him.

He sat on one of the bench seats—the kind that lifted for storage and would be a perfect mobile resting place for he and Sekhmet—and braced himself against the wood of the shelves bolted into the bus for supplies.

William swallowed the bitter taste in his mouth. He hadn't really expected anything else, but he'd hoped. He tried to stop the panic creeping up in his gut by reminding himself they didn't want her dead.

CHAPTER 30

William tore through the hotel door like a possessed thing and found exactly what he feared.

Nothing.

For a long moment, icy rage seemed to blot out his vision, and his wolf very nearly took control. The wolf wanted to rend and howl and tear the entire hotel to the ground.

He fought back the beast, determined to remain in control.

He needed to think, to come up with a plan. His wolf wasn't helping. If ever he needed a clear head, this was the time.

His teeth snapped together in frustrated fury and he tried to calm himself. With his eyes closed, he took a deep breath and let it out slowly to center his thoughts. Once he had some semblance of control, he began to smell the room, trying to catch the scent—some clue—of what had happened.

It was difficult since it was a hotel and there were so many different smells to sift through. Amber and Emily's scents were easy to find, but he couldn't locate Lycaon's. Maybe he hadn't come here at all. Or maybe he'd used the same magic to mask his scent the Coven used on Sekhmet.

He caught the distinct scent of silver and found himself fighting the rage in his wolf again. They'd used silver on his mate.

There was a blood trail, but it wasn't her blood. He used that knowledge to force his wolf back. She'd fought them and done serious damage to at least one wolf. There was no sign or smell of Emily's blood, which meant she hadn't been shot or stabbed. He didn't know what the silver would have been, but without blood, it couldn't have caused too serious an injury. It would have caused pain, yes. But no serious injury.

He couldn't stand to think of Emily being hurt by silver.

No, he chided himself and pushed the thought away.

He couldn't think about it, not if he hoped to have a clear enough head to find her.

Several other wolves' scents were there, though none he could identify.

He opened the door and stepped out onto the narrow walkway in front of the hotel room.

Emily's scent grew very faint, while Amber and the other wolves remained strong. It took a moment of consideration to determine they must have carried her through there.

He followed the trail until it ended in the parking lot, which meant they had a vehicle waiting. Small drops of blood littered the ground from the walkway all the way to where they must have parked. It was from a different source than the blood in the hotel room.

None of it was Emily's blood.

A swell of pride rose up, and a slight smile tugged one corner of his mouth. His mate hadn't gone easily or quietly. Which didn't help him find her, but it was good to know she was still in fighting shape.

His phone rang, and he snatched it out of his pocket and saw a number he didn't recognize. He ignored it and went back to staring at the empty parking space, trying to think of a way he could track the vehicle they were driving.

Maybe security cameras caught them on video and he could at least see which direction they went. His phone rang again, and he looked at the screen with annoyance. It was the same number. He hit answer and didn't say anything.

"William?" Empusa's voice sounded loud and worried.

"Where are you?" William jumped right into conversation without pleasantries.

He wasn't feeling particularly pleasant, and he would welcome a little help.

"Sekhmet messaged me and told me what's happened. I'm coming as fast as I can. Maybe another hour before I reach you. Have you located Emily yet?" Empusa wanted to know.

William shook his head even though the other man couldn't see him.

"I lost the trail in the parking lot," he growled.

There was a moment of silence, then Empusa swore.

"This is why I told Paoli you needed time with wolves when you were a fledgling," he said with heat. "You don't know nearly enough about the wolf side of who you are."

There was a long, irritated sigh.

"You have a mate bond with her. All you need to do is use it to track her," Empusa said in a much calmer voice.

William had never been one to reveal a weakness. He'd learned if the other immortals thought he was all-powerful, it helped to feed his reputation as an unstoppable killer and therefore keep their fear of him high. As much as he hated being seen as the boogeyman, it was a necessary part of who and what he was. But in this case, none of that mattered. He needed to get to Emily, and if Empusa could help him, he could stomach eating a little crow.

"I don't know what you mean," he said irritably.

To his credit, Empusa didn't make a sound of annoyance or impatience.

"What kind of connection does your bond give you? I've heard of some couples with true telepathy because of a mating bond, but they're rare. It would be nice if you guys had that, though. Then she could just tell you, 'Why yes, we're at 123 Help Me Lane,' and make this much easier."

William smiled grudgingly.

"I don't know about the mating bond or the wolf side of things, but I can feel her emotions at times," he said.

He didn't bother to mention he thought that was more connected to his vampire half.

"And we can share strength and emotion," he added.

"OK, good," Empusa said. "It's not exactly what I hoped for, but we can work with that. Clear your mind. Find the last feelings you got from her, and really focus on them. Then try to focus *through* them and feel for the woman beyond."

William took a minute to calm his mind and tried to do as Empusa instructed.

He remembered standing in the yard behind the house and the feeling that had come to him. It was a horrible feeling of panic; a sickening, helpless feeling. Then he focused on where it had come from and reached for her. When he did, the power of rage that swept through him nearly broke his control.

It took a long moment to realize it wasn't his rage he felt.

It was hers.

She wasn't cowering in fear, helpless and afraid.

Not his mate.

She was ready to kill.

A faint taste came to his tongue, and he realized absently it was the taste on hers.

Blood.

Scents came to him, and faint sounds.

With sudden clarity, he realized he could feel her direction.

"I've got a lock on her," William said with conviction.

On the other end of the phone, Empusa sighed in obvious relief.

"We need a plan. Start toward them, but don't run in without knowing the situation. If they get you both, it'll just be me and two vamps left to save you. That's *if* they don't stake them. I don't know about Paoli, but Sekhmet and I spent too many years at the Coven, and our fighting skills are rusty," Empusa said.

William was already headed back to the bus. He kept his mind locked with Emily's and pointed the vehicle in the right direction.

He tried to keep his speed low enough to avoid attracting attention, but in his need to get to Emily, it was a struggle.

"Can you track the GPS on my phone?" William asked.

"No," Empusa said.

There was a long pause.

"But I can always track Sekhmet," he added.

"You allowed him to take your blood?" William asked in surprise.

Empusa chuckled.

"It's not like I became his human familiar, William. We shared blood for a blood bond. That's how I'm tracking you now. Have you and Paoli never exchanged blood?" He asked as though it was a rhetorical question, but the truth was no.

Until Emily, William had never shared blood with anyone.

Most vampires shared blood with any number of humans they claimed as their own, but that was only to mark their familiars—the people they chose as their food source—so other vampires would know they were already owned and under protection. It was almost like marking cattle. It also allowed them to have some control of the human, and the ability to know where they were.

"No," William finally answered Empusa's question. "We've never shared blood."

Empusa made a frustrated sound.

"When I get to you guys, I may stake Paoli myself," he announced without heat. "I know he tries to keep as close to a human life as possible, but some things are just part of what we are and should be embraced."

William didn't comment.

He kept his focus on Emily and closing the gap between them. Now that he had a better understanding of their bond, he found he could reach for her at will and touch her emotions.

There was still rage and plenty of fear, but no pain.

He found that reassuring and allowed it to steady him.

CHAPTER 31

Emily sat in the cage in her wolf form and glared at the wolves around her. All seven of them were in human form, but there was no mistaking their scent. Thanks to William's training, she'd learned to discern many scents.

Werewolf was an easy one.

Interestingly enough, most of them looked at her with wariness and kept a good distance between themselves and her, especially after she'd nearly torn out the throat of the wolf who stuck her in this damned cage in the first place.

It gave her some satisfaction to see the fear in their eyes.

Part of it was fear of her—of her sheer size, since most wolves were about twice the size of an ordinary timber wolf, while she was nearly three times that and winged—a condition unique to her, if Paoli was to be believed—but most of it was their fear of William, she thought.

They knew he'd be hunting them and enraged, and *everyone* was afraid of William, even under the best of circumstances. If he caught them before they got wherever Lycaon arranged to meet up with him, they were all dead.

They knew it.

Which was probably why they'd thrown her into this RV and hadn't stopped driving since.

They talked to each other about how William wouldn't be able to start after them until nightfall. They were nervously confident the diversion would stall him until morning and he'd have to wait until sunset to give chase because of Paoli.

Somehow, Emily knew they were wrong. She wasn't sure *how* she knew, but he was coming for her and gaining on her captives.

She hadn't intended to shift into wolf form, but when she opened the door of her hotel room and a fine silver net was thrown over her, the burn was unbearable and she panicked. Her wolf had taken over without a thought or intent, and Emily found she was grateful for it.

In wolf form, the thick fur provided some protection from the silver. When she was stuffed into a too-small cage with silver-lined bars, it was easier to get comfortable. Plus, the minute someone opened the door, she was going to plow through it with all the force her wolf shape could muster and make her escape.

Once she got airborne, no one stood a chance of stopping her, including Lycaon himself. If she could manage to damage or dismember one or two of his followers in the process, more power to her.

Amber had—for the most part—simply ignored her, which was fine with Emily.

If she managed to get out of this cage, she had every intention of killing anyone who tried to stop her. If Amber thought she was safe, she was sadly mistaken. Many things had changed, and Emily now saw Amber clearly for what she was.

Damaged and dangerous.

While Emily had changed since she met William, Amber was exactly as she'd always been. Emily just hadn't been willing to face it before.

"Damn it!" The wolf who was driving suddenly swore and swerved the RV so quickly it sent Emily sliding into the side of the cage with a thud.

She quickly scrambled away from the bars, trying to catch traction with her claws.

"What was that?" Amber gasped from the passenger seat.

Emily could smell her unease, though she didn't see what caused it.

"A bird," the driver answered.

He turned on the windshield wipers and managed to smear blood across the windshield before it cleared. He glanced anxiously at the cloudy sky.

Emily got to her feet and watched in morbid fascination as another bird flew into the windshield with a loud thump, followed by another and another until they hit and bounced off like hail, almost obliterating the driver's view in a swarm of black, broken, feathery bodies.

Amber's head turned toward Emily.

"Are you doing this?" she demanded, as if the wolf could answer.

Emily lifted her lip and snarled in response.

A low whine caught her attention, but she wasn't sure which of the wolves it came from. They all stared nervously at the windshield, and the acrid stench of fear filled her nose and pleased the wolf.

"Should we call Lycaon?" someone asked.

"And tell him what?" Amber snapped impatiently. "It's raining birds?"

Silence stretched out. The only sound was the constant thump of birds and the pounding of hearts.

"There's someone standing in the road!" the driver cried.

The RV jerked to the side to avoid hitting the person in the middle of the highway. They'd been forced to slow down because of the lack of visibility, but they were still going too fast to bring the vehicle to a stop.

Amber grabbed the wheel and forced the RV back into the lane, keeping the man directly in their path.

"It's him," she said darkly. "It's daytime, so he's alone. Run him down."

She turned and gave Emily a cruel smile.

Emily slammed hard against the bars of the cage, mindless of the damage from the silver.

She had to get out, to help William before they killed him. Why would he be standing in the road?

Without warning, the window nearest to her crashed in and William landed beside her, rolling to his feet with the force of his entry. His growl was silent and deadly.

With a less-than-manly squeak, the driver jerked the RV to the side of the road and brought it to a halt.

By then, William had already decapitated three of the wolves before they even had time to process what was happening and was quickly making his way forward.

Fury emanated from him like a living, breathing thing.

Emily heard the explosive sound of a gunshot, and it caused her sensitive ears to ring painfully. She looked up and saw Amber on her knees, turned around to face the living quarters of the RV interior with a gun in her hand.

A quick glance at William showed the first shot had missed him, but the gun was now trained on his chest and he stood perfectly still, watching her carefully.

He and the rest of the RV were dripping with blood from the slain wolves, and his eyes glowed a dangerous wolf gold.

"Lycaon gave me this gun," Amber said bitingly. "It's loaded with silver bullets. He wants you both alive, but I'd be happy to deliver you loaded with silver and let him figure out what to do from there."

William growled low, his gaze locked with hers.

Amber looked away from his eyes and turned her head just in time to see the man who jerked her door open abruptly and grabbed her. A second shot sounded, and one of the wolves yelped as the stray shot hit.

William started toward the remaining wolves with enough speed to blur her vision, and Emily had to look away from him.

It wasn't his actions, which she not only understood but agreed with. If she wasn't stuck in the cage, she'd love to tear them apart herself. But the speed of his movement was enough to make her nauseous.

Whines and snarls fought with the sound of battle but were cut short one after another. In an almost disturbingly short amount of time, William, Empusa, and Emily were the only living things left.

Without a word, William searched for the keys to Emily's cage. It took a couple of minutes to find them, tucked into the pocket of one of the fallen wolves.

William knelt beside the cage, and for a long moment, uncertainty prickled him.

She'd seen him kill before, yes. But not like this.

She'd never seen him truly enraged, with his wolf in control, and he didn't know if he could bear to see horror in her when she looked at him.

The eyes that finally met his, however, were full of relief and impatience, without even a hint of the fear he'd been so sure would be there.

As soon as the lock fell away, she burst through the open door and into the safety of his bloody arms with enough force that he had to brace himself to keep from being bowled over.

He buried his hands in her thick pelt and breathed her in, letting her clean presence wash away the bloodlust and the need for violence.

They hadn't hurt her. He hadn't been too late.

He closed his eyes and heaved a trembling sigh of relief. If something had happened to her, if he lost her . . . He clenched his jaw and pushed away the thought.

Emily's eyes met his questioningly, and he could feel her confusion.

"I think I'd tear the whole world apart for you," he said around a sudden lump in his throat.

"I hate to break up this touching moment," Empusa interrupted. "But that woman got away from me, and we need to get someplace less conspicuous before the police come to check on an abandoned vehicle on the side of the road. That could really complicate things," he said with a look around the blood-soaked RV.

William gave a quick nod but never loosened his grip on Emily.

Empusa was right.

They needed to get moving and find a way to clean up the mess before Paoli and Sekhmet rose.

While neither of them would complain about the events, he didn't want them to rise surrounded by the scent of blood. Paoli's control was legendary, but he wasn't sure about Sekhmet.

Emily had seen enough of the dark side of their world for one day.

"If you guys want to take the bus, we can find a campground to park long enough to start getting cleaned up," Empusa offered.

William looked around and nodded.

Now that the immediate emergency was past, they needed to come up with a plan. Getting set up in a campground would allow them some time to wait for Paoli and Sekhmet. Then their little group could sit down and decide what the best course of action would be.

CHAPTER 32

Emily sat on one of the bench seats on the bus, feeling strangely satiated.

After they arrived at the small campground, the three wolves had taken to the wooded area that hugged the little clearing and gone hunting.

It was Emily's first hunt as a wolf, and it had been absolutely thrilling. Together, they brought down a buck that seemed huge to her, but she was later informed it was at best medium sized.

She would never have guessed how satisfying it would be to use her new big teeth—*the better to eat you with, my deer*, she thought with a chuckle to herself at her own play on words—to tear apart a carcass, still flanked protectively by the two males.

After the hunt, both William and Empusa showered in the RV that she would *not* go back into for *any* reason and joined her on the bus to wait for their vampire compatriots to rise for the long evening ahead.

Now she sat between William and Paoli, across from Empusa and Sekhmet, and even with the future ahead so unknown, she felt safer and more protected than she ever had before.

"The committee wants to meet with us," Sekhmet said.

It was not a surprising announcement.

William had been theorizing all evening they'd be called back to the Coven's castle in light of recent events. Apparently, Paoli had been expecting it as well, since his only reaction was a slight murmur of acknowledgment.

"It's known you didn't leave last time under," Sekhmet paused and looked somewhat sheepish, "the best of circumstances."

William gave a slight smile at the extreme understatement.

"To which the committee offers sincere apologies," Sekhmet went on.

Paoli snorted at that and fell into a mocking tone.

"'Sorry we tried to break your mate's arms, but hey, we're sorry now,'" he said in his most patronizing tone.

Empusa stiffened.

"The committee has acted as counterbalance for the Coven since the beginning," he said. "It was never an easy partnership. That's why Sekhmet and I both served; to watch for any signs of trouble within the Coven."

At Paoli's pointed look, he gave an exasperated sigh.

"We told them years ago Lycaon was up to some-thing, but we had no proof until he attacked Emily. It's when Lilith was informed of the situation that he attacked her and destroyed her current form," he said defensively.

"We served because we believe a lasting peace is possible. After so long on this earth, it's important to hold on to hope. *Any* hope," Sekhmet said passionate-ly. "Otherwise, we lose ourselves in the nothingness of time and forget that things *do* matter."

"You've made sacrifices you don't even know about," Empusa said, his clear brown eyes holding William's gray ones just for a moment before he had to look away. "You're a wolf, and wolves need packs.

Isolation eats at a wolf and eventually leads to madness. You were denied your right to a pack, partially because of your vampire blood, and because Paoli feared you wouldn't be safe if an entire pack could track you."

"It's also difficult to make a kill if you're tied to the condemned by pack bonds," Paoli said reasonably. "Executions can weigh on a person heavily. Pack bonds would mean he had to feel the loss himself when he carried out his orders."

"Paoli and I made the best we could from a bad situation," William said. "And he was right. By having no relationship to the condemned, it made my job possible. Not easy, but possible."

Empusa lowered his head, showing he meant no disrespect.

Emily watched the display carefully.

She felt the rising tension in William when he felt Paoli was being criticized, and she fought the urge to take his hand, for fear it might make him feel weak. Instead, she sent him feelings of calm.

He breathed deeply, and his muscles relaxed the smallest bit, but he gave no other sign that would have clued the others in to what had happened. It seemed so intimate to be able to share themselves without anyone else knowing.

"Yes," Sekhmet agreed. "But time brings change, and we must all change with it."

"That's something we all know. Time changes all things, and the only way to survive in the world is to flow like water with the changes. Immortals who hold too long to the past don't survive into the future," Paoli said.

Empusa nodded in agreement.

"A war is coming again. Not all of us here are wolves," he said.

Slowly, he met the eyes of everyone one by one.

"But we are all willing to follow you as a united pack. If you are willing to lead us," he told William.

He crossed his arms at the elbows and held his hands out to William, palms up.

William regarded him for a long moment, as if reading his face. Then he gripped the other man's arms fiercely in the same fashion and dragged his face close in a show of staunch solidarity.

"I will lead you as my brothers," William growled.

Then he released one of Empusa's hands and bit into his own arm.

Empusa took the bleeding forearm that was offered. He pressed his mouth to the wound and drank of the powerful blood that was unique to William. Sekhmet and Paoli followed suit, creating blood bonds that would hold them to each other.

Emily watched in silent fascination, wondering at the changes happening this night. Something told her she was witnessing an event that would one day become legend.

Whatever the future held, they were now all in it together.

When the exchanges were done, Paoli broke the ceremonial atmosphere by saying, "Now we go to the committee as a seriously weird pack. Hey," he said, as if an idea just hit him. "Can we be a herd instead?"

"We can be a flock for all I care," Sekhmet said. "As long as we're united."

Emily laughed. She couldn't help it.

"Now that's a title sure to inspire fear wherever we go," she said in mock seriousness.

Amusement danced briefly in Williams eyes before he turned his attention back to their current situation.

"We need to get moving," he said. "How far is the nearest crematorium the Coven has in this area?"

"Hold on," Empusa said.

He pushed a few buttons on his phone, then looked up with a grimace.

"Only one in this state. It's about three hours from here," he said.

"Any chance the committee could be persuaded to send people to pick up this RV, instead of us having to drive it there?" Paoli wanted to know.

"It's worth a try. I'll make a few calls," Empusa said, stepping out of the bus.

Within a half hour, they were all piled back into the bus. Paoli was driving them toward the nearest airstrip that would carry them back to the dreaded castle they had only recently escaped from.

A cleanup crew would take care of the RV, and the only thing they needed to worry about was getting to the airfield where a plane would be waiting for them.

When questioned, Empusa reported the car he had was one of the Coven's own, and it had GPS, so they would send people to reclaim it, as well.

Emily had so many questions to ask, but she held her tongue. Her curiosity could wait until she and William were alone.

She noticed Empusa watching her intently and held his gaze. She wasn't sure if she was supposed to drop her eyes the way she'd seen people do with William, so she didn't.

A faint smile touched his mouth, and he looked away briefly, then slid down on his seat until he was directly across from her.

He kept his gaze on the floor and his shoulders slightly slumped.

"I know it was your sister I fought today," he said. "I hesitated, and she escaped. But something tells me we haven't seen the last of her."

She hadn't expected his words and hadn't been braced for them. She stared at him.

"I'm sorry my relationship with her made you hesitate," she said and found she really meant it. "She hasn't been my sister for a long time. Not really. Please don't ever risk your own safety for her."

Empusa inclined his head slightly in acknowledgment.

Emily noticed William watching her from where he sat. She gave him a reassuring smile, and his mouth quirked just the slightest bit in answer.

CHAPTER 33

After a long night of flying, the five of them landed outside of the castle on the same runway they'd used to escape only a few weeks before.

The irony of that fact was not lost on Emily, and a part of her was expecting to see Lycaon and a whole army waiting for them in a twisted trap.

But all that awaited them were two ornate crates that looked as though they belonged in a museum of ancient artifacts.

Emily gave William a questioning look when she noticed the men loading them into the back of the plane.

With a gentle hand on her arm, William guided her behind him, and Empusa walked behind Emily, successfully blocking her between them as they all disembarked.

"It's daytime," William said in answer to her silent question. "They'll get Paoli and Sekhmet to the castle safely."

She eyed the strange men assessingly, uncertain if they could be trusted with the two vampires while they slept—or were dead for the day, which just gave her the creeps.

No, she decided.

They were asleep, no matter what Sekhmet said.

She had *not* just been in a little airplane with two dead guys.

If there were a trap, it would be a perfect way to rid themselves of two of their "flock," as Sekhmet had dubbed them. All they'd need to do is open the boxes.

William noticed her brooding look and seemed to follow her thoughts.

"They wouldn't dare," he said darkly.

She stepped off the steps of the plane and onto the runway.

"How can you be so sure?" she asked as the three of them walked toward the waiting car.

"Because they haven't been convicted of wrongdoing, so their deaths would be murder and I'd kill them myself," he said with absolute confidence.

"Besides," Empusa interjected as he opened the car door and waited for her to slide into the middle seat before he and William slid in on either side of her.

"The Coven was known for some surreptitious acts, but the Coven has been dissolved. The committee tries to operate as morally as possible."

Emily decided if neither of them were worried, she'd simply have to trust their judgement.

She settled into her seat for the short ride.

William's leg against hers was strong and solid—like the man himself—and she took comfort from the simple contact.

Her nervousness grew as they drew close to the looming ancient castle, and the nearness of both men with her was like a balm to her worried soul.

"Relax," Empusa chided gently when they walked through the massive doors and into the antechamber.

She looked at him in surprise.

Until then, she'd thought she was doing a good job of hiding her fear.

William's nose brushed the top of her head, and he whispered, "Werewolf, remember? We can smell fear."

"It's not fear," she returned hotly, though much of her heat was lost at a whisper. "It's . . . trepidation."

That sounded much better than fear, she decided.

Less cowardly.

William noticed the stubborn set of her chin and smiled in spite of himself.

He gave her a look that clearly said, "I surrender," and went back to searching the unusually empty antechamber.

"Besides, you're upset enough to feed the energy through our pack ties," Empusa said in the same low tone. "And I'm feeling it, too."

Emily had started to follow them further into the room but stumbled at his words.

"What do you mean?" she demanded.

She hadn't considered the side effects of the blood exchanges. Could he feel her emotions the same way William could?

Could *all* of them?

"I don't think this is the time or place for that conversation," Empusa said and continued forward.

"Where is everyone?" William asked of the silent, almost mausoleum-like atmosphere around them.

"When Lycaon attacked, it wasn't only Lilith that was hurt. A lot of others turned on each other, taking sides on the spot," Empusa said, shuddering at the memory. "Blood was everywhere, which only fueled the vampires more."

William and Emily followed him down the eerily empty halls.

Last time she'd been there, the entire area had been a bustle of activity. The empty silence seemed eerie now. Desolate, somehow.

"You still didn't answer my question," William said to Empusa. "Where is everyone?"

"Many of them were killed in the attack," Empusa explained. "Most of the survivors fled. Some joined Lycaon and left with him. Others ran for their lives. Lycaon destroyed Lilith, then strolled through the castle with a fairly large following, demanding allegiance from any wolf he came to. Those who refused were killed then and there."

"Where were the vampires?" Emily wanted to know, thinking of the overly flirtatious Mary.

Empusa paused and appeared decidedly uncomfortable for a moment.

"It was early evening," he said carefully. "Some of them had yet to rise, and many of the others were feeding."

His gaze darted back and forth from Emily to William, and she saw William give a small nod.

"I'm not a child," Emily said angrily, having noticed their silent communication. "I realize most vampires feed on people."

"*All* vampires feed on people. Some are just more selective about the process," Empusa disagreed gently.

Emily fell silent and continued to follow the men.

Empusa was right.

It had only been a couple of days since she'd noticed the dwindling supply of blood in the fridge. She'd given a lot of thought to the hunt that normally fed vampires.

"I didn't mean to upset you," Empusa interrupted her thoughts. "I was just pointing out the facts."

William hadn't said anything, apparently deciding instead to let her make her own conclusions.

"Where are we going?" he asked Empusa.

"To my side of the castle. We have a few hours before dark, so we might as well get some rest while we
wait. We have a meeting with the committee tonight."
Empusa spoke over his shoulder, but his attention was
fixed on broken bits of stone they passed.

William decided quickly it must have been done
by Lycaon's people, since Empusa had spent centuries
in this castle, and his notice meant it must be new.
Quietly, discreetly, he felt down the pack bond for
Empusa and found sadness.

William said nothing, sure Empusa would refuse
to discuss it. Empusa had come to the castle already
immortal, but it had been his comfortable and familiar home for a very long time. It must be hard to see it
damaged and empty and so different than it had ever
been.

William sent him strength through their bond,
and a very subtle calmness he borrowed from Emily.

He smiled to himself when he noted the decrease
in the level of sadness emanating from Empusa.

Empusa made no move to indicate he was even
aware of what William had done, which gave William
a great sense of satisfaction.

CHAPTER 34

E mpusa showed them into a room that was much smaller and less decorated than the one they'd had their previous stay.

Guard quarters, William realized.

The furniture was much the same type, with a decent-sized bed in the center of the room and a small table in the corner. It was just less decorative and more utilitarian.

His nose told him the room was clean, though, and that was good enough.

"My quarters are right across the hall. I'm going to grab some sleep, so I'll be easy to find if you need me," Empusa said.

"With everything going on around here, it's probably a good idea if we stick together and don't wander the castle alone," William said.

"That's my thought, as well," Empusa agreed easily. "Sekhmet and Paoli will come and get us when they rise, and we can go to the committee as a united pack."

"A flock," Emily corrected.

Empusa gave her an exaggerated wince and a smile.

"I am *not* part of a flock," he said with mock seriousness.

She gave him a slightly teasing smile.

"You are now," she returned.

William shut the door on Empusa's fading laugh as the other man headed across the hall to his own room.

William was glad for Emily's willingness to keep her positive attitude and humor. She was so similar in many ways to Paoli.

They all needed the levity in light of what they were facing.

"What's going to happen tonight?" she asked, the slightest hint of worry in her voice.

William watched as she moved toward the bed.

"I don't know," he said honestly, still watching her.

He'd nearly lost her, and he hadn't gotten an opportunity to reassure himself she was all right until now. They had a few hours to sleep, but first, he had other plans.

He surprised a squeak from her when he stepped behind her and spun her around to face him.

His gaze was hot and hungry.

"And I don't care about tonight. Not right now," he said, his voice rich and husky.

Emily stared into those dark amber eyes, and all thoughts of sleep and what was to come fled. She stood on tiptoe and met his seeking mouth, feeding his almost desperate need with her own.

When he pulled back to look at her, they were both breathless, but his touch was gentle when he caressed her cheek.

"I thought I'd lost you because I didn't know how to use the bond," he admitted, his voice raw.

He looked so vulnerable.

It gave her pause that a man so powerful, so dominant, would look at her with such emotion, as if he was lost without her.

"I'm fine," she whispered, holding his gaze. "We both have a lot to learn about the blood bonds," she admitted. "But we can worry about it later. For now . . ." She leaned back in his arms and pulled her shirt over her head, determined to give him something else to focus on.

Her sentence went unfinished. Before her shirt even touched the cold stone floor, William bent low and captured a bare breast in his lips to tug and tease the peak. His tongue rolled across her hardened nipple and she gasped, throwing her head back.

William had every intention of taking his time to worship her beautiful, soft body.

She evidently had other plans, though, since she pushed him back and began her own onslaught of kissing his neck with open-mouthed kisses. Torturously slow, she kissed her way down his chest to his belly, making the muscles jump beneath her lips, until she knelt in front of him.

With her eyes locked on his, she freed his thick manhood from his jeans. When her soft mouth kissed the throbbing tip, he sucked in a breath through his teeth. He fought the urge to put his hand on her head, but nothing could stop his hips from rocking helplessly foward.

She took as much of him into her mouth as she could.

She began to suck, and he was nearly undone.

Guttural sounds escaped him, and he wasn't even aware of it. Being in her mouth was sheer ecstasy. Far too soon, he had to pull her to her feet for fear of being unmanned too soon.

He stripped her remaining clothes in frenzied movements.

With his body, he pushed her down onto the bed and entered her quickly, burying himself to the hilt in her softness.

Emily's gasp was one of sheer pleasure. She locked her legs around him and met each thrust with equal abandon, raising her hips to meet him and take him in just a little further.

Her climax tore through her like a freight train, fast and almost violent in its intensity.

William returned her cry with his own gasping groan as he finally allowed himself to reach fulfillment as well, pulsing inside her as he was gripped by release.

Afterward, he cradled her in his arms and listened to the even sound of her breathing while she slept.

His.

The force of his possessiveness rang through him. After so many years of isolation, of having no one in his life except Paoli, she had come into his bleak world like a whirlwind and everything had changed. He would do whatever, kill whoever, to keep her safe and by his side.

Where she belonged.

They were about to find themselves in a battle of predators and territory, just like the wolves in the wild. It was a battle that had long since grown unnecessary since the human population had grown so large. But territory and hunting rights were almost instinctive for both species, and with Lycaon dividing the wolves, they were left with little choice but to follow.

He sighed and pulled Emily closer to him. He brushed a gentle kiss across the corner of her forehead and inhaled the sweet scent that was his mate.

Whatever the night would bring, they would deal with it together. All of them. As a pack.

Or a flock, as Emily was determined to call them. He drifted into sleep, still smiling.

CHAPTER 35

William and Emily stood side by side before the committee. Paoli stood on Emily's other side, and Sekhmet and Empusa flanked the group. They presented a united front of strength and power.

William was proud to stand surrounded by his people.

No matter that some of them had come to him at the behest of the committee itself. They were his now, with blood bonds to unite them, and that was all that really mattered in the end.

Unconsciously, he felt for the people connected to him and found some comfort in his ability to do so. He could feel the nervousness and turmoil of each person, and without even giving it a thought, he sent them strength and calm.

Afterward, he smiled a little to himself as he watched the posture of each of his people relax almost imperceptibly. It was only seen in the set of their shoulders and the dimming of their scents.

It was enough.

He'd done what he could for the pack.

His pack. His flock.

He had to focus to keep his blank mask in place.

"It's good to see you, executioner," a young-looking woman with strawberry-blonde hair said very seriously.

While she appeared to be in her midtwenties, his nose told him she was vampire. She could be older than Paoli, for all he really knew. All her appearance could tell him was she was turned around that age, while his nose informed him she was old.

"I did not expect to be welcomed back here after our last departure," he returned carefully. "At least not in the capacity of allies."

A short silence fell over the ten members of the committee. In contrast to the formal atmosphere of the Coven, the committee sat in a half circle at a large table that looked as though it belonged in a boardroom.

"We were informed of the situation of your last departure after the fact, I'm afraid," the woman said. "We hope you realize Lycaon was acting on his own as a rogue, and not with any support from us."

William inclined his head very slightly in acknowledgement. He intended to remain silent as much as possible.

"You were bound by the Coven," said a young-looking man who was werewolf. "But the Coven is no more. Your bargain has been fulfilled, and you're no longer bound."

William audibly sucked in a breath at the unexpected announcement.

He'd been bound to the Coven his entire life.

In bondage.

With those simple words, he was freed.

It was enough to set his head spinning.

With far more emotion in his eyes than he would have liked, he glanced at Paoli, who met his gaze with a very slight smile of shared relief and understanding.

It hadn't only been William who'd been bound all these centuries.

William turned his attention back to the werewolf who'd spoken.

"Thank you," he managed to say past the emotion that threatened to choke him.

Emily brushed his fingers lightly with her own in a subtle show of support.

"You are much more powerful than you understand," said a woman seated toward the center of the committee members.

Again, his nose told him she was far older than she appeared, and werewolf.

"We're aware of Lycaon's plan. He intends to turn as many humans as he can and use them to force the vampires into submission. As always, he wants to be the single ruler of the entire immortal world. He's not opposed to killing any who oppose his will. He believes you're the key to uniting all. We think he's right."

William scoffed aloud before he could stop himself.

More than one committee member gave him a look of surprise at his reaction.

Subtle and diplomatic, that was him, all right.

Paoli stepped on his foot in response.

Hard.

It was a slight movement no one else was likely to notice, but it took a lot of effort to keep from reacting to his suddenly smashed toes.

"You're no fool, William," one of the committee members said, pulling his attention from his pained foot.

It was the first time he could remember anyone in the castle using his actual name.

The speaker was vampire, and he'd been turned later in life. His hair was thinning on top, and he had lines of age on his face.

"You may be the only way to ever truly unite the wolves with the vampires," the man said.

"Just because I'm a combination of the bloods doesn't mean my existence will make everyone lay down their arms and embrace one another," William disagreed.

He was getting tired of everyone acting like he could walk by and make raging immortals start singing campfire songs together simply because of his presence.

"These battles have raged long before my time on this earth. While most wolves no longer hunt humans, they're still territorial," William said.

"We are aware the changes will take time, but they must be made. Both species can learn to coexist. Everyone will have to give a little for us to survive in this changing world," said the strawberry blonde.

"What is it you require of us?" Paoli asked.

It was apparently the right question, because the woman smiled.

"Before we can ever have lasting peace, Lycaon must be stopped," she answered carefully.

Her eyes rested on William, who groaned inwardly.

"Can Lycaon even die?" he asked. "And if he did, what would happen to the wolves?"

"We aren't sure if Lycaon can die, but it's doubtful. We constructed a special way to hold him. All you have to do is capture him," said the middle-aged vampire.

He made it sound so simple.

Sure, just go grab the oldest living wolf on the planet and bring him back.

He was sure to be easy to capture.

Right.

"Lycaon is amassing an army, as you already know," Emily said.

The young-looking male werewolf nodded in agreement.

"Yes, but the attack on your home was nearly all the wolves he has. His following is not large, and most of the wolves are young. We expect him to try making more to add to his ranks, but without time and proper training, the new ones may very well prove to be more trouble than value. And each wolf not given the proper time to adjust raises the risk for us all," said the werewolf.

Which was true.

A new and untrained werewolf could easily lose control at the wrong moment and in the wrong place. It would only take one person with a cell phone and the humans would descend on them from everywhere. Humans may not be as powerful as the immortals, but their sheer numbers would be impossible to defeat.

"We're asking you to begin collecting your own army. Track Lycaon and clean up the messes he's bound to make. Dwindle his numbers until you're confident you can defeat him. Then bind him with silver and bring him to us. He draws most of his power from the wolves bound to him, so each kill will weaken him," said the balding vampire.

"We agree to provide you with all the resources you need," the strawberry-blonde added. "Right now, most of the loyal guards have been dispatched in similar missions," she said, nodding slightly at Empusa and Sekhmet.

"You're not alone in this mission. Only working together do we stand a chance of stopping this before it's too late. We aren't fighting for control any longer. We're fighting extinction," the woman continued.

Those words rang in William's ears.

He glanced at Emily, who was the mate he hadn't even known he could have, and was swamped by his fierce need to protect her.

If Lycaon didn't get stopped quickly and quietly, it was only a matter of time before they would be fighting battles they couldn't win. It was no longer about who was the more powerful species.

This was a battle for survival.

Staying out of it was simply not an option.

He turned his back on the committee and faced their group.

One by one, he met the eyes of everyone who stood with him.

They had chosen him to lead them, and the blood bonds they shared cemented their connections for all time. He wouldn't make a decision of this magnitude without conferring with them.

As expected, each person solemnly nodded agreement until Emily gave him a brave smile and a little shrug.

"I follow where you lead," she said.

And thus, with his pack's support and agreement, they entered into a blood-bound pact with the committee. Each pack member took their turn getting their finger pricked with a long dagger and added a single drop of their blood onto an ancient sheet of parchment that spelled out the agreement in specific detail.

They were told it was simply to allow the committee to locate them in case something went wrong. William suspected it was more a show of loyalty than anything else, but he had no objection.

CHAPTER 36

"What do you suppose is the effect of what we've just done?" Empusa asked when the group gathered in Paoli's room.

Empusa was lounging casually on the bed with his legs crossed at the ankles and his hands folded behind his head, looking for all the world like a man without a care.

"You're the expert on blood binding around here. You tell us," Paoli returned. "My only experience with blood bonds has proven to be questionable at best. Maybe I did it wrong."

He shrugged carelessly, but his face looked more concerned than anything.

Empusa gave him a wide-eyed look of surprise.

"I'm a wolf with understanding of pack ties. Here in the Coven, I was a spy to watch Lycaon and report to the committee. I don't know anything about parchment agreements and blood contracts. That's more in your wheelhouse, being a vampire and all," he said.

Sekhmet came into the room with a rosy glow on his cheeks.

Paoli narrowed his eyes at him.

Sekhmet grinned in return.

"Don't look at me like that," he said with a dismissive shake of his head. "I can feed without killing. Smell me for death if you want."

He held his arms out in invitation, but Paoli just continued to give him a dirty look.

"You may be able to get all your blood from those little bags, but it doesn't compare to fresh," Sekhmet said.

When they'd left the committee, Sekhmet had broken off from the group to visit what he referred to as "the buffet," apparently deaf to Paoli's objections on the matter.

"Your worldviews are going to have to change. I'm a vampire and I fed. We don't *all* kill our prey," Sekhmet assured him.

"It's dangerous," Paoli said.

Sekhmet rolled his eyes in exasperation.

"I'm not a new vampire. I know the risks of getting too comfortable with the kill. But I know what I am, and I'm OK with being a vampire, Paoli," he said.

Paoli opened his mouth to argue further, but Emily had evidently heard enough.

"All right, you two," she interjected crossly. "Let's agree to disagree and move on," she said, stepping between them. "I have no intention of sitting back and watching the testosterone fest escalate. We have more pressing concerns at hand than Sekhmet's feeding habits."

"Tell that to the human he just munched on," Paoli mumbled under his breath.

Emily shot him a dark look, which he returned with an innocent smile.

She heaved a heavy sigh and turned her attention to William.

"What do we do now?" she asked.

"Now we head out into the world in search of Lycaon and his minions," William said.

"So, it's the five of us against the world," Empusa announced cheerfully. "Look out, world!"

He laughed, which started a domino effect that led everyone else in the room to join him until they were all laughing just because they were laughing. It broke the tension in the room completely.

None of them had much to pack, having arrived with not much more than the clothes on their backs. It didn't take them long to be ready to travel again.

William had the names of a few cities, which gave them a starting point.

Paoli paled when he saw the list and announced they needed to go to Virginia first and leave immediately. His reaction earned him a few questioning looks, but he ignored them.

Since they didn't exactly have a schedule to keep, no one was opposed to Virginia.

They made plans to travel there first, then head over to Louisiana.

Empusa knew a few wolves in that area, and Sekhmet knew of some vampires, as well.

It seemed as good a place as any to begin.

William considered the people in their party as they walked shoulder to shoulder through the massive doors of the castle.

So many things were different now.

He glanced at the beautiful woman who walked on his right side, and tender feelings filled his chest.

She was such a miracle.

He considered Empusa and Sekhmet, both of whom were now permanent fixtures in his life.

He had to admit Empusa may have been right. For so many years he'd been isolated, with only Paoli in his world and the never-ending deaths he was forced to bring. Now he had a pack and a purpose, and it was a vast improvement.

They faced nearly insurmountable odds, but for the first time he could remember, he was at peace. They all had a lot of adjusting to do to find their way together, but he had no doubt they'd manage, one way or another.

He decided not to worry about it now.

Who knew, after all?

Tomorrow could find them all dead, defeated at the hands of their enemies.

But for today, they were together. They were strong and going off on an impossible journey. He smiled a little to himself. After so many years of monotony, he couldn't wait to see what tomorrow might bring.

ACKNOWLEDGMENTS

I want to give a special thanks to Tom Reale and the wonderful team at Brown Books. They've been truly amazing through this journey. There's no telling where this wild ride will lead, and I'm grateful to have them as my guides.